BEAT

A NOVEL

RICHARD LEWIS MATER

Boulevard 55 Books
Los Angeles 2022

Lyrics from "Suicide Child" by The Nuns
are used with permission.

Cover Design by Cakamura
Interior Design by Jess LaGreca, Mayfly Design

ISBN 978-1-7368230-0-2 (e-book)
978-1-7368230-1-9 (paperback)

Printed in the United States of America

1 fiction 2 San Francisco 3 Counterculture 4 Haight Ashbury 5 Beats

NOTE: This story is set in San Francisco, circa 1976.
The attitudes and language of the narrator and other characters
regarding sex, drugs, gender, sexual preference and presentation,
and other issues are contemporary to that period and don't necessarily
reflect current values and attitudes, including those of the author.

*This book is dedicated to a time and a place
and a group of people who passed through it.*

1

ONE

S he could be the reincarnation of Veronica Lake in *This Gun for Hire*: the delicately refined features, the cascading honey-blonde hair draped over an eye peek-a-boo style, the sideways smile. Regal in a sleek designer chair, she conjured the film noir femme fatale while sheathed in cream slacks with matching fuck-me pumps. A small adoring audience surrounded her as I watched from across the room.

The party's ostensible guest of honor, Warhol "Superstar" Holly Woodlawn, wandered the loft space, virtually ignored in a T-shirt announcing, "Holly Woodlawn is a Man." She appeared unsure of herself, her once-long, unruly black hair cropped into a shocking, shorter cut—a seeming rebuke of her male-to-female gender switch recounted in the lyrics of Lou Reed's "Walk on the Wild Side." Woodlawn walked past Pristine Condition who was in full drag and holding court in a corner, his mannish features still obvious under garish makeup, a platinum wig, and a fruit-festooned Carmen Miranda hat.

I turned my attention back to the blonde seated across the room. She shifted her legs. The slacks drew a crisp line through the meeting place of her thighs, the snug fit suggesting the surgery had been completed.

Manny was hitting on a cocktail waitress, but I caught him rubbernecking the epicene beauty. Even Manny seemed stymied, perhaps intimidated. Something about that made me feel good. He broke it off with the cocktail waitress and wandered over, speaking above the music.

"God, isn't she something?" He smiled and looked over at the blonde. "She has an uncanny resemblance to Candy Darling, don't you think? Ah, to 'live fast, die young and leave a good-looking corpse.'"

He moved past me, and without thinking, I grabbed the shoulder of his motorcycle jacket.

"Are you serious?" he said.

I pulled away my hand. "Sure. Go for it."

Manny inserted himself into the little group surrounding her, making remarks I couldn't hear. I could see her fail to smile, to laugh, to react to him at all. Manny backed away, returning to me.

"Jesus. She's a shiksa goddess."

"Too bad you struck out."

"What's wrong, Billy? You seem a little on edge. I thought you did a lude."

"I did," I said. Truthfully, I could feel the effects of the Quaalude flagging. I'd taken the pill too early in the evening. Sometimes it was just so hard to wait.

"You know, this should be part of my 'Night Scene' piece," Manny said, glancing around at the crowd. "Ah, San Francisco! The land of Cockettes, misfits, and adorable hyphenates." He chuckled, took a small notebook and pen from a pocket, and started to jot down notes.

I stood against the wall, my eyes half-closed, feeling the beat of the music, content to just experience the exotic swirl around me. After a few moments, I opened my lids and looked at Manny as he put away the notebook and pen.

"Back in the realm of the doable," he said, "Shelley seems to be ready, willing, and I'm able. I won't be needing that ride to my place."

"Have fun," I said.

Manny went back to the cute cocktail waitress. She held a tray filled with rows of jittery champagne glasses and smiled at some quip from him. Her hair was chopped indifferently about the shoulders, with a thin, tightly-twisted brown braid running from the nape of her neck and down a bare back revealed by the cut of the French maid's uniform. I recognized her, I realized. She worked as a waitress at the Palms. A few nights before, as Manny and I were enjoying the cabaret antics of Leila and the Snakes, she brought us our drinks.

I was used to this being the pattern. Sometimes I was jealous of Manny's successes, but after all, he was better looking than me and charming as hell when he wanted to be. Besides, after his initial charm had worn out its welcome, sometimes the women next gravitated to me. By not needing a ride, he'd freed me up to keep my own rendezvous tonight without having to manufacture an excuse.

With nothing further for me here, I crossed the room, waved goodbye to Manny, and headed down the staircase. A slender Cockette with show makeup on slipped past me coming up. He appeared very feminine, perhaps Filipino or from some other part of that region of the world. I paused and turned to watch him for a moment.

At the bottom of the stairs, I hung a right out onto Broadway and into the Saturday night bedlam. Music pounded from open car windows, barkers yelled their pitches from strip club doorways, and just up ahead, red lights flashed as two cops threw a guy against a car and patted him down. Making my way through the commotion, I glanced back with an uneasy feeling in my gut. As they cuffed the guy, I wondered what he'd done wrong.

At Enrico's, I spotted Carlos, David, and Monique sitting at one of the tables outside, along with Constantina. A railing with a single opening separated them from the sidewalk.

"Hello, Billy!" David called, French-accented, over the noise of the street. "Come join us!"

I advanced into the area of packed tables. Carlos pulled up an empty chair for me. As I sat down, he tried to put an arm around Constantina. I caught her lean away. Then, she lifted her legs up in front of her and wrapped an arm around them as she smoked a cigarette. Her chestnut hair fell from beneath a worn men's dress hat; a striped club tie hung loosely around her neck, and she wore black jeans with the usual paint splatters from her acrylics.

"Got any, Billy?" David asked from across the table.

"Uh-huh."

"How about three, one for the each of us?" David looked over at Constantina. "Would you like one too? My treat."

"No thanks," she said, resting her chin on her knees.

I tried to give David the pills discreetly at first, bending down and reaching under the table. It suddenly didn't feel discreet at all. I sat back up and looked around for cops. There was a pair on motorcycles across the street, and the police cruiser pulling out with its prisoner. To hell with it, I thought. I passed the pills directly to David over the table, and he handed me the cash.

"Where's Ti?" Carlos wanted to know.

"I was with Manny," I said, as if that explained it, stuffing the bills into a pocket.

"I don't think being with Manny is quite the same thing," he said, leering.

"Ti and I aren't wedded at the hip, you know."

"She thinks you are. I cut her hair; I hear it all."

"Actually, I think she's someplace with her new roommate," I said. "Girls' night out."

"I've met that new roommate," said Monique. "She's very inter-esting." Monique had an annoying habit of looking anywhere but at you as she spoke. Right now, she seemed preoccupied with the oc-cupants of a nearby table, a couple dressed in formal eveningwear.

"Besides, there is also lovely Lannie, isn't there?" Carlos said. "I wonder what Ti would think about that?"

I wasn't sure how to respond, so I held my tongue.

"Where is Manny?" David said, passing one of the Quaaludes to Monique and one to Carlos. "He is quite an entertaining fellow. I enjoy our encounters."

"Down the street. We were at a party. Lots of Cockettes."

Monique swallowed the pill with her wine. "They were such a fun show," she said. "Even if so many of them are unfeminine. That Pristine Condition, for one. It is a farce."

"Maybe that's the intent," said Constantina, flicking cigarette ash into her empty drink glass.

"Really?" said Monique, poking at her salad.

From behind her, the waiter approached me. Tall and thin, he ap-peared contemptuous. "Are you going to order something tonight?"

"Maybe just a gin and tonic. Separate check." He headed off, and I asked, "What are you guys up to?"

"We were at that art-house theater on Bancroft for a *Nouvelle Vague* retrospective before a night out in the city," said David.

"I enjoy the deft *ennui*," said Monique. "How are things with your new place over here, Billy?"

"The apartment is fine, but my roommate—who was already there before I moved in—is a strange guy. Keeps to himself."

"When you answer an ad, it's the risk you take," Carlos said. He adjusted the cuffs of his silk shirt as he spoke. "Myself, I live solo on Telegraph Hill with a great view of the city. Now that's the life."

There was a pause. My drink arrived, and I took a gulp.

"How's the boutique doing?" I asked Monique.

"It went out of business."

"Oh. Sorry."

"Believe me, so am I. I enjoyed the work and being around fashion, and the benefit of the discount." She indicated her chic dress with a downward look. Then, she began watching something. I turned to see Spencer and his girlfriend Zora sitting down at a table in a corner.

Spencer got up immediately when he spotted me and ambled over as Zora remained behind. Walking in his silver-and-black cowboy boots, he towered over the seated diners, a rock musician's swagger to his step, his long, stringy reddish-brown hair topped by a gaucho hat. As he knelt beside me and I did my business with him, I saw his eyes glazed and suspected he'd already shot up. David and Carlos acted as if he wasn't there, and Monique was especially obvious with her disdain. Spencer must have sensed it and made no attempt to stay and talk.

"So, are you doing something new?" I asked Monique.

She took another sip of her wine and made as if she hadn't heard me over the sound of the street and a passing bus.

"She's working as the hostess at Le Bateau Ivre," David said.

"It is temporary!" Monique replied, stabbing her salad. "I will find something soon."

"Maybe Berkeley isn't the best place for a boutique," said Carlos, slicing a generous portion from his steak. "Or," he continued, "even a French restaurant for that matter."

"We are planning a move across the bay here into the city," David said. "When we do, we will rent a nice place and start a business."

"What about you?" Constantina asked, catching me off guard. "What's new?"

"Still managing that T-shirt store in the Haight," I said, inflating my salesclerk position as always. For her, I wished I could have also said something about the writing. But what was there to say? I would get back to it one day, and then there would be something to say.

"How's business?" Carlos asked me. "My salon is doing well, but I know things can be tough."

"The store is probably going to close by September after tourist season."

"Try not to think about it," advised Monique.

I played with the silver spoon from the table setting in front of me. It was smooth to the touch and had a crest design where the stem met the bowl.

"Yes, one should live very much in the present anyway," said David. "Besides, that leaves you several months. You will find something else, not to mention you have your sideline. Maybe you can do it full time," he laughed.

"I already call you *le drugstore*," said Monique. She smiled, and I thought maybe she was feeling the pill already.

David continued. "You will be successful if you run it more like a business."

"You could use invoices and give out receipts," said Monique.

"Open a storefront," said David, and everyone shared a laugh, even Constantina.

"I can give you my old pads from the boutique," Monique said. There was another round of laughter. "Be sure to stay in touch, Billy, whatever happens," she added. "We value your company." She was no longer looking away, but right at me. I wondered if she might be flirting, but with her, it was hard to tell. Besides, David was very good-looking.

"Yes, be sure to let us know if you have any cocaine," David said. "That's the business to really be in. You could make a lot of money."

"Count me in on that," said Carlos, sucking at a piece of meat visible between his front teeth. "I'm up for a couple grams anytime."

"It's dangerous to get into that line of work," I said.

"Dangerous, really?" David replied.

"You're talking lots of cash, and things can happen."

"Things can always happen," said Carlos.

"But you have greatly increased the odds," I said. "People get hooked and greedy besides. Sometimes they act crazy."

For a few seconds, no one spoke, and there was only the noise of Broadway and the people talking at the tables around us. I glanced down and realized I had bent the spoon rather severely.

David and Carlos began placing bills in a little pile in the middle of the table. I downed the last of the gin and tonic, swallowing the other half of the Quaalude I'd begun earlier, and settled up also. As the waiter approached, I covered the damaged spoon with a napkin.

"Hey, Billy, if you ever want to cut that hippie hair of yours and become respectable, let me know," Carlos said. "We could work out a trade."

"Anyone know what time it is?" I asked.

David checked his watch. "Pushing midnight. Where to next? We could dance for a while at Earl's, and there's Dance Your Ass Off."

"Dance Your Ass Off is my favorite," said Monique.

Constantina tapped an unlit, unfiltered cigarette against an antique silver case and turned to Carlos. "You can just drop me off at my place," she said.

I got up. "I'm going to head out."

"If you get any more pills or anything else, let us know," said Monique, smiling and looking happy, feeling the lude for sure.

"Everyone remember, if you ever want a T-shirt, drop by Aquarius Shirts." As I finished saying this, I was looking only at Constantina. She peered up at me, her eyes gray-blue and arresting. She wore no makeup. Next to Monique whose face was heavy with makeup under her dark bangs, Constantina should have paled, but she didn't.

"Isn't it all just Grateful Dead shirts?" Carlos said, putting aside his knife and fork, leaving a large portion of the steak on his plate.

"There are some other choices," I said, annoyed. "I can give you guys a discount."

"Well, maybe," said David, tossing his napkin onto the table, but I could tell he was just being polite. "Are you on foot?" he asked. "Perhaps we can offer you a ride."

"That's okay. I have Kozmic parked around the corner."

"Kozmic?" Costantina asked.

"My VW Bus."

"You have a name for your car?"

"Well, it's a VW bus, but yes."

"How utterly charming!"

"Well, see you around," I said.

"*Au revoir*," David and Monique said in unison. Constantina gave me a nod, more with her eyes than her head, her chin still resting on her knees.

Reaching the sidewalk, I looked back at them seated around the table, still trying to formulate their plans, I supposed. Spencer and Zora sat in their corner, his head resting against her shoulder and her long jet-black hair. There was no food or drink in front of them, and I had the thought that perhaps the tall, thin waiter was ignoring them, hoping they'd just go away.

TWO

Outside Enrico's, I turned right, walking past the Condor Club. I glanced at the posters of headliner Carol Doda, with stars over the nipples of her silicone breasts. People were gathered at the door of the notorious strip joint to see the show.

As I walked, I thought about my roommate Noel. Likely he had something he could teach me about the writing. He'd once had a story published in *The Paris Review*. The literary magazine's cover, along with the story's now-yellowed first page, hung framed in his bedroom. It must have been terribly exciting for him at the time. Unfortunately, I could never talk to him about it, since I wasn't supposed to have seen it in the first place. He had given me strict instructions never to enter his room.

Gerold, the creepy guy across the hallway, had hinted about other writings: poems, more short stories, possibly a novel. Even that Noel was somehow tied to the Beats. I imagined a young Noel at poetry readings, perhaps in the audience for Ginsberg's legendary unveiling of *Howl* at the Six Gallery, not far from our apartment. Kerouac swigging from the jug of wine Cassady passed around, yelling drunken encouragement from the back of the room. Michael McClure, Philip Whalen, and Gary Snyder also giving readings; Lawrence Ferlinghetti in attendance. To have been there and witnessed it, that would have really been something.

I turned up Grant, past small stores, Caffe Trieste, and clubs with their doors open and music filling the crowded, narrow sidewalk. Perhaps music was the key to getting to know Noel better, bridging the gap of the dozen or more years that separated us. He played classical records for hours behind his closed bedroom door. I could ask him about a composition when he emerged. Maybe get him to show me the album with information about the orchestra, the conductor, the recording of it. I could then spot the framed *Paris Review* cover and its companion page on the wall as if I'd never seen it before and start a conversation about writing. Yes, that was a plan. With a little more time, I could gain his trust. And time was one thing I had plenty of.

I reached the Savoy Tivoli and stepped inside. Ti sat sideways to the bar, her legs crossed. She had strawberry hair in a pixie cut and wore a pink summer dress that had the appearance of being from a thrift store, along with the worn blood-red flats that set off the white of her bare calves. A girl who I assumed must be Karen was beside her and turned away to talk to another woman as I approached.

"Hi," I said. Ti spun around on the barstool.

"Good to *see* you, Billy!" she said. She grabbed me behind my neck and drew me to her for a kiss. "You're late," she added.

"Business."

"Ooh. Then do you have some fairy dust?" she asked. She sipped some of her drink and I gave her a smile. "Great! Have you met Karen?"

I put out my hand.

Karen turned and fixed me with slack eyes. A conspicuous crystal mounted on a stud pierced one of her nostrils. She said nothing to me and went back to talking to the woman on the stool beside her. I stood against the bar next to Ti as she took a hat from her lap and placed it on her head.

"Like my hat?"

"Adorable."

"It's Karen's but feels right for me."

The bartender came over. Flinging a white linen cloth over her shoulder and placing her hands on the counter, she said, "What can I get you?"

"Thanks," I said, "but we're leaving in just a minute."

"You're not joining us for a drink?" Ti asked as the bartender stepped away.

"I've already had some of this, some of that. Besides, you said you wanted to go dancing tonight."

"It can wait, Billy. Everything can wait if you're having fun. It's all rather simple. You know what Manny says."

"What does Manny say?"

"'To be happy, all I need is a latté, a looker, and my friends.' And isn't that what it's all about? Friends and just having fun!"

"Maybe."

She turned to Karen and said loudly, "Isn't it all rather simple?"

"Sometimes," Karen said, looking me up and down.

Ti tugged on the hat and pulled it low as Karen turned away again to the other woman who was older and paid her close attention.

"Manny used to say I was his looker. Am I your looker, Billy?"

"Sure."

"And am I mysterious?" she said, peering out from under the brim.

"Not really." She was clearly a bit loopy from drinking, I decided.

"But I so want to be mysterious! The Mata Hari of—where are we? North Beach? The Mata Hari of North Beach! Who shall we spy on?" She picked up her glass and took a gulp to empty it. Turning the glass around, she looked through the bottom as if it were a telescope. Then she leaned against me. "Take me, I'm yours!" she said, laughing. Worried she might fall off the barstool, I put an arm around her to steady her.

"What say we go?" I said.

"But I'm not ready to go home!"

"Not home. To Dance Your Ass Off."

"Oh my God! Yes! Great idea! Karen?"

Ti handed her the hat, and Karen said goodbye to the woman next to her. I realized Karen was going with us.

"I have a new improved fake ID, Billy," Ti said. "I will *not* embarrass you this time by getting busted at the door. It worked just fine here." With a conspiratorial expression, she put a finger to her lips and whispered, "Shush. Don't tell anyone."

Once outside, I said, "Do you guys want to walk over or drive?"

"I vote for a ride," said Karen, standing close to Ti.

"I could go either way," Ti said, putting her arm through Karen's and bursting into laughter.

I set off for Kozmic, then turned my head and saw them chatting with some people. Ti feminine, even with shortness of her hair; Karen, taller and sturdy in jeans and Doc Martens, with her own close-cropped hair now hidden under the hat. They looked comfortable together, if an odd couple. I turned the corner and walked faster up the hill, concerned they might not be there when I returned.

Up ahead, I spotted Kozmic covered in hard-to-miss psychedelic swirls of fading colors. I drove back to the Savoy, having to loop around and deal with the one-way street, the traffic, and people crossing the pavement in front of me. Ti and Karen were still talking to the strangers. I hit the horn, and the two of them got in, Ti in the passenger seat, Karen squatting in the walk-through space between the front seats, holding the seatbacks on either side, her knuckles close to my face.

We drove north, took a left, and then a right onto Columbus, and went on for several blocks. Neon brightened the exterior of Dance Your Ass Off, and a line stood waiting to gain entrance. We got lucky as a car pulled out, and I grabbed a spot. As we sat there, we all did some coke from my vial with its miniature silver spoon attached to the twist-off cap by means of an elegant strand of chain. I wasn't happy about having to share it with Karen, but she only took a little, as if to avoid being indebted to me. At the door, Karen paid for herself, and I took care of Ti, her phony ID working fine.

Inside the cavernous club, thumping sound inundated us. It was almost impossible to talk. Spotlights cut through the air, reflecting off the silver disco ball suspended from the high ceiling. Colored bulbs pulsated above the dance floor, the crowd moving as a throbbing mass. We checked our jackets and sliced into it, barely avoiding bodies, making our way to the center of the room.

Ti moved in front of me, her hands held overhead like a flamenco dancer. Karen made it a three-way. Ti yelled to me over the music. "You know, I had lessons as a child. I wanted to be a dancer!"

I nodded. She had told me this before. As I watched, she closed her eyes, going off, I imagined, on a journey to someplace where she was on stage. Karen danced close to her as if I wasn't there. Then, the two of them put on a performance right out of the Anna and Giulia dance floor scene in *The Conformist*, complete with the crowd parting to make room for them. For a few moments, I became an observer along with everyone else.

Next, we danced together for another song, and one after that, and one more still. Sometimes Ti faced Karen, sometimes me. The songs flowed from one to another, no one leaving the dance floor. Barely feeling my body now, I floated along and moved with a freedom, feeling the lude. Feeling happy. At some point, Karen shouted something into Ti's ear, and Ti frowned. They kissed on the lips, and Karen wandered off.

I spotted David with Monique, Karen now by their side. Ti gave them a nod. David smiled back, his face rakish in the lights, all French Jean-Paul Belmondo cool. It was hard not to just watch him. Like some suave visitor from the past, he was timeless in his handsomeness and masculinity. He danced sedately amid the wildness of the fashions and colors and movement surrounding him. Monique glided serenely by his side, chic in her dress. Karen was next to her, also dancing.

After more drinking and dancing, by design or chance, David and Monique exited the club at the same time as Ti and me, along with Karen. We all stood together, blocking the sidewalk near the door. People had to make their way around us like we were some kind of cool gang ruling our turf in the night.

"Want to share a cab?" David asked Ti.

"We're fine," I said. Karen and Monique were chatting together. It was the most animated I'd seen either of them. I took David aside, putting a hand on his arm. "Could you do me a favor, and not mention to Manny that you saw me with Ti?"

"Oh, he does not know?"

"I'll tell him soon. Here." I slipped him a Quaalude.

"Karen will share a cab with us," Monique called over.

"Oh, really?" said Ti. "Karen, won't you come with us?" I wasn't sure what she thought we were going to do with her, although I was open to almost anything in my state.

"It's okay," David said. "We'll get her home."

Ti made a pouty face.

David stepped to the curb and flagged down a cab, and he, Monique and Karen got in.

"See you at the apartment!" Ti called after Karen as David shut the car door. Karen sat in the backseat between the two of them, their arms around her.

"So, Karen and Monique know each other?" I asked Ti as we began to walk.

"It was news to me."

"David too?"

"Yes, she didn't know him. Of that, I'm sure. God, I'm jealous. He was *so* handsome tonight."

Just then, two electric buses went by in opposite directions, passing each other very close, blue arcs flashing through the air with a noisy crackling and popping, their poles slapping against the web of wires at the intersection.

"Yes, he was," I said.

"Do you have any more fairy dust?"

"I think there's a little left."

"Oh, goody."

She wobbled on her feet and slipped her arm through mine. We arrived at Kozmic, and I unlocked the passenger door for her. I helped her up with a hand on a slim hip, the fabric of her dress soft to the touch.

"Oh, am I an invalid now?" she said. But then she stumbled. She would have fallen had I not caught her. She was a feather in my arms.

THREE

heard the apartment door open and close. I checked the clock next to the bed: 3 AM. Noel's boots thumped across the thin living room carpeting and thudded into the kitchen.

Ti asked, "Is that him?"

"Yes."

"How come I've never met him?" She propped herself up on an elbow. "Are you afraid he might steal me away?" She stroked my bare chest with a hand. "Love is the Drug" throbbed from the stereo, a solitary candle illuminated the darkness, the scent of sandalwood incense thick.

"He's gay," I said.

"Even better. My kind of guy. Alexander calls me his 'fag haggala.'"

"Besides, he spends most of his time alone in his room with the door closed."

"Doing what?"

"Playing records and writing, I suppose. Listen, I'm going out to say hi."

I gave her a peck on the cheek and got out of bed. I pulled on my jeans and opened the door to the living room, taking my empty drink glass with me. In the kitchen, I found that Noel had gone into the bathroom. Through the all-but-closed door, I could hear the noisy jet as he relieved himself. I put the glass into the sink and sneaked a peek into a brown shopping bag on the counter. Inside was a bottle of gin, some cigarettes, a chocolate cake visible in a box with a cellophane window, and a little packet of birthday candles. The gin struck me as odd. That Noel was a recovering alcoholic was one of the few things I'd been able to glean from him. When I moved in, he'd asked me to keep my Kahlua and bottle of vodka stashed out of sight in my bedroom. Feeling guilty about my intrusion, I slipped back to my room. Closing the door behind me, I pulled off my jeans and got back under the covers, the heated waterbed now in motion.

"So, darling," Ti said to me, "how's the reclusive *artiste*?"

"I'm doing fine."

"Ha! Really? Have you been hiding something from me? You know I love a good secret!"

"Shhhh, he's still in there," I said, pointing to the other door from my bedroom that led to the bathroom. "Besides," I said in a low voice, "then it wouldn't be a secret, would it? Anyway, I didn't get to see him."

We heard the toilet flush and Noel leave the bathroom.

"I've got a secret, too, you know," Ti said. "It's a really good one. You tell me yours, and I'll tell you mine."

"Doesn't work that way."

"That's not fair. Anyway, don't you want to know my secret?"

"I thought you were about to tell me."

"Well, then, if you won't tell me yours, do you at least have some more fairy dust?"

"We finished it."

"Damn it all to hell. Then what do I get for my secret?"

I reached for the joint in the ashtray on the orange-colored plastic crate that served as a nightstand and also held the candle, an incense holder, and Ti's White Russian. I passed the joint to her. She placed it between her lips, and I put a match to the candle. The sulfur flared, and I shifted the flame to the joint. In the glow, Ti's pale skin took on a golden tinge, her hair a shade of crimson around the edges.

She exhaled and smiled at me. "That girl you met tonight, Karen, my new roommate? She has the secret, actually." Ti took another hit and, with her free hand, reached for her drink, a tuft of blonde-red hair in an armpit revealing itself. She took two sips, the second longer than the first.

As I waited, I lit a fresh stick of incense off the candle and deposited it into the holder. Ti passed me the joint, and I took a hit. I exhaled and said, "Okay, what about Karen's secret?"

Ti moved closer, her bare skin glistened, and I smelled a touch of perfume mixed with sweat. Her face near to mine, she said, "She goes by 'Delaney' and works at the Black Door."

"Isn't that some kind of S&M club?"

"So she tells me! Last night, she gave me the details. She gets a hundred bucks an hour to act out fantasies with middle-aged men. She has a closet full of getups. Leather bras with holes cut out for the nipples, or even an entire cup missing. Thigh-high black leather boots. Whips! She says she doesn't even have to really have sex, per se."

"'Per se?'"

"Well, there's Diaper Guy. He gets yelled at and spanked in diapers. He pees and shits in them, too, while he sits in a playpen. She tells me it's a gas whipping stockbrokers, bankers, and lawyers."

"So, she's a dominatrix."

"That's what I'm not exactly sure about. I get the impression she's sometimes on the receiving end. Master Robert puts a leash and dog collar around her neck and makes her lick milk out of a bowl."

"Delightful."

"I think she has a bit of a crush on me. A couple nights ago, she had on some of her gear. We'd been drinking. She grabbed my wrists like I was her prisoner, and nailed me up against the wall, and kissed me on the mouth. I felt helpless to prevent it. It was all *so* very arousing."

I rolled over on my back. I imagined Ti in thigh-high black leather boots, whipping some fat banker.

"You're so quiet," she said. "Did I say something wrong?"

I glanced over and then wrapped my arms around her. She held me back so tight there was no separation between our chests.

"Oh, Billy, I do love you so," she whispered, smiling up at me, her eyes opening wide. "I want us to be perfect, like in the movies. Kiss me!" She closed her lids and pursed her lips. I kissed her lightly on the mouth and gave her a lick on the nose. She made a face and giggled. I waited for her to open her eyes again. But the eyes remained closed, the smile melted into repose, her breathing slowed.

I lay there, intertwined with her. The eight years I had on her sometimes seemed like eighty. I wouldn't even be seeing her to begin with if Manny hadn't brought her by the T-shirt store that day. "Ti," she'd said from across the counter, with an outstretched hand and a laugh too big for her size. "Like in 'bi.'"

I was unable to sleep. Maybe it was the coke we'd shared along with everything else. I stared over at the flickering candle flame. The old and poorly framed bedroom window always let in too much air. It would be really bothersome come winter. Maybe I should try to fix it. The arm of the stereo retracted. Silence came over the room. The incense streamed its thin rope. I heard Noel out in the kitchen, his footsteps retreating across the living room, the closing of his bedroom door.

Easing out of the entanglement of Ti's arms, I got out of bed slowly so as to avoid disturbing her and found a Valium. Crunching it up between my teeth for faster effect, I washed it down with the watery remains of Ti's drink. I heard scratching noises. The closet door had swung closed. I opened it and Cat emerged, and I rubbed him behind the ears. A shaft of light slipped past the edge of the window curtain, the full moon reflected in his golden eyes. I kissed him on top of his furry black head.

"Love you, little guy."

I lifted Cat and brought him under the covers. He purred up against me. I set the alarm for 7 AM as promised, to get Ti up for her breakfast waitress shift. Blowing out the candle, I rested my head on the pillow, my mind churning. I kept thinking about Noel and that bottle of gin.

FOUR

The angry buzzing of the alarm clock shocked me awake. Ti jerked herself into a sitting position as I slammed the off button, and Cat jumped off the bed.

"Jesus!" she said. "Have you ever considered a clock radio with some fucking music?"

"Feel free to take a shower," I said. "You can get the bus down the street at the corner. It'll take a couple transfers, but it'll take you there."

"You won't give me a ride?"

"Your shift starts at eight-thirty. I don't open up 'til ten."

"God, I hate it when I have to go in early to help out with breakfast prep. What about some coffee?"

"There's some instant in the kitchen."

"Christ, I like you better on drugs."

I gave her a conciliatory smooch on the cheek. "I'm sorry," I said. "I'm fried and really need more sleep."

"What about Noel?" she asked.

"What about him?"

"Well, I feel a little strange wandering around naked. Using the shower, not to mention the toilet."

"Just lock the door from the kitchen if you're worried."

I sneaked a peek at her boyish ass as she walked through the doorway into the bathroom. After resetting the alarm, I drifted off to the sounds of her showering.

I awoke with a start from a surprisingly deep sleep. Ti stood over me in last night's clothes, shaking me.

"Do you have any ones?" she asked. "For the bus and some real coffee. I'm short."

I got up, naked, retrieved my wallet and gave her a few bucks. I could see through the partially open curtains that it was one of those indeterminate San Francisco mornings when it was hard to tell whether the gray outside was clouds or fog. I escorted Ti out into the living room, as the familiar sound of classical music came from behind Noel's door. Sometimes I would also hear his typewriter clacking away. I imagined him hard at work on stories, worthy if belated successors to his *Paris Review* publication. Or perhaps the novel hinted at by Gerold.

At the door, Ti hugged me and said, "I'm so glad you rescued me from Karen last night. My feelings for you are so special. I—"

I pinched her ass and whispered, "*Ma cherie*, I want to do this again very soon," and I stuck my tongue into her ear.

"Ew!" she said, laughing.

"I'll be thinking of you," I said.

"God, I've got to get some fucking real coffee."

"There's that little café on the corner."

"Maybe I'll bring you some later at the store after my shift."

"Sure," I said, and she kissed me on the lips. Then she headed down the stairs, and I locked the door behind her and went back to bed. I woke up a couple hours later to the alarm and heard the same music coming from Noel's room. Every time the record ended, it began again, apparently stuck on endless repeat.

After feeding Cat, showering, and eating a bowl of cereal, I prepared to leave to open the store for the day. I wondered if Noel was even home. I knocked on his door. Getting no response, I opened the door slowly and took a tentative step inside. The music engulfed me with grim power.

Noel lay on his back, naked and white, the sheets and blankets rumpled at the foot of the bed. His arms were outstretched, palms facing up; his legs were together and jutting straight from the torso, feet crossed at the ankles. The drained bottle of gin stood upright on the nightstand. Alongside it was the amber prescription pill vial from me, now empty.

Goddamn. Goddamn. Goddamn.

I backed out of the room and walked quickly to the kitchen. I searched for the emergency numbers on the neat handwritten list Noel had posted next to the phone. I dialed the number for the police. A man answered. I formed words with great difficulty. My voice quivered and shook, my throat so constricted I could barely speak.

"My roommate is dead," I managed to say. "Suicide."

"What's your name and address?"

I gave it to him, and he said, "Someone will be there soon. Don't disturb anything."

I hung up and stood there. A fly buzzed against the cantilevered glass of the window. I walked back to Noel's bedroom and entered slowly. Remains of chocolate cake littered a plate in the middle of the floor. Four wax birthday candles in bright colors lay askew, wicks unlit. I walked around the foot of the bed. Next to the typewriter on Noel's desk sat an ashtray overflowing with half-smoked cigarettes, stubbed out hard and turned in on themselves at sharp angles. The music continued to play loudly from large speakers resting on the floor. Should I turn it off? No. Leave everything untouched for the police. I walked over and looked at the spinning disk: "Prokofiev's 6th Symphony."

I went over to Noel. I debated touching him. You could tell he had once been quite handsome, with piercingly intelligent blue eyes. Now his eyes stared uselessly, his mouth slightly open, teeth yellow. Some drool escaped right then. His belly hung pasty around his middle, his penis lifeless below it, curled in its brown nest.

I considered the pill vial on the nightstand. I'd already stripped the label with its information before I gave it to Noel. Still, I wondered if there was an issue of fingerprints. Was there some further action for me to take before the police arrived?

The doorbell rang, startling me. I moved rapidly from the room. Pushing the buzzer to release the lock for the downstairs door, I stepped out onto the landing.

"Where's the body?" asked a heavy-set black cop, breathing hard as he climbed the last of the stairs. His partner, Asian, was right behind him. The drugs in my room suddenly concerned me. Suppose they wanted to search the apartment?

I managed a mangled "This way, officers."

"A suicide?" the Asian cop said.

"Uh-huh," I said, standing at Noel's door.

The black cop walked over to Noel, shined a flashlight into his eyes, and felt a wrist for a pulse. The Asian cop went to the stereo. He glanced over as he turned down the volume. "Wait in the kitchen, sir."

I left the doorway and sat at the kitchen table. The black cop came out, sat opposite me, and pulled out a notebook and pen.

"Your name?"

"Billy Johnson."

"No nicknames."

"William Johnson."

"Middle initial."

"H."

"When did you discover the body?"

"This morning."

"What time?"

"About 9:30."

"Do you have any contact information for the next of kin of the deceased?"

I pointed to Noel's neat handwritten list of numbers on the wall next to the phone. The cop went over and began writing. The helpless fly continued its buzzing. I stood to open the window's crank handle. The cop turned, "Sir, I'm going to have to ask you to remain seated while we conduct our investigation."

I placed my ass back on the chair.

"It just says 'Mother' and 'Father,'" the cop said. "Do you know their full names?"

"No. Noel's last name is Edwards. That's all I know."

How would Noel's parents take the phone call from the police? Would there be a scream from his mother? A businesslike handling of things by his father? Would there be a funeral I was supposed to attend? No, that was silly. I barely knew the man.

"What can you tell me about him?" the cop asked.

"Almost nothing. I've been his roommate for only a month. But he works at the State Unemployment Office."

The cop came back over and sat down facing me.

"Age?"

"Mine or his?"

"Don't be a wiseass. His."

"I don't know. Maybe forty?" I stared at the dark blue of the uniform. I read the numbers on the shiny silver badge and examined the words "San Francisco" curved across the top and "Police" below. He had sergeant stripes on his shoulders.

"I think it was his birthday," I said. "There's a cake in his room."

"Any reason why he would commit suicide?"

That struck me as very funny. But the cop was serious. Jesus. Where to start?

"Was he laid off or something?" the cop said. "Depressed? Anything traumatic happen?"

"I'm not sure," was the best I could muster. "We didn't know each other very well."

"You were his roommate."

I felt as if I had been derelict. "He spent a lot of time alone in his room with the door closed," I tried to explain. "Yesterday was no different. It was a day like any other."

The cop took a card with a phone number out of his shirt pocket and placed it on the table between us. "Don't disturb his room. Coroner's on the way."

I remembered I was supposed to be opening the T-shirt store.

"I need to call my boss," I said.

"No problem."

I got up and went over to the phone and called Miranda at home, using the number she'd written in blue ink on the back of the business card of hers that I kept tucked in my wallet. A woman I presumed to be a housekeeper answered. "Stein residence."

"Miranda, please?" I said. I watched the fly buzz against the glass. Outside was now bright and sunny.

"This is Miranda."

"It's Billy. My, uh, roommate committed suicide. I'm here with the police."

"What? Are you serious?"

"I just don't think I can make it in."

"That's okay. Damn. I'll get over there and open up. Or I'll see if Laurel or somebody else can do an extra day. Listen, I'm really sorry. Take your time. Just let me know later what's up."

"Okay." I hung up. I went over to the window and cranked the handle. The fly flew up against the screen, where a tear in the corner would permit freedom.

When the coroner arrived, the cops left. The coroner was a slight, prematurely balding guy with a tired face framed by black glasses. I judged him to be in his fifties. A tall, muscular young assistant followed, dragging a collapsible gurney upstairs, its wheels bumping over each step like a bulky piece of luggage. I led the two of them into Noel's bedroom and left them there. After a while, they emerged with a black body bag strapped to the gurney. I opened the apartment door, and they pushed it to the landing.

After raising the wheels up underneath, they began to carry the gurney down the stairs, stretcher-style. They struggled due to the sharp turn halfway down, where the ceiling was so low it forced the assistant to bow his head. Unable to go any further, they returned to the landing, unstrapped the body bag, and laid it on the floor. The assistant collapsed the gurney, took it downstairs and outside, and then came back.

The coroner asked if I would be willing to help, and the three of us carried the body bag down the stairs. The assistant was below, supporting one end, and the coroner and I held the other. I could sense from the shape and feel that I held the end with Noel's shoulders, his head against my hand. Rigor mortis had set in, his body stiff. I began to sweat. As we slowly negotiated the turn, I lost my grip, and my side of the body bag banged hard against the stairs.

I felt like an incompetent pallbearer.

I swore under my breath and picked up my corner. We made our way outside and placed the body on the gurney. The assistant strapped Noel's corpse in place, and he and the coroner loaded it into their van. I watched them drive off and returned up the stairs.

By now, it was early evening. I pondered my options. Without Noel, I had the apartment to myself. This made for less motivation to go out. Besides, I was in no mood to go anywhere and especially not interested in talking with anybody. Instead, I sat on the living room couch. I looked around the sparse room. No TV. No decent furniture. Nothing to speak of on the walls. I thought how I should improve it. Get some posters from the Print Mint, I decided.

I got up and paced for a while. Then, I sat back down on the couch. Cat jumped up, and I petted him with extra-long strokes from the top of his head to his tail as he purred. I lost track of time as the sun went down and the apartment descended into darkness.

Finally, I turned on some lights. Cat followed me to the kitchen where I filled his bowl from the bag of dried cat food, some of it spilling to the floor. I made myself a sandwich from Noel's bologna, white bread, and mayonnaise. I chewed it mechanically as I stood at the counter.

I needed to alter my state. Going into my bedroom, I retrieved my stash box from its hiding place between the waterbed frame and the wall. I put it on the coffee table in the living room and sat back on the couch. Originally, the box had been a fancy container for a large-sized bottle of Amaretto Disaronno. The expensive liquor, long since consumed, had been a gift from my acquaintance Nick James, an ambitious grad student who had worked for a time down the street from me on Haight and who valued the appearance of being able to afford such things.

Under its convenient lift-off cover, the rectangular receptacle was filled with vials of pills, as well as varieties of pot in baggies and various little containers, each with a tiny handwritten Scotch-taped label indicating the strength and nature of the high and the date procured. There was also a small wooden pipe, extra screens, rolling papers, matches, and even an old hit of blotter acid that I'd been loath to throw away.

I took out a pinch of pot from a small baggie with a label promising a "clean great head high"—a beautiful resinous bud of Columbian fit for a *High Times* cover shot—and smoked a little piece of it in my pipe. As I got stoned, I immediately regretted it, given the circumstances of the day and my own culpability. I quickly took a Valium, crunching it up with my teeth for faster impact. Without even waiting, I decided that wasn't enough and took a Phenobarb.

The phone rang. I ignored it. I went back to my room. The sounds of the city filtered in through the partially raised window. I left both doors open, the one to the bathroom and the one to the living room. Turning on the old black-and-white TV that was balanced on a stack of books, I crawled under the covers of the waterbed.

By then, it was past midnight. Naked and warm with Cat curled up beside me, I floated. I watched an old Barbara Stanwyck movie, the one where she and Fred MacMurray end up at a farm somewhere in the Pennsylvania countryside at night. Then, I drifted into sleep, just the way I liked it: a slow numbing coming over me and shutting down my brain without me having to think about it.

FIVE

I was startled out of some nightmare. Someone was ringing the doorbell and wouldn't stop. I got up and threw on some jeans. "Alright, alright, I'm coming!" I said out loud, no matter they couldn't hear me. I buzzed in whoever it was, went out onto the landing and peered over the banister. A uniformed Western Union guy climbed the stairs. It was the first time I'd ever received a telegram. After he left, un-tipped and appearing annoyed, I read the piece of paper:

BILL CAN YOU PACK NOELS PERSONAL EFFECTS FOR US IN THIS TIME OF OUR DEEP SORROW. LETTERS CLOTHES COLLEGE DIPLOMA WRITINGS AND IMPORTANT DOCUMENTS. PLEASE SHIP THEM TO US AT THE ADDRESS BELOW. WRITE OR CALL WHEN READY. I WILL WIRE YOU THE MONEY IN ADVANCE PLUS SOMETHING FOR YOUR EFFORTS. ANYTHING ELSE IN NOELS ROOM YOU ARE WELCOME TO DO WITH AS YOU SEE FIT.

JONATHAN J EDWARDS ATTORNEY AT LAW 339 BROAD STREET PHILADELPHIA PA

The thought of gathering Noel's things and boxing them up felt daunting. It also struck me as odd that Noel's father knew my name. Perhaps the police had provided it. On the telegram, there was a phone number just below the address. I could always call and ask his father to handle it himself, but he was going to pay me, and I could sure use the money.

I fried up two eggs and ate wheat toast with marmalade. The eggs and marmalade were Noel's. Normally, I just ate a bowl of Wheat Chex.

I went first to the shared bathroom. Picking up a can of shaving cream, I read the label and placed it on my side of the sink. The aftershave was unfamiliar. I opened it and took a sniff. Too sweet, like perfume. I dropped it into the trashcan. The last items on Noel's side were his toothbrush and an old, traditional double-edge razor with a gruesome blade. I chucked them also.

We each had a small wooden drawer under the sink. My drawer was almost empty. Noel's was full and immaculately organized: tweezers, nail clippers, a hand mirror, dental floss and toothpaste, Q-tips, aspirin, cough drops, a little stack of small packets of Kleenex, extra razors, and a small pair of scissors, all neatly lined up in parallel formations.

I transferred all of those things into my drawer, then found a half-filled vial of Librium hidden inside an opened box of cold medicine. That made my efforts worthwhile right there. I counted out nine of the black-and-green capsules into my palm and pocketed them.

I thought I'd emptied the drawer, but I reached beyond what had been visible to double-check. I found a washcloth wrapped around something. I pulled it out. A pair of twin metal mechanical devices fell to the floor. I picked them up. They looked like car battery clamps held together by a length of chain. I had no idea what they were. Inspecting one of them up close, I noted it had a thick moveable screw. I turned the little knob, and the ends of the apparatus adjusted closer together. There was a trace of what appeared to be dried blood on cold steel. Some sort of clamps? For nipples? In any case, what to do with it? I thought of Noel's father's request to ship important personal effects back to him and laughed out loud, the sound eerie. I tossed the clamps into the trashcan, where they landed with a loud clatter.

I carried the trashcan down the old wooden staircase from the kitchen backdoor, wincing at the brightness of the sun. Shirtless, wearing only my jeans, the air warm against my skin, I walked around the side of the building. I dumped the contents into one of the metal garbage cans next to the tool shed. Cat had followed me and now lay in the grass at the center of the small garden bordered with flowers. He twitched, watching birds fly in and out of bushes. Noel had done a nice job of maintaining the garden. Our neighbor Gerold leaned out his window, his ruddy face an ugly thing in the sun.

"Isn't it a shame about Noel?"

"Yes," I said.

"Will there be a funeral?"

"Up to his parents, I guess."

"Can you let me know?"

"If I hear anything."

I hiked back up the stairs, returning the trashcan to its spot near the sink. I walked into Noel's bedroom, a certain perversity to the moment. After all, Noel had been such a guardian of his privacy. It struck me that the room was almost twice as big as my own, yet I paid half the rent. For all I knew, I paid more than half. I took it all in. There was the large wooden desk with its typewriter, the dresser, and the closet. There was no TV. A worn light-brown carpet covered most of the scuffed hardwood floor. The stereo system sat opposite me, its speakers breaking up a long row of albums running the entirety of the floor along the wall. Up above were three sagging wooden shelves filled with books: used hardcovers and paperbacks of differing sizes. A degree from Yale hung framed nearby.

I walked over and examined the turntable. "Prokofiev's 6th" sat silent, its red label encircled by ebony vinyl. I went back to stare at the framed *Paris Review* cover hanging near the door, running the tips of my fingers over the glass and reading Noel's name and the title of his story, "Failing to Fly." Then, I read the page next to it, which started out innocently enough. Did it qualify as personal effects? "Writings," as the telegram specified? I supposed, after some consideration, that it should go back to the family. Still, I thought about keeping it. I could hang it in the living room—part inspiration, part memorial.

I wondered if I would find evidence of Noel's writing beyond the framed cover. The desk was of substantial size and beat-up. Three drawers with old brass pull handles were on the left side all the way to the floor. Another thinner drawer ran along the underside of the desktop. I went over and did a quick opening and closing of the drawers. All were neat and organized, with pencils, a stapler, extra staples in a long narrow box, paper clips, magic markers, postage stamps, envelopes, and a ream of typing paper. The thin top drawer contained a ring of keys with Noel's work picture ID clipped to it. In the photo, Noel wore a beard and looked like an unhappy college professor. The bottom drawer was big and deep, filled with hanging file folders that were marked by labels for utility bills and other business.

I stepped over to the lone window and pulled the cord for the Venetian blind. I raised it as far as it would go, then hooked it in place. This brightened the room considerably. Stepping back, I scanned the expanse of books above the records. Maybe I would pick out a few of the volumes to add to my own limited collection then sell the rest. I would also sell what must have been the several hundred classical albums. After all, the telegram hadn't said anything about books and records.

I walked over to the closet and opened the door. Stepping inside, I pulled the dangling light string, and a bright overhead bulb lit up. All was again exceptionally neat: starched shirts hanging stiffly, pressed pants in a row next to them, shoes and boots in a line along the floor, polished if somewhat worn. It was as if Noel surrounded himself with some outer manifestation of order to mask his inner turmoil. I inspected the clothes I would need to pack. I wondered why his parents wanted them to begin with.

Behind the shirts, an ironing board stood straight up against the wall. A can of spray starch sat visible on the outer edge of a shelf above me. I couldn't get a clear view of the rest of the shelf's contents. Rolling the chair over from its place at the desk, I brought it in for a better look. I clambered onto it, balanced myself precariously with a hand on a wall, and found myself eye-to-eye with a stack of spiral notebooks.

I took the top notebook from its place, flipped open the cover, and examined a page. It was a journal. I carried all of the notebooks to a spot in the middle of the room and placed them on the floor. Sitting cross-legged, I leafed quickly through the most recent journal until I found the entry I was searching for, and I began to read:

April 3rd

I don't know why I did my laundry on the day I decided to die. There, at the all night laundromat down the street, I was alone with my workmanlike motions and pocket full of coins. I have arranged everything: I have obtained the pills from William; I have the fifth of gin, bringing an end to a year of sobriety. It is Gilbey's, which I used to drink daily prior to AA. I do not remember why it became my brand of choice, or even if I particularly liked it. Only that it was affordable and perhaps that alone explains it.

This year as I achieve forty, there is no longer any escaping it. I am an adult, and it is time to be judged as an adult. There are no excuses anymore; I am crushed with despair. At my age, Flaubert had completed "Madame Bovary," Miller had left America behind for Paris, Rimbaud was long dead, and always there was Mozart.

Jesus. A chill ran through me. I returned to the top of the page. "*I don't know why I did my laundry on the day I decided to die.*" I thought about how Noel wrote this while I slept, or perhaps as I talked with Ti. Then, I read the part about me supplying the pills, ripped out the incriminating sheet, folded it up, and stuck it in a pocket.

I plunged into more of the journal entries throughout the afternoon, sensing there was a reason for reading it all. There were poems rich with unusual juxtapositions and striking imagery, fragments of what I guessed to be fiction, and sixteen or so pages of what, as best as I could make out, was an absurdist play starring his father. There were authors read and critiqued: Andre Gide's *Corydon*, Celine's *Rigadoon*, and more prosaically, Fitzgerald's *This Side of Paradise*. There was theater attended and also music: *Dances: Sacred and Profane* by Claude Debussy, other classical works, opera, and jazz.

All of it was written in Noel's neat, artful cursive, other than when he was utterly past the point of control on alcohol before he had achieved sobriety. There were accompanying details of his unhappy days and tortured nights.

Late in the day, after many hours of reading, I came upon Noel addressing "*you, my dear reader.*" That and a reference to future editing made me think the journals were intended to be read, even published. Noel had, after all, left them behind, undestroyed. He must have known someone would discover them, perhaps even wanting them to be found. I had the unnerving thought he planned for that person to be me.

Sensing, finally, the need for a break, I closed the notebook and took a deep breath. After immersion in the journals, my thoughts and feelings no longer felt like my own. Noel's aura shrouded my psyche. Glancing up at the window, I was surprised to see it was dusk. Cat lay patiently beside me, awaiting dinner. I hadn't eaten since breakfast, yet I wasn't hungry. I stood, overcome by an urge to escape the suddenly claustrophobic confines of Noel's bedroom and the journals.

Cat reached the kitchen ahead of me and meowed. I filled his bowl. Throwing on my old thrift-store World War II bomber jacket, I opened the living room door and descended the stairs. Outside, I filled my lungs with the freshness of early evening air and began to walk, my boot heels echoing.

Cars whizzed by me as if slingshotted. A MUNI bus went past like a giant aquarium full of white light, sallow people staring out from its windows. Buildings appeared to be made of cardboard; pedestrians came at me from odd angles; reflections followed me on store windows. My movements felt wooden. I walked uneasily, my head down, anticipating the coming of the night.

I wanted to be invisible.

My mind tried to process what the journals and Noel's suicide imparted about life and death, success and failure, talent and lack of talent. Noel had been smarter than me. Much, in fact. He'd gone to Yale, after all. But even with his superior intelligence and his erudition, Noel was dead, and I was alive. Something intrinsic was not fair about this. I'd passed the suicide test; Noel had not. "We the living," I thought. At least for now. But my hoped-for mentor was gone, and I was complicit in that calamity.

I was walking east. I wanted to see if Manny was home. Why hadn't I thought to call before leaving? Yes, I needed to find Manny for comforting familiarity. For human contact. More simply, for a destination. I laughed out loud at that, and a nicely dressed woman passing by looked at me oddly.

I waited at Van Ness, impatient on the curb. Should I walk against the light? No. Engines revved as cars picked up speed for the charge up the hill. I felt a coldness inside me, despite it not being cold. I shivered. My teeth chattered.

The light changed, and I crossed the boulevard, cutting south and walking the short steep hill up to Polk. There, the level street gave my legs a break. Dodging cars, I crossed against the light. I hiked up the hill on the other side, which was stacked with three-story apartment buildings. Finally, I reached Larkin and turned right. My teeth stopped chattering.

Before Manny's apartment, I thought to first check Café Le Petit. Manny often wrote there; in fact, he almost never wrote at his place. I reached the café and peered into the window. Manny indeed sat at one of the small tables in back. Relieved since I had no alternate plan, I pushed open the door and walked in. Closing the door behind me, I gave the extra pull required, and the cozy warmth of the café enveloped me. I was interrupting Manny and two young women seated at the table next to him. They all smiled and laughed together. I felt as if I'd entered some other world.

I proceeded slowly toward them until Manny spotted me.

"Billy! Ladies, meet my good friend Billy. This is Brigit and—?"

"Miriana," the blond one answered with what I took to be an Italian accent.

I nodded in their direction. I supposed them to be in their very early twenties, if that. Brigit, a pretty brunette, seemed only mildly interested in my arrival. Miriana barely gave me a glance.

"So, what's new, pal?" Manny said expansively.

I sat down next to him, keeping my jacket on, my hands plunged deep into the pockets, slouching low in the chair, my legs spread under the table. "I need to talk to you," I said quietly. It was odd to hear myself speak.

Manny brokered the awkward moment. "Well, we can go for a walk in a bit if you'd like. I was going to make my way over to North Beach. I need to review a triple punk bill at the Mab. The Nuns are headlining." He said that last part louder than he needed to, with a touch of self-importance. Brigit seemed impressed and whispered something to her companion.

"How about a cappuccino?" Manny hinted in a verbal nudge. "Joaquin," he called out, "can you fix up a Cappuccino Royale for my dour friend? Something is making him require a sampling of the best coffee the city has to offer. Put it on my tab."

That was rich. Joaquin played along. "Yes, *Monsieur* Manny," he said, cheerfully. I slouched even lower in my chair.

Joaquin brought the oversized cup, placing it and the latest issue of the *Bay Guardian* before me. "Thanks," I said, sipping at the coffee and pretending to read a film review. It was either that and wait for Manny or get up and leave. That was no choice at all, really. Discreetly scooting my chair away from Manny, I moved out of the social-engagement line of fire. Something by Johnny Hallyday—the "French Elvis"—came from speakers suspended in the ceiling corners. Joaquin and Felix had hung a big poster of him on the wall behind the counter. His blue eyes bore into me, his brown hair combed back handsomely. He wore a jacket like the one James Dean had on in *Rebel Without a Cause*.

Meanwhile, Manny launched into a convoluted tangent about the Justice League of America, focusing on how Wonder Woman came to join the all-male ensemble, reading out-loud snippets from the latest issue of the comic book open before him. He did it with such panache—as if giving a performance on stage, inserting jokes and amusing tidbits referencing superhero mythology—that even I was caught up in it. Hard as I tried not to, I smiled once or twice. As he went on, I read the film review for real, then became increasingly impatient. Finally, after what seemed like forever, the two girls prepared to depart.

"Perhaps you would like to go see some music one enchanted evening?" Manny asked Brigit as she rose. I watched her more closely now. It was impossible not to. She was very pretty and young. She doubtless thought Manny was funny and charming. She said, "Yes. You can reach me at this number," writing on a napkin. Manny smiled, pocketing the treasure as they left the table. Laughing, he called out, "*Au revoir*," and in unison, they responded, "*Ciao*." He turned to me as they gave waves from outside the café and strolled off arm-in-arm.

"San Francisco, it eez such a wonderful zitee," he said. "It is full of chicks. Foreign, domestic, young, beautiful. And since half the good-looking guys are into each other, it is quite the playing field."

"Much more than half," Felix said from behind the register.

"The more the merrier, chum, and the better my odds." Manny turned to me. "Okay, Billy, why so glum?"

"Noel committed suicide."

"You're shitting me!" His black eyebrows furrowed behind the glasses.

"I found him yesterday morning," I said. Then I gave specifics: the Christ-like pose, the classical music, the telegram from his father, me going through Noel's things. I didn't mention the journals or my own unwitting involvement in his death.

When I was finished, Manny said, "But Billy, it was only Noel."

"I found the fucking body. Naked and dead," I said, raising my voice as if that alone would give it meaning, instead of telling him the whole story.

Joaquin brought Manny some soup and French bread on a tray.

"I thought we were leaving," I said, unable to hide my annoyance any longer.

"One must eat, my impatient friend," Manny replied.

"I couldn't help but overhear the tragic news," said Felix. "Here's some food, on the house." He deposited soup and bread in front of me, a sympathetic smile on his face. "And don't worry about the Royale."

"Thanks," I said to him.

"So, what did the body look like?" Manny wanted to know.

"Dead."

"Well, how about a little more than that?"

"Pasty white. Flabby around the middle."

"Guess if you don't hit the gym, dying in the nude is probably not the smartest thing to do," Manny said. "What did his dick look like?"

I shrugged.

"Circumcised or uncircumcised?"

"Uncircumcised."

Manny leaned closer. "I've heard of dead guys with erections."

"I think that's maybe if you hang yourself."

"Not to mention you should be well-hung." Manny laughed, sitting back, his arms folded across his chest. "So, he was play-ing classical music," he continued, regaining his composure given I wasn't laughing. "No suicide note? I would leave a note. Name names: everyone who had done me wrong and driven me to this. Make them feel like shit and personally responsible."

"No suicide note," I said. Never mind that the journals were, in their way, nothing if not one long suicide note.

Manny gathered up his things. There was his large writing note-book and the small one, the comic book, and the thick little stack of notes and phone numbers he always traveled with, wrapped in a rubber band and jammed into a pocket. We got up and said good-bye to Felix and Joaquin. I left my food almost untouched, other than a few token sips of the soup and a bite of the bread.

SIX

Outside, night was falling. The air was cool. A breeze blew in from the bay.

"Where did you park?" Manny wanted to know.

"I'm on foot."

"Really? Well, it's mostly downhill from here, my hapless friend."

Manny and I walked, ready to traverse the remainder of the immense hill that separated us from North Beach. At Hyde Street a cable car rumbled past, its bell clanging. The last of the steep climb was via a pedestrian stairway cutting a narrow, zigzagging swath skyward between backyard fences, garden walls, and small apartment buildings.

As we navigated the concrete steps single-file, I pulled up my jacket collar against the cool night air. Where the steps came to a little cobblestone square, I stopped and took a joint and a book of matches from my jacket pocket. To light up, I had to escape the breeze, so I stepped into the doorway of one of the small buildings bracketing the square on two sides. I took big puffs, the joint palmed and burning out of sight when not between my lips.

Manny leaned against a low brick wall enclosing the small square, his back to the bay. He perused the *Justice League* comic under an old-fashioned streetlight, the glowing glass orb mounted on a pedestal a few feet above his head. I smoked and thought how I had done nothing about the writing. How I was going to have to deal with finding a new roommate. Between that and the store likely closing by the end of summer, I was screwed. Plus, there was the perilous state of my finances to begin with, always threatening to push the whole off-kilter mess completely over the edge. Just as I finally established some sort of stability, it was coming down like a house of cards.

I walked over to Manny. "Hit?"

"No thanks."

The little square had a view between the buildings. As I stood next to Manny, I looked to the west and the north at the lights coming on below us. The setting sun was almost completely gone behind the Golden Gate Bridge, with its airplane warning beacons blinking red.

"So, what are you going to do?" Manny said, his eyes still on the comic book.

"About what?"

"The apartment."

"Are you kidding? Keep it."

"But isn't it going to be kind of weird living where somebody offed himself just across the living room?"

I wondered sometimes if Manny wanted me to fail.

"You know how hard it is to find a decent place in the city," I said.

"Yeah, another week on my couch and I would have had to start charging you rent."

"Escaping stagnation in Berkeley was a major victory." I took another hit off the joint.

"Dashed youthful revolutionary dreams die hard. 'Power to the people,' sis-boom-bah!"

"Those were different times," I said, exhaling.

"I'll say, firebombing the—"

"Hey! Don't ever talk about that!"

"Geez, sorry. Cone of silence."

"Besides, nobody got hurt."

I took another hit. I was barely holding them in now.

"Noel left behind a stack of journals in his closet," I announced. "I found them when I started going through his things for his parents."

There. It was out.

"And?" Manny said, handling the comic book gingerly, as if it were a rare artifact, his palm and fingers spread under it, making sure not to crease a page. "God," he said, "this artwork is amazing."

"They're really intense," I said. "I think—" I wasn't sure how to explain it to Manny. It was a mistake to bring it up. He stood there, leafing through the comic book, barely paying attention.

"Finding a new roommate is going to be a hassle," I said instead. "I'm tempted to avoid it until the rent is due. God, it's so great to have your own place."

"Tell me about it. Charlie's shooting China White. I'd like to figure out a way to get rid of him if he doesn't manage to do it himself. Hey, do you suppose if they added some more contemporary superheroes to the League, it would create a fan backlash?"

"You know," I said, "if Aquaman drowned tomorrow, nobody would give a shit."

"He can't drown. He—"

"Yes, of course, Manny. Besides each and every member of the Justice League and assorted super-pals is essential to the survival of American pop culture as we know it."

"Exactly."

"Bring back fucking Captain Marvel!"

"Shazam!"

I laughed. I didn't want to fight with Manny.

"Let's go," I said.

We began to climb the last of the stairway to the crest of the hill looming above us. I inhaled from what was left of the joint as we walked, a huge lung-sucking-from-deep-inside-fill-it-up-completely toke, holding it in as long as I could while we hiked the final steps. At last, I exhaled, lightheaded, smiling with the body rushes that were likely propelled as much by oxygen deprivation as they were by the mediocre weed.

"Geez, you are quite the doper tonight, Billy. Once a hippie, always a hippie."

I turned for a final look at the view behind us. The Pacific—normally dominating the horizon during the day, allowing you to even catch sight of the rocky outposts of the Farallon Islands on an exceptionally clear morning—was now a mass of blackness beyond the city lights.

"Watch out, Billy. Next step is the big H."

"You do coke."

"Yes, I do. And pot on occasion. Mostly to lure the ladies. Drugs can be veritable pheromones. But I refuse to spend any coin on them."

I put out the remains of the joint against the sole of my boot. Retrieving the matchbook from my pocket, I placed the roach snugly inside, between the cardboard base and the bottom of the soft cover. Closing the matchbook, I returned it to my jacket pocket as we continued walking down to North Beach. Coit Tower rose opposite us on Telegraph Hill, glowing ivory in its bath of spotlights.

"You know," I said. "The one and only time I ever went into Coit Tower was when Honey and I first came to California. There were these floor-to-ceiling social-realism murals on the lobby walls. Images of daily life in San Francisco back in the 1930s. And there was this door that wasn't locked. We sneaked in and found narrow stairs winding upward. The walls around us were covered in more murals, ones that had been hidden from public view for years. As we climbed, we saw this Powell Street fresco full of people on their hill alongside us. There was this family and a little girl staring right at me—"

"Ever the art enthusiast, huh, Billy?"

I chose to ignore Manny and remembered how Honey and I had made it to the top of the stairs and found three small rooms filled with yet more murals. Some depicted children and families, and there was one with a deer in a peaceful meadow. Honey and I hugged and kissed as if enchanted, as if we'd found paradise in San Francisco after our cross-country journey together in Kozmic. Then, Honey reached up and whispered into my ear, like it was the most truthful thing she had ever said in her life: "*Honey and Billy forever.*" I wanted to believe it. I wanted to trust in it, and for a time, I did. But in the end, it was just a sucker's Shangri-La.

Manny and I walked in silence as we continued our descent. Finally, I spoke. "I cried for the first couple hundred miles of the New York Thruway after I dropped Honey off back at her mother's."

Manny appeared surprised that I'd shared that. On a normal night, I wouldn't have. Somehow, it was because of Noel and the journals.

"Why?" he said.

"I was in love. And it was over."

We connected into Columbus Avenue. Crossing and turning right, we strolled past small restaurants spewing young couples onto the sidewalk. Sometimes, a maître d beckoned at a doorway like a strip club barker. I'd barely eaten anything all day and felt gaunt inside, yet still had no appetite. Manny stopped as we reached Caffé Roma.

"Wanna go in?"

"I'm not sure what I want to do."

"Well, my stoned latter-day hippie friend, I'm supposed to meet Shelley. Take her over to the Mab. That's why I didn't follow up immediately with Brigit back at Café Le Petit. Ah, juggling the endless female possibilities. A tiring, but at the same time, most enjoyable task. It is my duty, my cross to bear in life, my *tres grand bur-done*," he said with dramatic mock puffery, bringing a fist to his chest with a flourish. Even as he did so, he glanced through the large plate glass café window, presumably for potential women to chat up before Shelley arrived.

"You're welcome to join us at the Mab," he added. "I think can get you in for free."

"Thanks. I don't know." We milled at the entrance.

"Hey, any chance you could spare a lude? For Shelley."

"Okay." I gave him the only one on me.

"Thanks. You're a pal."

"Maybe I'll see you at the club," I said.

"Look for your name at the door. Meanwhile, if in your current state, you find God or some reasonable facsimile, be sure to let me know. Or, Billy, think of San Francisco as Oz." With a sweeping motion, he indicated the city shining around us. "You're off to see the Wizard. If you find him, tell him what you're missing." He chuckled and slapped me hard on the shoulder.

I couldn't think of a rejoinder, so I left him with a mumbled "see you later." I continued along Columbus, turning back to observe Manny through the window as he smiled at a young guy behind the café counter. Sometimes, I was jealous of his embracing all human contact, not just women. I wondered what kept me from being like that.

At Broadway, I crossed with the crowd, then entered City Lights Books, passing through the main room with its novels of the moment, browsing tourists, and perishable magazines in their racks. I walked into the little room beyond it, climbing the wooden staircase you almost had to know was there to find it, ascending to the Beat collection. There, I came upon two guys and a girl by herself.

They were reading. It was peaceful. I gazed at the woman. She was of uncertain age, perhaps slightly older than me, with glasses and long, thick, brown hair. She sat on a chair, appearing engrossed in the book open in her lap, unaware of the males in the room.

I went to the shelf housing *Go*. There were three copies. There were always three copies. I found the one with the top right-hand page corner turned down. I began reading where I'd left off, sitting cross-legged on the floor. Jack Kerouac, only half-hidden behind a pseudonym, declared that people should walk around naked.

The two guys in the room left, their shoes clunking against the bare wooden stairs. The woman hadn't moved. I wondered what her story was. Glancing up, she caught me staring, and I immediately looked back down at the page before me.

Paul Hobbes—*Go* author John Clellon Holmes' own alias— gave his apartment key to Kerouac's character so the latter and a girl could consummate their passion. I wondered about Ti and what she was doing. Should I call her? No, she would get in touch soon enough. Then, I thought of Constantina. That was odd. We barely knew each other, yet she came to mind. And always there was Lannie and her frustrating elusiveness.

I sat and persevered through the book for a while, eventually skipping ahead and finding that Allen Ginsberg's namesake confessed his homosexuality to his father with predictably hostile results. I went back to where I was supposed to be.

Finally, I called a halt to it. Under the influence of the pot, my eyes were weary. The lighting in the room felt too bright. I folded the top corner of the page and got up, my legs a bit stiff, my ass sore. As I put the book back on the shelf, I realized the woman had somehow slipped out. I perused the other volumes on the shelves, noting titles. They had everything Kerouac wrote, even an obscure publication of *And the Hippos Were Boiled in Their Tanks*, his early collaboration with William Burroughs. Then I headed down the stairs.

I didn't want to go to the Mab with its noise and its crowd. Instead, I turned right, crossed the alley and went into Vesuvio for a drink. Once inside, I looked around at the gloomy interior, the Tiffany lamps, the former hipsters going gray. I changed my mind. Back outside, I was annoyed I didn't have Kozmic parked nearby. I could call Asher and go score some more ludes in Berkeley. Instead, I faced the long walk back to the apartment alone.

Turning left at Broadway, I passed a couple strip clubs, including one that boasted a man and a woman performing simulated sex acts. Next came some stores and restaurants marking the northernmost fringes of Chinatown, the sidewalks a crowded racial mix as people with purpose hurried places. I wondered if I should just turn back and go to the Mab? I stood there, not moving, people pushing around me, sometimes bumping into me. I wished I'd taken the Quaalude instead of giving it to Manny. I wished I had a girl with me. I wished Noel was still alive back at the apartment. Most of all, I wished I'd never sold him the pills.

2

SEVEN

By the time I parked Kozmic around the corner from Aquarius Shirts, it was almost 10:20 AM. Abe, the old guy who ran Flower Power next door, was unloading a shipment of fresh roses from his white Ford Econoline van. I called over a hello, but he either didn't hear or ignored me.

Miranda always said Abe was a grouch. She called him "the *tsoris* next doorus" and told me not to pay any attention to him. After she explained that "*tsoris*" was Yiddish for "pain in the ass," she went on to give me some specifics. They had a dispute over who was responsible for taking care of the large metal trash basket out front. The city emptied it once a week, which wasn't often enough. A couple days before the garbage truck rolled by, the trash basket would be filled to overflowing, spilling onto the sidewalk. Every time the city emptied the trash basket, they put it in front of Abe's flower shop, near the corner. As the week progressed, it mysteriously migrated to a spot in front of the T-shirt store, just in time to overflow. We got stuck with going out periodically, picking things up, and trying to stuff them back in.

As I turned onto Haight Street to open up, I passed the trash basket, which was only half-full and still close to the corner. A grumpy-looking Deadhead awaited me at the entrance to the store. "You're supposed to be open at ten, man," he said. Once inside, he plunked his money down for three *Mars Hotel* silk-screened T-shirts. I rang up two and pocketed the cash for the third.

After the Deadhead departed, I retrieved the broom and began sweeping. I started behind the polished wood counter, pushing dust and errant price tags ahead of me. The counter made an L-turn and ended a dozen feet further at the dressing room, which looked like a wooden outdoor shower stall with a green curtain across it.

Sweeping around the L-turn, I arrived where the countertop lifted up in front of the bulky iron-on decal heat press. I dodged the long metal handle that brought the two halves together to attach rubbery decals to shirts. The press serviced mostly tourists and some students too foolish to not buy one of the more expensive, genuine Kelley-Mouse silk-screened shirts that could last for years. My favorite was a T-shirt with hard-to-read psychedelic lettering across the front. Only if you looked really closely could you figure out that maybe it said, "FUCK."

The decals did offer a wide assortment of pictures of the Golden Gate Bridge and of the San Francisco skyline with the Transamerica pyramid featured prominently. One was an imitation R. Crumb cartoon of a wasted hippie sitting against a wall below lettering that read, "I Was Groovy in Haight Ashbury." It was the store's second biggest seller. The biggest seller was a picture of the famous connected-at-right-angles Haight and Ashbury street signs. The real signs should have been visible a couple blocks away, but they had been stolen so often the city had given up on them.

Raising the top of the counter, I swept the little pile of debris toward the door, where, after a check to make sure Abe wasn't watching, I would send it flying out onto the sidewalk. Rudy— owner of Feed Your Head, the shop on the other side of Aquarius

Shirts—could care less. I regularly sold him Quaaludes cheap; in return, he gave me my pipe and kept me supplied with free screens, rolling paper, and incense.

As I neared the door with the broom, Ti marched in. "Hi, hi, hi!" she announced.

"Hey! Nice to see you," I said.

"Like my new haircut? Carlos cut it for free!" She did a little spin for me to see. The close-cropped red hair, shorter now, made the freckles on her face more prominent, and the tightness of her top emphasized the smallness of her breasts, her jeans the boyishness of her hips.

"Very Jean Seberg," I said, pausing in my sweeping.

"Who?"

"Never mind."

She pulled a scone out of her handbag. "I brought something sweet for my sweetie." She placed the scone and a napkin on the counter. "I also brought you a nice, healthy organic sandwich from the restaurant." She set it on the counter as well.

"Thanks."

"How come no music?" she wanted to know, nodding at the small shelf where the radio sat silent.

"I was about to read before things got too busy."

"Read what?" She stretched over the counter, checking underneath where she knew I put my things.

"*Steppenwolf.*"

"Oh, I've heard of it. It's by that guy, what's his name?" She picked up the worn paperback from its place atop a copy of *The Dharma Bums*. "Hess?"

"Hess-*eh*."

"What's it about?"

"Alienation from bourgeois society. Internal confusion. Suicide. Maybe you should read more."

"Well, ex-*cuse* me! Much as that sounds like a blast. I do read, you know. My mother had most everything Frank Yerby wrote. Ever read *The Saracen Blade?*"

"No. But it's hardly the same thing," I said, jettisoning the debris out the door with the broom.

"You seem awfully subdued," she said. "Something up?"

"Sometimes life throws you a curve."

"You mean Noel?"

"You know?"

"Miranda told me when I came by with your coffee that day. Tried to call you at the apartment, but you never picked up."

Ti placed the book on the counter and walked over to me, blocking my path as I held the broom upright before me. She put her arms around my waist, the stiffness of the broom between us. "Frank Yerby was my porn when I was ten," she said. "Whatcha doin' tonight? Maybe I can cheer you up."

I was struck by the beauty of her bright blue eyes gazing up at me. There were moments when she really was quite exquisite, her aggressiveness appealing.

"Whatcha got in mind?" I said.

"Dinner at a nice restaurant one of these nights?"

"I don't know. Kind of expensive."

"Well, how about lude-treats and another foray into clubland?"

"Okay," I found myself saying. It was hard to resist when they made the first move, when they made it easy. "Pick you up at your place?" I felt things getting lighter inside me, the day changing.

"I'm working dinner, love. How about we meet at Adriano's? Like about eleven. Then, we can go over to Dance Your Ass Off. Or maybe Buzzby's."

"Okay, it's a deal." Truthfully, I would rather not meet at Adriano's. She'd never gone until, foolishly, I took her one night.

Now, she showed up any time she wanted, with or without me. That they were lazy about carding only encouraged her.

"Perhaps you might even have some fairy dust?"

"I think we can probably come up with something."

"Works for me, dahhhling," she said brightly. "Now, I have to go meet Delaney—I mean Karen. God! It's so confusing! We're supposed to have coffee before my lunch shift. She promised to let me touch her boob job. The swelling's gone down. Maybe someday I'll get one and stop looking like a boy, or do you prefer me that way? Ta-ta!"

She headed for the door, turning around to blow me a kiss. Walking backwards, she tripped and fell on her ass. She let out a yelp, covering her mouth with a palm, making as if embarrassed.

"Oops!" she said, getting her feet. "Hey, listen, I just had a thought. Maybe we can move in with you! Karen can rent Noel's room." She turned and, with a bounce to her step, paraded up the sidewalk.

A bit later, I took my lunch break, flipping around the sign on the door after setting its clock hands to 1:00 PM. I walked along Haight Street, which was broad and spacious with a jumble of architecture, some of it old and fancy even if a bit faded and in need of new coats of paint. There was a string of rudimentary one-story commercial structures where the T-shirt store was located, but that changed to two and three-story wood-appointed buildings at intersections. Those had a distinctive, quasi-Victorian character, with ornate facades and bay windows above the storefronts.

I negotiated sidewalks that were increasingly crowded with street vendors and pedestrians as I got closer to Golden Gate Park. At Cole, I passed the Dog Lady, her three unfortunate little black mutts tugging at the end of their frayed ropes. I felt sorry for the animals and made my way into Raffe's.

"Here," the girl serving my cappuccino said with a smile. She was young, perhaps a student. I took my coffee and walked over to Manny who was seated at a table by a window with a sidewalk view. He glanced up from whatever he was working on, a sheaf of typewritten pages beside him. Smiling over to the counter girl, he toasted her with his glass of café mocha, licking his lips and mouthing, "Yum-yum, good!"

She smiled back at him.

"How's life in the world of T-shirts?" he asked as I sat down.

"Miranda still asks about you."

"Yeah, well, the less said. Just be glad you got a job out of it." He took a sip of his coffee and added, "You just missed Ti and her pal Karen."

"Oh. Too bad."

"That Karen's quite the little minx, if you like them a tad on the butchy side. Her nose stud is kinda cool—as long as it doesn't snag on something during sex. Anyway, I think she's more into the sisterhood. The Manny charm seems to incinerate upon contact. Did get her laughing at one point with a titty joke at Ti's expense."

I searched for something to say. The subject of Ti made me uncomfortable. Just then, two women walked by outside. A short, pretty brunette wearing a Judy Chicago flower-vagina T-shirt, and a taller, plainer female with a T-shirt that read, "So Many Women, So Little Time."

"Do you think they can be converted?" Manny said with a nod towards the cute brunette and her friend as they continued out of sight. "Ti once told me I unleashed her first orgasm ever from a man."

"That must have been very flattering," I said, evenly.

"Read the *Kama Sutra* when I was twelve. Learned a thing or two. Though the illustrations were a bit strange. All the wangs looked like curved bananas."

Manny removed his beret and, using the window as a mirror, primped his curly black hair with an Afro-Pick. "Mine is straight as an arrow," he added as if explaining something I should know. "Speaking of which, how's it going with Lannie?"

"Well, we still just got it on that one time."

"Congrats, pal. Although I must admit, I do insist on at least a little personality in my women. And brains are a definite plus."

I stumbled around for the right words. "She's not so bad. She's really attractive and a sharp dresser." Realizing how shallow that sounded, I quickly added, "Besides, we go way back, and it's nice to take it to another level."

"True. But when all is said and done—especially done, as in talking—she lacks that spark in those baby blues of hers."

"Brown."

"Myself, I like a touch of the scamp and some ability at verbal repartee. I find an impish quality most endearing."

"But you'd sleep with her."

"Who?" Manny was staring past me. I turned to look as a girl in Birkenstocks and a flowing batik dress walked past.

"Lannie."

"Oh. Not while you're hot for her. Male bonding and all that."

"I appreciate it."

"Listen, I need to give this one more read, pal," and he picked up the sheaf of typewritten pages.

I sipped my coffee and gazed around at fresh-faced college students, radicals and revolutionaries, miscellaneous longhairs, and an older black guy with a stringy goatee who wore a dashiki and wrote on a yellow legal pad.

"Maybe I *will* do her," Manny said without looking up.

"I don't think that's funny," I said.

"Yeah, it would be pretty low, pal, wouldn't it?"

The edge to his voice made me wonder if he knew about Ti, or if he was referring to one of the others.

"Enough of this chit-chat," Manny said to my relief. "Let me tell you what I've written so far." He sat straight in his chair, holding the typed pages up in front of him, his voice rising as he commenced a punchy read.

"The Nuns can be best summed up by two songs performed at their packed Mabuhay Gardens show, 'Suicide Child' and 'Decadent Jew.' The former poignantly laments the death of a girlfriend, only to obliterate mawkish sentiment with a punishing chorus: 'You slit your wrist. You, fucking bitch!'"

Manny paused, looking to me. I nodded. He continued: "As blond chanteuse Jennifer Miro—a punk-meets-beatnik art-goddess—chunks out the chords on her Farfisa organ, the Nuns dropkick the Fab Mab crowd with 'Decadent Jew.'"

Manny chuckled.

"It's a performance done with tongue firmly planted in cheek—not to overlook Miro's sardonic solo turn on 'I'm Lazy (Too Lazy to Look for Love),' a Nico reincarnate moment if ever there was one. The Nuns remain, along with the Avengers, at the top of this reviewer's list of the most exciting new Bay Area bands."

Manny looked to me, questioningly.

"Absolutely. Nails it. Love the 'Nico reincarnate' line."

"Yeah, gotta say I think I'm pretty happy with it. There's more, but you get the drift. You sure about the Nico thing? Is it a mistake to put them, even by implication, in the same league as the Velvets? Am I setting them up for some sort of audience over-expectations? I mean, after all, Lou and the gang are the Godhead."

"But Nico isn't."

"Good point. And quickly gone from the band with the passing of Warhol's puppetry. So, you don't think it's too laudatory?"

"No. At their best, they're terrific."

"You're right, Billy. As usual. I'm dropping it off at *San Francisco Lifestyle*."

"Where exactly are their offices?"

"Just over on Ashbury at Oak. Wouldn't be schlepping over here on city buses for my health you know," he said with an almost a patrician sniff, glancing around the room. "Hanging out with the hippie *hoi polloi* and Haight-Ashbury acid casualties. Although select hippie chicks are not without appeal." He looked over at the girl behind the counter. "Young Heather being a case in point."

"She just start?"

"Yep. Pure as the wind-driven snow. Down from Oregon and falling hard for the Manny charm." He caught her eye. With a grin, he pantomimed a downward motion with his hand, mouthing, "The fifties go *under* the cash drawer."

She smiled back.

"Is she a student?" I asked, and I thought how it was like we were back in the college cafeteria, eyeing the incoming freshman class for prospects.

"Only of life. Though she's thinking about attending Cal Arts in the fall."

"What happened to Mary?"

"You mean my former muse? She still works, mostly weekends."

"By the way, who do you turn your articles into?"

"Ed Bernstein, the editor. Why? What's up, pal?"

"I was wondering if you could give me an intro. You know, I did a little writing in school."

"Yes, for that alternative campus rag, what was the name?"

"*Up Against the Wall, Motherfucker.*"

"Yeah." Manny laughed. "I remember that hilarious article they ran on Radical Chic. All that stuff about new blue jeans and crisp work shirts, factory boots and berets. The whole uniformity of your fellow upper-middle-class, suburban, supposedly rebel-lious ones, and their sloganeering buttonmania. Now, berets are less about 'Che' and more about 'Chez,'" he said, adjusting his own beret via the reflection in the window.

"And the only buttonmania is bandmania," I said, pointing to the Flamin' Groovies button on the Triumph motorcycle T-shirt that peeked out from Manny's black leather jacket. Manny peered down at his button with its picture of the band. "The new Mods already, Billy. Ever more pop culture recycling is upon us. At this rate, we should have a rebirth of acid-rock by next month."

I laughed appreciatively.

"Anyway, do you have something in mind you want to write about?"

"Maybe," I said.

"Ah, playing it close to the vest. A caution that band reviews are my turf, pal."

★ ★ ★

That night, I stood in Noel's room and pondered the daunting task before me. I'd brought half-a-dozen cardboard boxes from the store to start the job of packing up his things. The boxes sat empty and scattered around the room. I would need to confirm a date with Noel's father and how shipping was to be handled. I was surprised I hadn't heard anything further from him. But it had only been a few days, and frankly, I was in no rush. I was still making my way through the journals, and if I decided to send them along to the family, I wanted to finish reading them first.

Noel's typewriter sat in its place on his desk. Originally, I'd thought about selling it. Now, as I considered, I decided it would come in handy for my own efforts. For the moment, I would leave it in its place.

I pushed one of the two nightstands from Noel's room into mine. It replaced the orange-colored plastic crate, which now became the stand for my old black-and-white TV with its small screen, freeing the stack of books that had been supporting it. The books joined the others on their cinderblock-and-wood shelf.

Back in Noel's room, I picked up a journal, made my way through its pages, and read one of his poems. It made me wonder about his family. There wasn't much to go on in the journals. He had a sister, Evangeline, but it was clear he detested her. His relationship with his father was, by all appearances, turbulent; his mother was barely mentioned, a furtive shadow.

I walked back into my bedroom, grabbed the glass from the closet, and mixed one-part vodka to two-parts Kahlua. I went into the kitchen to add some milk and a couple ice cubes. Returning to my room, I took a half-lude with the White Russian, and put on a Roxy Music album, playing it loud and with both doors open, enjoying the freedom of my new solitude. I sang along to "Out of the Blue," even doing a little dancing and air guitar.

Then, I made my usual preparations for the night: pills in their container into the front pocket of my denim jacket, along with a couple condoms, a book of matches, and two pre-rolled joints, plus my little coke vial sequestered in a side pocket of my pants. I already had on my jewelry, rings on four of my fingers, and I added my silver turquoise bracelet. Heading into the bathroom, I brushed the tangles out of my hair and secured it into a ponytail.

EIGHT

Constantina gave me a little wave from across the main room at Adriano's. Her younger brother Alexander sat next to her on the couch. If you didn't look closely, you could mistake him for the woman: lips covered in coral lipstick, cheeks heavy with rouge, lids thick with eye shadow, his long hair teased. I had the thought perhaps Constantina didn't wear makeup because the competition was too stiff.

Ti sat on the other side of Alexander, engaging him in animated conversation, as yet unaware of my arrival. Beside her was Karen, dressed in black, looking supremely bored. Now that I knew the truth about Karen, I was intrigued, even if she was sullen, her face surprisingly tough for one so young.

I gave Constantina a discreet wave back and slipped into the other half of the room, separated immediately from the four of them by the shoulder-high partition running the length of the space. I wondered how long it would take for Ti to find me. I'd arrived early, hoping for time first without her, flush with a fresh supply of pills from Asher and ready to do business.

Carlos motioned me over to where he sat alone at a table, a cocktail glass in front of him.

"Let me buy you a drink," he offered as I pulled up a seat. "David and Monique should be here soon."

"I noticed Constantina," I said, taking a pretzel from the bowl in front of us.

"Word to the wise: Not worth the hassle," Carlos said and nudged me with an elbow, adding, "But that Ti's a fox, not to mention fun in the sack."

I didn't react, making as if I already knew this piece of unwelcome information about the two of them.

"Hey, can you deal me a half-dozen?" he asked.

"I can only spare a couple, and the price has doubled."

He frowned. "Spotted a couple narcs in here earlier," he said.

"You sure?"

"Yep. Two plainclothes cops trying to blend in."

"Shit."

"Yeah. Better watch yourself."

I glanced around, but it was only the usual crowd. I took the pill container from my jacket pocket, shook out two of the white tablets into my palm below table level and passed them to him. Carlos slipped me the cash.

A cocktail waitress breezed over. "I'm Gina, and I'll be your server." She was healthy looking, with a tan and bright teeth.

"Did anyone ever tell you that you look like Lauren Bacall?" Carlos asked.

"Actually, they usually say Charlotte Rampling," Gina replied dryly, making me like her immediately. "What can I bring you gentlemen?"

"I'll take another gin and tonic," said Carlos. "Bombay."

"Rum gimlet," I said.

Carlos nodded in my direction. "You and Billy must buy your clothes at the same place." He said it as if we were in competition for her already, making a put-down to knock me out of contention.

Taking in my tight, dark-blue stretch top mirroring her own, Gina said, "Then he's got good taste." For good measure, she added, "I like your bracelet, Billy. That looks like Arizona turquoise."

"Thanks. It is."

"Be back soon," she said.

I turned and watched her go.

"Listen, anytime you get more ludes, I'll take them off your hands," Carlos said. "I'll match or beat what anyone else is paying. My clients at the salon are always asking."

"I'll do what I can."

"I'm gonna hold you to that. Now, I need to hit the john." Carlos stood up, took off his brushed denim jacket, and placed it over the back of his chair. A black bolo tie ran through a silver clasp, set against the white of his shirt that was buttoned at the collar and tucked into the brushed denim jeans—the other half of his suit. He wasn't sturdy on his feet.

As he left, I surveyed the room. The furniture was a mix of small square tables and large round ones, with a scattering of couches and armchairs. Ferns hung in pots above the twin, large plate-glass windows on either side of the entrance. Tiffany lamps and quasi-macho kitsch adorned the walls. There were framed reproductions of posters from long forgotten boxing matches, early-1900s black-and-white posed photographs of onetime local luminaries, and a pair of purloined Haight and Ashbury street signs suspended from the ceiling.

Fat Stan sat at his usual place on a plush red couch in a corner, his long gray hair combed past his collar, his skin appearing jaundiced. Rumor had it he kept a fountain pen filled with coke in the inside pocket of the brown leather trench coat he never removed, and that he shared it with boys as well as girls. Johnny Starr sat close to him, looking like a young Keith Richards in black leather pants, striped jacket, scarf—the whole nine yards.

Spencer and Zora walked over from the direction of the bar. They carried bottles of beer and sat down on either side of me.

"Can you do us some?" Spencer asked.

"How many?"

"Four, two for the each of us," Zora said, smoking a cigar barely larger than a cigarette.

"What are you guys up to?" I said as I gave Spencer the pills, charging the regular amount, keeping an eye on the room.

Zora tilted herself towards me, her wrist hung with bracelets, her arms tattooed, her breasts spilling out of a black V-top. "We're on the prowl for the yowl."

"Well, those should get you yowling."

She gave a harsh laugh and got up.

"See you later, Billy," Spencer said, also getting up. "Got a gig coming up next week at the Keystone. You should come by. I'll put you on the list."

"Cool. Maybe I'll do that."

The two of them headed over to Johnny Starr and Fat Stan.

Gina returned with my rum gimlet and Carlos' drink. "Your friend has had a few," she said. "He keeps telling me what a big-time stylist he is and trying to get my phone number. Says he'll cut my hair for free."

"Actually," I said, "he's more of an acquaintance."

I paid her for my drink, held out a lude between my thumb and forefinger as a tip.

"Thanks!" she said, and I pressed it into her palm. It was hard to take her friendliness as much of anything as she moved on to another table with her tray of drinks. But it felt good, and I could believe it meant something more.

I heard the jingle of the bell mounted above the front door that announced each new arrival. I turned to see if it was Nick James coming for his pills. Instead, Lannie made her entrance in a swirl of smiling sensuality. She strutted into the room in high-heeled black leather boots, skin-tight jeans, an emerald green satin top, and a black velvet form-fitting jacket open to the waist. Her long brown hair hung straight and glistened, a purple beret perched rakishly on her head. She was alone but wouldn't be for long.

I wished I didn't have Carlos returning to the table. I was sure he'd been dying to screw her for months. Being a hairdresser with his own salon gave him a legitimate career to dangle in front of women. Gina might not care, but others certainly did. There was also the matter of my date with Ti.

Lannie spotted someone she knew and stopped. I stood to check who it was over the partition. I saw a guy I didn't recognize and a woman, apparently his girlfriend or a date. Lannie bent over, chatting, not sitting. The guy obviously wanted her to stay; the girl appeared surly.

Then, Lannie was on the move, breezing through the room. Male heads turned; my pulse quickened. Lannie called, "Hey, everybody!" to Zora, Johnny, and Spencer. Ti wasn't looking in my direction, so I gave Lannie a wave, but she didn't see me. Passing Ti and the others on the couch, she headed for the bar in back, and I felt like a bit of an ass standing there. I covered my drink with a napkin and walked in her direction.

Out of the corner of my eye, I could see Ti, her back turned to me, the gesticulation of pale hands. Her brash laugh cut through the din as she talked with Alexander and Karen. Constantina tapped a cigarette against her antique silver case, eyeing me.

"Hello, you," I said to Lannie, coming up behind her as I heard the words "on the house" from Jerry the bartender.

"Billy!" she said. "Where can we sit down? Do you have a table?"

"Sure." I pointed, and she followed, snagging her drink. Turning to check that Ti hadn't spotted me, I caught Jerry giving me a dirty look as I pulled out a chair for Lannie. She thanked me and sat down. I saw Constantina, Ti, Alexander, and Karen get up and head for the rear exit and the alley running behind the building. Relieved they were leaving, I sat next to Lannie, turned to face her, and removed the napkin covering my drink.

"You know, I was hoping to find you here," she said. "Wade wants me to move back in with him. I don't know what to do." She said this with her earnest intensity, ripe with naivete and girlish charm, as if desperate for the advice she would surely follow this time.

"Well, you need to make that decision," I said non-committedly. The silver glitter in the makeup on her eyelids sparkled before me.

"But I don't know what to do!"

"You only just got your own place and your new job."

"Yes, and they love me at I. Magnin! And I can get designer clothes for a third off. It's *so* cool! Maybe I can make this job last for a while!"

"If you can avoid temptation."

"Yes, Billy. Gosh, the clothes are *so* gorgeous, and I have been *so* tempted. But I've been good." She smiled at me, aware that I knew how effortlessly and often she lied.

"So, do you have anything?" she said as she polished off her drink. "Boy, I would die for a lude."

The bell over the door jingled, and Nick James came in with his girlfriend Summer. I saw them head for the bar.

Gina came over to take Lannie's drink order. It was as if Gina and I knew each other now and shared something unspoken. I was glad she was seeing me with someone so attractive. Lannie asked her for a glass of white wine. Gina left, and I turned my attention to Lannie who reached for her purse, then applied bright red lipstick to her mouth, looking into a small hand mirror. She brought her lips together the way women do, her breasts dangling against her sheer top. Memories of our night together flooded back.

"Do you have plans?" I asked as vaguely as I could manage.

"For tonight? Not really. I just want to forget about my un-appreciating boyfriend."

Her wine arrived. She made a motion to go to her purse, but I paid. Gina received two ones as a tip and said, "Thank you, Billy." Lannie gave her a closer look this time.

Carlos returned and sat down. "Lannie," he said, "You look lovely tonight." To me he said, "Did you already pay for my drink?"

"No, she's coming back." Leaning in close to Lannie, her per-fume in my nostrils, I whispered into an ear. "I have ludes with me. And coke. First, I need to do a little business in the other room. Would you like to keep me company?"

She positively beamed. "Of course."

We picked up our drinks, said goodbye to Carlos, and walked around the partition. A couple was vacating a small table near the front door, and I moved fast to secure it, Lannie trailing. We sat down, Nick James came over, and we did the transaction as he crouched next to me. "Thanks," he said, adding, "I could use some lids for the guys at the house."

"How many?"

"A half-dozen."

"Sure. Come by the store, or else my place." Then, I introduced him to Lannie. We chatted for a few minutes before he returned to Summer at the bar.

I broke a 714 down the scored line in the middle. I was feeling really good, operating right out in the open, buzzed on the half-lude I'd taken before I left the apartment. I gave Lannie a half. She looked disappointed. But with the outcome of the evening still unclear, it made sense to limit her.

Lannie popped the half into her mouth, drinking some wine with it.

"Trust me," I said, "you should wait. You can have the other half later." I placed it in my jacket pocket.

She stuck out her tongue. "Do I get a reward for behaving myself? Or do you?"

I chuckled and said nothing, thinking how I needed to find a way out of my date with Ti. Lannie took another sip of wine, finishing off the glass. The room around us swelled with conversation and music, enveloping us. Perhaps I should simply get up and leave with her? Make up some excuse later to Ti?

"Do you want to go do some coke?" I asked.

Lannie smiled and stood, and I did likewise. I had her right where I wanted her, which also happened to be right where she wanted to be. The bell jingled, and the front door flew open. A giggling Ti and grinning Alexander barged through, upon us immediately, Constantina and Karen close behind. Constantina passed without breaking stride. Karen hesitated, gave me an annoyed look, and followed her.

"Billy!" Ti said, standing arm-in-arm with Alexander. "I've been wondering where you were. Are you ready to go over to Dance Your Ass Off? I've already found some fairy dust!" Alexander smiled at me and broke free of her, weaving on red high heels as he runwayed the room. I turned my attention back to Ti who stood before me, her hands on her hips. Lannie remained next to me, wearing a frozen smile.

"So, Billy, who's your friend?" Ti said.

"Ti, this is Lannie."

"Nice to meet you," Lannie said, appearing unsure of herself as the two of them stood toe to toe. Lannie was several inches taller and, in her boots, taller still—not to mention almost a decade older. But Ti held her ground.

"Weren't we just leaving?" Ti asked me.

Lannie's face turned hard. "See you, Billy," she said, and she spun around and walked off toward the bar.

"Bye," Ti called after her. Placing an arm through mine, she waved after Lannie with the other. The door jingled behind us as Ti pulled me outside. I tried to tell myself it was a plus in the long run for Lannie to see me taken away by another woman. But if Carlos ended up with her, I would be pissed.

NINE

Leaving Adriano's behind, we walked the two blocks to Kozmic, my boots echoing in the stillness of Union Street, Ti's heels making quick, sharp strikes.

"This fashion photographer is the real deal," she was saying. "He works for *GQ*, *Vogue*, *Interview*, all sorts of magazines. He gave Alexander a business card while buying a pair of shoes from him today. Alexander told me the guy said, 'Promise me you will star in my shoot.' As if Alexander was the only one who would permit it to go forward. And he gave Alexander some coke! Isn't life grand?"

"Uh-huh."

"Oh God! I want to go somewhere. Let's just go somewhere! I want to see the world! Japan especially. It *sooo* fascinates me. There's this Japanese fashion designer, Kansai Yamamoto, who has some items on exhibit at the Palace of Fine Arts."

"Isn't he the one who did Bowie's Ziggy costumes?"

"Yes! He was influenced by the concept of eccentric and extravagant excess."

I was pleasantly surprised to hear her knowledgeable about something so esoteric.

"Maybe I can work in fashion," she said, "Alexander and I can do some ads for those boutiques on Maiden Lane. Who knows? By the way, I bought this dress just for our date. I got it at the store Constantina works at. Isn't it out of sight?"

I glanced over at what looked like an old flapper outfit from the Twenties, pale green with a matching jacket.

"Far out."

"You're taller," she said. "Are those new boots?"

"I'm going to sell off Noel's record collection and his stereo, so I decided to splurge."

"Well, they really suit you. I like a taller man. Although you should have just gone all out and gotten them with higher heels and in red leather, like Johnny Starr's platforms."

"That's hard to pull off unless you're in a band."

"I suppose. You know, Alexander wants me to move in with him when he gets his next place. Of course, if a better opportunity came along, I could be swayed." She looked at me, pointedly.

I said only, "I'm surprised there was any blow left by the time you saw him."

"It wasn't much. We polished it off in no time flat and shared it with Constantina and Karen besides. But I'm always ready for more!"

"Does Karen work tonight?"

"She keeps crazy hours. Later, I think. What about the fairy dust?"

"We'll see."

Her lips turned into a pout. If I was lucky, Alexander's generosity had permitted me to preserve most of what I had left for when I next encountered Lannie.

"Oh, come on," she pleaded.

"Maybe."

She smiled as if I'd said yes. We reached Kozmic. I unlocked the passenger door, and Ti stepped up and in. I went around and I mounted from the other side. The engine turned over on the second try. I would need to do a tune-up soon. Ti took a cigarette from her purse and lit up as we pulled out from the parking space. Yanking open the ashtray from the dash, she slid the passenger side window a crack and dropped her purse to the floor between the walk-through seats. "Gee, it looks awfully empty back there," she said.

"I moved Nick James into his new place. I put the plywood platform and the mattress in the garage at the apartment. It's kind of cool to have all the extra room."

"Aren't there supposed to be seats?"

"I left them on the East Coast a few years ago."

"The curtains are still up. Makes it kind of homey."

"For the moment anyway. But I think the last cross-country journey has been done."

"That sounds so sad."

"It's time. By the way, since when do you smoke?"

"They're Karen's. It's fab to have her as my new roommate after Zora left me in the lurch and moved in with Spencer."

"Zora's interesting in a strange sort of way," I said.

"She's a pig and a whore. Anyway, since it's only a one-bedroom, Karen's sleeping on the couch, but she's a godsend. She takes good care of me." At this, Ti gave me a look. "I used to smoke occasionally, anyway. It's a nice stress reliever." She looked over at me again as if she'd asked a question.

"You're stressed?" I said.

"Yes. Listen, there's something I've been wanting to say."

"Uh-huh."

"You're pissed about leaving that *woman* you were with back there, aren't you?"

"No. It's okay. You and I had a date."

"Oooh, a 'date.' That sounds so romantic. I thought at the store you called it something else. You said, 'It's a deal.'"

"Force of habit. Business, you know."

"Very funny."

"But it's a date," I said. "We agreed, and here we are."

"Well, don't sound so goddamned happy about it." She gazed out the window as the shops on Union Street flashed by in a stream of neon and glass. She turned to me. "Have you had sex with her? No, to hell with that. Do you *like* her? Besides, what were you doing, hiding from me?"

I didn't respond. She remained silent in return, which for her was rare. Something was up.

I answered finally as we reached Van Ness. "Everything's fine. Just forget about it."

"Speaking of forgetting about it," she said, "the other night I said something I didn't exactly mean."

So, it wasn't really about Lannie. I pressed the accelerator to the floor to prepare for the approaching hill, shifting gears. Kozmic struggled with the steepness, and I had to be careful how hard I pushed him.

"Do you even remember what I said?" Ti asked.

"I always remember."

We made it to the top of the hill, and I placed my foot on the brake and downshifted for the dangerous descent.

"Yes, but I want to make sure we are talking about the same thing. We were both pretty loaded."

The brakes squealed, the beginning of metal on metal, as we came to the end of the long downhill. Damn. One more thing I needed to do. I turned left with the light, onto Columbus and its crowded sidewalks.

"I always remember," I said again. "Even loaded. It's a blessing and a curse."

"Well, then what am I talking about, Mister 'I Always Remember?'"

I searched for a parking spot on the busy streets of a Saturday night in the city, concentrating on the task at hand.

"Billy, it's important!"

"If it's so important, just spill it."

"Jesus. That's really helpful. I'm trying to communicate, fuck-face."

I laughed out loud. I couldn't help it. But Ti didn't laugh or even smile. She just peered out the window and remained silent as I turned right off Columbus and slowed down. There were cars parked everywhere; the streets were lined with them.

"Sorry," I said.

She stared out the window still.

"Please, Ti, apology accepted?" I said, trying to manufacture some contriteness. She turned to me.

"Okay," she said. "Listen, I didn't really mean it. I was really wasted, and it just sort of slipped out."

I didn't look at her. "You didn't mean what?" I would make her say it. After all, Lannie was gone in the night because of her.

"I thought you said you remembered?"

"Now I'm not so sure."

She stared out the window again for a moment and then spoke, as if reluctant, her voice soft. "I said, 'I love you.'"

I let it hang in the air, driving very slowly, scanning the parked cars for a space. "Actually, you said, 'I *do* love you *so*.'"

Ti's head snapped around. "Bastard!" She took a sharp drag from the cigarette and stubbed it out hard in the ashtray.

I watched the parked cars on my right. We were two blocks from Columbus, so there should have been an opening soon.

"You didn't say anything back," she continued. "I didn't even think you heard me."

There it was, a space. I put on the turn signal and pulled up.

She collected herself. "Anyway, I was very high. It was just an expression of, well, appreciation for, I guess, the sex. After all, I know we are just 'fuck buddies,' right?" She was forcing it now, I thought, passing through the dark tunnel of the lie.

"Sure," I said. "It cuts both ways. You have the freedom to do as you wish."

"You don't care if I screw someone else?"

I backed into the parking space. It was tight, and once in, it would be difficult to maneuver my way out.

"Well, I wouldn't quite put it that way," I said, my voice calm and deliberate.

"How *would* you put it?"

"You've put it just fine. I would add only there are no emotional demands. We're both free spirits."

"Oh, that's you. A veritable fucking free spirit!"

I put the gearshift into neutral and applied my foot to the brake.

"Yep," I said. "'My costume is translucence. My soul passes through endless dark passages of time. Fearful of my destiny, navigating the waters of my resplendent glistening isolation, I plummet to the earth for the nightly ritual of the dance.'"

"What's that?" she asked.

"Something I wrote a long time ago."

"It's very interesting."

"You don't have to flatter me. It was part of an assignment in college for a creative writing course. I was on acid, and we were reading Byron and some others that week. I got what was described at the time by the professor as a 'generous C.'"

I put Kozmic in reverse and finished backing up, stopping just short of the car behind us. Twisting the wheel hard and pulling forward, I ran up and over the curb, almost nicking a parking meter. A ding in Kozmic's swirl of every-color-under-the-sun paint job wouldn't really matter all that much, but it was still nice just the same to have missed the iron sentinel. I backed off the curb, having parked neatly between the two cars. The light from a streetlamp caught Ti's fingers, her rings shining. She lit another cigarette and took a long drag, leaning against the door. I shifted into first, pulled the parking brake, and held up a hand heavy with my own rings.

"We match," I said.

"You wear more fucking jewelry than Alexander. Are you sure you aren't a faggot? And don't change the subject, mister." She exhaled out the crack in the window, her head resting against the glass. "You know," she said. "I was the one who ended it with Manny."

I turned off the engine.

"He was a mediocre lover," she said, turning to me. I had no idea of the truth of it, one way or another, but that she said it at all pleased me. I remained silent, sitting behind the steering wheel.

"Maybe we could try a three-way," she said, "to see if Manny might be willing to share me more directly."

I tapped the steering wheel, keeping time to a tune in my head, staring out at the periodic pedestrian. If the radio was working, I would have turned it on for distraction. Deciding to end the stand-off, I pulled the vial of coke from my pocket. Ti watched as I heaped a white crystal mound onto the small silver spoon. Carefully, I held it to her face, and she snorted it. She took the next one up the other nostril. We repeated the ritual several times. I had a couple hits myself.

"God," she said, "I feel so alive!" She smiled at me and laughed. It was as if our previous conversation had occurred a very long time ago, or perhaps not at all.

I busied myself screwing the black cap onto the vial, the spoon hanging by its miniature chain. Ti pressed out her cigarette in the dashboard ashtray and slid the window closed.

"Ready to dance, mister?"

We got out of Kozmic, and I locked the doors behind us. Ti took my arm, and we began to walk. I stopped us, kissing her on the mouth, catching her off-guard, I could tell, caressing her cheek with a hand. We stood there, the city falling away around us, snug in our embrace, like any other pair of lovers in the night.

TEN

Jowly and balding, what was left of his dark hair oily and combed straight back, Ed Bernstein sat across from me. He wore a yellow bowtie against a rumpled, striped blue dress shirt, smoking a cigar as he finished reading something on his desk. Manny sat in the chair next to me, leafing through a copy of the latest issue of *San Francisco Lifestyle*.

"So, you want to write for me?" Bernstein said, looking up.

"Yes, I—"

"Manny here has done some good stuff for me. What are you pitching?"

"You know about Dance Your Ass Off?"

"I've seen that billboard they have up when you come over the Bay Bridge."

"Well, dance clubs have gone from being mostly a gay thing to mainstream," I said. "I'd like to write an article about the whole scene and include a club directory for readers."

"He's right, Ed," Manny said. "It's hip—more or less anyway— and it's happening."

"I'd like to cover the straight places over on Clement, some clubs in the East Bay, plus the gay and the mixed ones," I said.

"And, of course, Dance Your Ass Off, which is pretty much the epicenter."

"Okay, so it's not a bad idea. Have you written before?"

"Back in college for the school paper."

"That's it?"

"And he helped me out with the band survey piece," Manny chimed in.

"You know, I'm knee-deep in writers, Bobby."

"Billy." I tried to stay upbeat.

"Writers are a dime a dozen. They walk in here every day of the week. They send me stuff, unsolicited. I'm sorry, but I think I'll have to pass."

I stood to leave. Maybe the *Guardian* was worth a try. I wasn't going to take no for an answer this time.

"What I really need is somebody to sell ad space," Bernstein said. "Ever sell?"

"I've been managing Aquarius Shirts on Haight."

"So, you're in retail. A *schmatta* salesman!"

"I guess," I said, not familiar with the term.

"Full or part-time?"

"Part-time."

"Good. Sit back down."

Manny, to his credit, had never left his chair.

"Tell you what, I'll read this article of yours and see if it's any good. If I take it, after that, you sell ad space for me part-time. Maybe we can do more articles if you make me some money. Stay in touch with my Debbie."

Manny and I got up and headed out of the office past Debbie at her desk. She peered up at Manny, and I saw him give her a wink as she smiled and squinted, which made her glasses ride up the bridge of her nose.

"What did I tell you?" Manny said out on the sidewalk.

"Thanks," I said.

"No problem, pal. Now get to work, and don't make me look bad."

We walked up Ashbury, then split up, Manny going off to Raffe's to write while I reopened the store. I imagined portions of the article in my head as I folded T-shirts. Each shirt had to be done just right. Miranda had instructed me on my first day with her exacting precision and mother-hen intensity. Lay the T-shirt flat, front down; smooth out any wrinkles. With both hands, take the side nearest and fold it away from you halfway into the middle. Turn the sleeve toward you. Fold the shirt from the other side, so it lay adjacent to the previously folded half. Turn that sleeve away from you. Flip the bottom third up and over itself twice. Turn the shirt over, so the label faced up, for a crisp, neat presentation.

I did all the shirts on both display tables. I felt surprisingly productive. There'd been dozens of shirts in disarray from the day before, and now there were none. I returned behind the counter as Lannie came. She was wearing designer jeans so tight I wondered at her ability to move in them.

"Hi," she smiled.

"Hey, what a pleasant surprise!"

"I need to buy a shirt for my younger sister's birthday. You know, we were only born a week apart."

"Must have been tough on your mother."

"No, I meant—oh, it's a joke, isn't it?"

"So, it's going to be your birthday soon?"

"Yes, twenty-seven on Friday in two weeks. Ooh, I like that one."

I turned around to the display on the cabinet behind me and found she was admiring a shirt with Susan Hayward's photo in black-and-white. Under it, in hot pink, as if scrawled with lipstick, it read, "*I Want to Live!*"

"I love that movie!" Lannie said. "It was on TV a few nights ago. It's so heart-wrenching. She dies in the end."

Lannie continued to stare at the shirt as if hypnotized. Her hair was brushed back that day, her ears exposed with their delicate curves and dainty lobes from which dangled emerald earrings set in gold. If the earrings were real, I wondered how she could afford them.

"So, it's for your sister?" I said.

"No, this one would be for me." Her lips were bright red, the lipstick glimmering. She wasn't the same in the daytime, shy and a bit nervous, but not so much today.

"Are you okay?" I asked.

"What do you mean?"

"Well, did you take something?"

"What would make you think that?"

"You just seem a little different," I said, feeling control between us shifting, as was our pattern.

"Well, I did have a Valium."

"Just one?"

"Yes." She looked at me with what I took to be the utmost sincerity she could muster. She really was quite good.

"Blue or yellow?" I said.

"Blue. It relaxes me. I have a prescription."

"Maybe have a cappuccino before you drive home."

"Oh, I didn't drive, I took a cab. Can I have my shirt?"

"Tell you what. Let's see, do you take a medium?"

"Small. I like them tight." She blushed a little.

"Okay."

I picked out a small from the cabinet. She held the shirt up in front of her, Susan Hayward's face rippling over her chest, the words below it reading as if now attached to Lannie.

"You can try it on if you like," I said. "There's a changing booth in the corner with a mirror."

I stared after her as she walked to the dressing room, elevated from the floor by the thick plastic soles of her shoes with see-through high heels. Yellow stars floated in clear liquid inside one, red stars hung suspended in the other.

She took off her jacket and placed it on the corner seat inside with the curtain still open. She began to unbutton her blouse, and for an instant I thought she might change without closing the curtain. But with the blouse open down the middle and wearing no bra, she pulled the two halves of the curtain together.

Play it cool, I thought. Unlike other men in her life, I didn't loan her money she would never repay. I didn't ask her to go out directly. I never told her how beautiful she was.

After a few minutes, she opened the curtain and came back holding the shirt.

"I'll take it," she said.

"Then it's yours."

She pulled a wallet out of her purse.

"No, it's yours," I said. "Early happy birthday, Lannie."

"Really?"

I nodded.

"Thank you, Billy." She bent over the counter and kissed me lightly on the lips. "You're such a friend," she said, tearing up a little. Then, she reached across with a finger and wiped away what must have been a trace of lipstick on my mouth.

"What about your sister?"

"She can be your friend, too," she replied earnestly. "She's supposed to come out over the summer."

"I meant what about her gift?" I asked, sure now she had taken more than one pill.

"Oh! Gosh, I'm such a goof. It should be something that says 'San Francisco.'"

"Well, what about the Golden Gate Bridge decal?"

"That would be good!"

"What size does she take?"

"Medium."

"Let me put it on a shirt, and you'll be all set."

"How much?"

"Well, let's just call that one half-price."

"Great!"

I took a plain white T-shirt to the heat press. She followed on the other side of the counter. I went through the box on the shelf below. I found the decal and placed it on the T-shirt between the two halves of the heat press. Lannie stood near the counter, and I could smell her perfume. I remembered myself inside her and the scent of her on me. Applying pressure to the handle, I brought it down and held it there.

"Listen, Billy. You want to maybe say 'hi' and celebrate at Adriano's on my birthday? Like about midnight? A Quaalude would be really nice and especially some coke."

The handle rose stiff in my grip, the top half of the press along with it.

"I'll make an excuse to Wade and come by. Assuming, that is, your little friend Ti won't be around. How is she, by the way?"

"It's sort of on-again, off-again," I said. "Besides, you're with Wade."

"That's different."

"How so?"

"I don't know!" she said, laughing, definitely silly from the pills.

"Okay. I'll be there," I said. I handed her the shirts in a bag, and she left, strutting in her shoes, the stars in her heels bobbing up and down.

ELEVEN

Noel had been dead for almost two weeks. I stood inside his room, leaning against a wall, arms folded. Two guys from Larry's Used Books and Music finished packing the records and books. I'd kept a few volumes but none of the records. The entire collection netted me two hundred dollars cash. Plus, one of the guys had paid me ninety dollars for the stereo system. I was flush, fifties and twenties thick in a pocket of my jeans.

After they departed, I walked over to the desk. I'd moved the typewriter into my bedroom, where it resided on Noel's old nightstand. I had also placed his framed *Paris Review* cover on a wall in the living room. Sitting at the desk, I pulled open the long flat drawer underneath the writing surface. Inside was Noel's keychain, his work photo ID attached by means of a metal clip. I put the keychain and ID on top of the desk, off to one side.

I moved to the large bottom drawer with its hanging file folders. I pulled it open, and it scraped noisily, wood on wood. I walked my fingers along the tops of "Bank of America," "Bell Telephone," "Employment," "Health Insurance." I went back to "Bank of America," the bulkiest of the folders, and it took both my hands to pull it free. I opened it on the desk, and a thick stack of monthly statements greeted me, the top one for March. The balance was thirty-six dollars and twenty-three cents. How had Noel planned on paying the next rent? Perhaps there was also a savings account. I searched, but the remainder of the contents consisted of deposit slips and old checks. I picked up the checks and thumbed through them until I found a rent payment. As I suspected, I'd been paying well over half the total. Perhaps I could rent out Noel's room for the lion's share of the amount.

I went back to the folders in the drawer, bending over further for a closer look. I removed "Employment" and laid it on the desk. The first item inside was a letter from the State Unemployment office, a termination notice dated three months previous.

Noel had been fired. Didn't that beat all? And Noel had lied to me. Saying he still worked half-time, he would disappear for hours on the days I was off from the store. Now I wondered where he'd gone. With a sense of urgency, I explored the other files. I came upon a letter attached by a paper clip to an envelope in a folder marked "Rent." It read:

Noel:

You are in arrears for this month's rent. Per our phone conversation, I suspect it will become clear to me in a few days that the same will hold true for April as well. Due to our previous problem in this regard, if the total sum due is not paid in toto as part of the rent due May 1 (i.e. three months' rent as a lump sum), I will be forced to begin eviction proceedings immediately. I know our friendship goes back a long time. But you leave me no choice.

Bob

What happened to the rent money I gave Noel? My looming financial difficulties became instantly insurmountable. There was no longer any question that a roommate was imperative. Not only would my freedom be gone—intruded upon by some as yet unknown stranger—but whatever money I had as well. Sagging in the chair, I felt as empty inside as the room surrounding me.

I had the address from the envelope. I needed the phone number. Maybe I could stall for time? I looked through the rent folder for the lease. There it was: a two-page form signed by Noel. The front page included the landlord's name, address, and telephone number. There was a second lease behind it, with an address on Vine Street in Berkeley. I supposed it to be where Noel lived prior to moving to San Francisco. It was close to where I used to live.

I returned the "Employment" and "Bank of America" folders back to their places, closed the file drawer, and sat there. The room needed to be emptied, with Noel's remaining things thrown out or shipped to his father. Any money earned from doing that could be added to my limited resources. I got up, taking the rent folder and its contents, along with the ring of keys and the ID from the drawer. I would need an apartment key for whoever moved into Noel's room. In my bedroom, I tossed the folder and keys on my bed, inadvertently startling Cat from a nap. I sat down next to him, putting the water into motion, the bed moving us gently up and down. I stroked his flank, and he stretched himself, his paws extended, his torso trembling slightly at the apex of the stretch.

I got up and stormed Noel's room. I stripped the bed, yanking everything off as I swore out loud, throwing the bedding to the floor. On a whim—and based on my own tricks—I lifted the mattress. I discovered photos: men masturbating, men in black leather with chain devices affixed to their genitals, men wearing black hoods, men committing sex acts upon each other. These last ones shocked even me.

I lifted the mattress still higher and found a black leather hood with metal zippers, one where the mouth should be. Jesus.

I bundled all of it up in my arms: the sheets, the blankets, the pillowcases, the worn bedspread, the black hood, the photos. I carried the whole bulky mess down the back stairs. Ramming it into the trashcan, I cursed Noel out loud for screwing me over so thoroughly from the grave.

TWELVE

I posted "Roommate Wanted" flyers on community bulletin boards in the Haight and a couple places on Union Street. Manny had run them off for free at the copy center. The dollar figure listed covered most of the rent, and frankly was exorbitant. If the flyers didn't work, I would try again with a more reasonable amount.

Calls didn't come flooding in. Gerold from across the hall accosted me one day on the landing. He had a pimply, skinny young blonde with him, which made me wonder. She stared at the floor and fidgeted as he spoke.

"I could move in," he offered. "I always liked Noel's bedroom more than mine."

"That's okay. I've already got somebody in mind," I responded quickly. In fact, only a few serious candidates emerged. A pair of male lovers were the first to make an in-person appearance. They were nice enough, and I had no problem with them, but I would first try to limit the invasion of my privacy to a single individual.

The only other serious candidate was a guy who was friendly on the phone and who belched loudly several times as I showed him around the apartment, including a side trip down to the garage. I was inclined to reject him out of hand, but after we sat down to talk—he took the couch, I got the armchair—he said, "I'm a businessman. I like the bedroom. There's a secure garage for my pickup and tools. I'm doing pretty well with freelance electrical contracting. I got a job lined up that'll bring in a thousand dollars. I'll do some stuff to fix this place up. What would it take to make this work?"

"First and last month's rent," I said. "Plus, a three-hundred-dollar refundable deposit. We split utilities, and by the way, the desk comes with the room. The bed too."

"Okay, we could do that," he said, "if you make the deposit two hundred and give me the garage parking space on the right. It's a little bigger, and I could use the extra room along the side to store my tools. Also, both the bed and desk are mine to take with me if I move. By the way, I notice you don't have a TV out here. Got one in your room?"

As if on cue, my bedroom door opened, the old television set visible for an instant on its orange-colored plastic crate, and Ti emerged sleepy-eyed, hair tousled. "God, I need some fucking coffee!" she announced. Noticing the stranger, she added, "Oh. Hi," and she padded into the kitchen, naked except for one of my T-shirts barely covering her ass.

"Yeah, an old black-and-white," I continued. "What was your name?" I had to ask him again.

"Tim Lipschitz," he said, staring after Ti. "Oh, man," he said under his breath. "Is that your girlfriend?"

"Sort of."

He waited, apparently for something more. When it was clear nothing was forthcoming, he said, "Now what were we talking about?"

"Televisions."

"Oh yeah. I got a new color TV I could put out here in the living room."

I was vaguely aware that this would turn the living room into an extension of Tim's bedroom.

"Mind if I smoke?" he said, retrieving a pack from a shirt pocket, along with a lighter. I slid one of Noel's old ashtrays across the coffee table towards him as he lit up. "And I'll get an extra phone line put in for my business stuff, so it won't tie up the regular phone."

"Deal," I said. He stretched out a puffy hand and grasped mine hard as we shook.

Ti leaned against the doorframe to the kitchen in my T-shirt, sipping her coffee, watching us. Each time she raised the cup to her mouth, the shirt lifted, exposing the golden red of her pubic hair.

"Okay, I'll move in next weekend," Tim said, looking past me at her. I saw moisture now on his upper lip, perspiration on his brow.

"Fine," I said.

"What are those boxes?" he said, pointing to the stack in a corner.

"I need to ship them. They're stuff that belongs to the guy who used to be here."

"So where do you live now?" Ti asked, taking another sip of her coffee.

"With my brother, over in the Sunset," Tim responded. "Here's the phone number." He wrote on a business card, jokingly making as if to pass it to Ti before turning to me. "Hey, my brother can be my reference. Wanna reference?"

"That's okay," I said, watching as he pulled a bent checkbook from a back pocket and began to write.

"Hey, bum a cigarette?" Ti said.

"Sure," Tim said, dropping everything.

She sauntered over and took a cigarette from the pack he held up to her. While I watched, annoyed, he fumbled with the lighter, and she bent down, her breasts visible as the T-shirt separated from her chest. Finally, they got the cigarette lit, and he went back to the checkbook. I would mail a money order to Bob, squaring everything. Half of me celebrated solving the immediate financial crisis; the other half dreaded life with Tim.

"Got a key?" he asked.

"Sure. There's one for the downstairs front door and one for the apartment, plus the garage key." I got up to retrieve the extra keys from my room. As I pulled them off the keychain, Noel's face on the ID card stared up at me. It looked like a prison mug shot to me this time.

I could hear Tim talking with Ti, asking her questions about her life. She chatted away, giving him answers, sounding friendly. I went back into the living room and handed him the keys.

"Okay, roomie," Tim said, grinning. "See you next Saturday."

THIRTEEN

I noticed Constantina wore no rings. There was nothing on her slender wrist, not even a watch. A dark sweater hung shapeless as if swallowing her, and the men's dress hat was perched on her head, tilted back.

"Cheers," she said to me. Adriano's was barely half-full, and music came through the speakers at a reasonable volume.

"Back at you," I said, our glasses raised but not touching. "What are we toasting?"

"Life, love, and the pursuit of happiness." Her speech was filled with delicious inflections as if she were originally from another country.

"If I didn't know any better," I said, "I'd think you were born in Europe."

"Never been." She flicked her cigarette into a copper ashtray on the low table between us.

I bent forward, elbows on my knees, holding my rum gimlet with both hands. "You're kidding."

"No. I grew up in a rambling house just outside of Geyser. Wine country. I tell myself, perhaps one day I'll have this grand adventure in Europe, especially Paris. I want to drink aperitifs and idle away my time strolling along the Seine and visiting art galleries. It will be wonderful beyond words."

"Why haven't you been?"

"Money, honey, as they say, doesn't grow on trees. Truth be told, I've never been out of California."

"I would never guess that. You seem so sophisticated."

"Well, thanks. I'll remember that as I sell used glad rags and baubles for minimum wage."

"I know the feeling."

The second-hand clothing store where she worked was nearby. I'd been there once, seeing her surrounded by old designer dressers, hats, and jewelry. Somehow that environment suited her, as if she herself had lived in the past.

"And you, I'm guessing, have seen Europe?" Constantina asked. She crossed one leg over the other, tight at the knees, a beat-up black sneaker twisting around its twin at the ankle.

"My mother's French, so we visited often."

"Well, you are a lucky duck." Then, she said something in French.

"I don't know what you said."

"Do you not speak French?"

"I'm afraid not."

"You and your mother must not be close."

"It's complicated."

She exhaled and looked at me directly. "Neither do I—speak French, that is. At least not all that well. I did learn some in high school. What I said was a line from an Edith Piaf song, 'La Vie en Rose.'"

"I think I know it. Wasn't she a singer from pretty far back?"

"Yes, from the 1930s and '40s, and for a while still after the war, even well into the 1950s. She died in '63."

"I'm pretty into music. But more what's happening now."

"Yes, punk has a certain ragged *élan*. But the last thing I really liked was probably recorded in 1955."

"A very good year. 'Rock Around the Clock.' Seminal, in fact."

"I was thinking more along the lines of 'Three Coins in the Fountain.' Sinatra, in fact." She gave a wry smile, holding the cigarette perpendicular to her cheek. "Actually, come to think of it, maybe that was '54."

Her eyes flitted around the room. Then, she tilted herself forward as if she wanted to share something, an elbow perched on the back of a wrist, her legs snaked together. I noticed the ends of her fingernails were truncated and uneven from chewing, and there were bloody little scabs at her cuticles along with some paint traces.

The doorbell jingled, and Manny came in, pausing for hellos with some people I didn't recognize. Then, he came over to us. Looking at Constantina, he said, "Don't you know smoking stunts your growth, chippie?"

"Better stunted than none at all," she replied.

"Yowch!" Manny said, placing his fists one over the other around the shaft of an imaginary arrow shot into his chest, staggering like he was mortally wounded. Constantina burst out laughing as if despite herself.

"*Au contraire, ma petite fleur,*" Manny said. "It is my plan. I'm going to start the Peter Pan Club. Print up cards at the copy center and hand them out. You two can be charter members. Everyone has to put aside thoughts of adult foolishness and join me in my quest."

"Sign me up," Constantina said.

"Pal, I'm ready for that ride," Manny said to me. Glancing at Constantina, he added, "Want to join us and go to the Palms?"

"Thanks anyway, but Alexander's coming by. I promised I'd attend a party with him and provide moral support in the pursuit of his latest object of doomed desire."

"Suit yourself," Manny said, and he headed for the door as I stood to follow.

"You know, Billy," Constantina said, making me stop in my tracks. "There's a terrific little orchestra at the Starlight Lounge on Divisadero that plays nothing but old standards. We could meet there one night."

"Okay," I said, surprised at the invitation.

"Then, let's," she said.

"Alright." I caught up with Manny at the door.

"A tad caustic, that one," he said.

"She's sassy," I said. "I like that. She's sassy, and she's smart."

"Yeah, she's not without appeal," Manny said, looking back at her as we headed outside, the bell above the door jingling behind us. "Can we stop off at my place first? Need to retrieve my press pass."

"Okay."

I drove us east across Van Ness and up the hill to Manny's apartment. I parked in the driveway out front, blocking the side-walk and the door to the garage with its sign: "Warning! You will be towed!"

"Don't worry, we'll make this fast," Manny said. Once inside, we walked down the narrow hallway that ran the length of the flat in typical San Francisco fashion. We reached the kitchen, where there was a door to Manny's bedroom.

"What are those holes from?" I asked, looking at the walls.

"Charlie shot up a speedball a few nights ago and decided Martians were invading through the back door. Then he shot up the place. I was in the bedroom with Debbie. Startled the shit out of us and ruined a night of good sex."

"Debbie from Bernstein's office?"

"Yeah. She's more fun than you might think. Still waters run nympho-deep. Plus, she tells Bernstein how great my stuff is. She's got a masters in English lit from Stanford, and he regards her opinion highly. So I need to keep up our little *tête-à-têtes*."

Manny opened the door to his bedroom and negotiated his way around the rows of free albums he'd been receiving from record labels in his role as an entertainment writer. Already, they covered a substantial portion of the floor, crowding against his bed, which was a mattress on the floor with a sheet and a blanket. There were also press kits stacked along with copies of newspapers and various music publications, plus comic books, some inside protective plastic sleeves. I waited at the doorway as Manny retrieved his press pass from a desk-top cardboard standup display of the Ramones, where it dangled from Joey's arm.

We walked back down the hallway, the walls hung with Charlie's oil paintings full of morbid people with dark eyes who moved through sunken streets devoid of cars and much of anything else.

I said, "A little scary Charlie's got a gun, no?"

"Very."

"Maybe you should move."

"I don't think so. Did you do a lude yet?" he asked as we reached the front door.

"Not yet."

"Want to before we leave?"

"Wasn't planning on it quite yet."

"What, do you time these things?"

"Yeah, kind of."

"How about you get started?"

We went to the flat's cramped bathroom. Manny ran a glass of water and handed it to me. I took a half-lude while he watched as if I was taking my medicine and he was the parent making sure. Then, I waited as he primped in the mirror.

"Do you have anything alcoholic?" I asked.

"Just an old bottle of Bailey's Irish Cream."

We went back to the kitchen, and Manny retrieved the liqueur from the refrigerator. "You might as well finish it," he said.

I took a swig and almost gagged at the sweetness. I polished it off anyway and left the empty bottle on the counter.

Outside, Kozmic sat parked in the driveway, still blocking the sidewalk. I'd been concerned about a ticket—or worse, getting towed—but the windshield was clear.

"By the way," Manny said as we got in, "Shelley will be working tonight, and there's fun to be had. Got a lude you could spare? And how about just a taste of coke for *moi* first."

I pulled us out into the street and said, "Listen, I'm a little short. I'm picking up a couple grams and a bunch of pills tomorrow. I'd like to hang on to the coke for Lannie. We're supposed to meet up later tonight."

"Hope she's worth it," he said. Then he added, "I wonder what Honey would say."

I turned onto Greenwich and plunged us down the hill. Manny grabbed the dash and muttered under his breath. At the bottom, the brakes squealed as we pulled up to a red light. When it changed to green, I released the brake, shifted, and pressed the gas pedal, and we picked up speed as I turned left.

Manny said, "Before the Palms, I suggest we first hit the comic store."

We headed east on Broadway, and I found parking off Columbus near Dance Your Ass Off. There was a line outside, and I thought about how I would describe the place in my dance club article. I'd begun to make notes for it in a large notebook.

We walked toward the comic book store. As if it were a pronouncement of import, I said, "I've been reading Noel's journals."

"Why?"

"I don't know. Maybe searching for truths."

"Don't think you'll find them there, pal."

I decided to try a different tact. "You know, Noel had a bizarre sex life."

Manny stopped walking and turned to me. "Like what?"

"I found nipple clamps in his bathroom drawer."

"Ouch. 'Don't Touch Me There!' to quote the Tubes."

We entered the comic store. I started to think about where I was going to get a real drink to trigger the lude.

"Anything else of interest?" Manny wanted to know as he examined various comic books.

"A lot of pained suffering-artist stuff."

"Wouldn't know about that. I consider myself an artist of sorts in the commercial sense of the term, but not pained. No plans to cut off an ear or any other body parts anytime soon."

"Mostly," I said, "he led this life alone in his bedroom. And all he had was his writing and listening to his music. You know, nobody came to visit him in the month we were together." Damn, I thought. "We were together" sounded strange.

"Hey, want to get a capp?" Manny said.

"He became obsessed with time passing," I continued, "and his failure to achieve something of significance with his writing. There's page after page of stuff on it. I think maybe—"

"Caffe Trieste?" Manny asked.

"Jesus. Okay. I could use something alcoholic. Maybe the Savoy instead?"

"Just a sec." Manny examined the latest *Batman*, so I contemplated an old copy of *Superboy* on display in a clear plastic wrapper. On the cover, Krypto and Supergirl joined Superboy in flight over Smallville. "I think I had this one when I was a kid," I said.

Manny glanced over. "Considering it's worth a couple hundred bucks, too bad you didn't keep it. How's it going with that roommate search?"

"Got a guy who's moving in next weekend. At least I'm not going to get evicted. But money's still tight."

"And what's the latest store closing deadline?"

"Not much past the end of summer, I suspect. You know, they're still going to have the Sausalito store, not to mention Fisherman's Wharf. That's the one closer to where I live anyway. They just won't give me a job there."

"How come?"

"Not sure. It's not like I haven't dropped hints. Miranda says it's because they're already fully staffed."

"What do you think?"

"I don't know what to think. And, Jesus, it's not like it's the greatest gig in the world to begin with." I picked up an issue of *Uncle Scrooge*, remembering how much I enjoyed it as a kid and how it wasn't cool to admit it at the time.

"Don't fool yourself, Billy. Where else could you get a job as good as the T-shirt store? What with that long hair and all, and your cheery good-natured self? Besides, maybe you better fit the expectations of what someone should look like selling T-shirts in Haight-Ashbury, rather than to visiting tourists from the heartland at Fisherman's Wharf."

"Are you saying you agree with her? Besides, there are tourists in the Haight."

"Just that I can see her point, chum. She told me as much when she hired you. Plus, you're not exactly Mister Sunshine, you know. Hard to think of you as the hail-fellow-hearty-sales-guy-of-the-month sort."

"Thanks." I considered leaving him there.

"It's not necessarily a bad thing. It's just not your field of endeavor."

I got the feeling again that Manny was sometimes glad to be witness to my personal trials. He picked up a *Superman*, flipping gingerly through the pages. "Hey, don't feel too bad," he said. "Things aren't swell at the copy center either. If I'm lucky, I could last another month or two. I've already been written up twice for an 'attitude problem.' Mira, that pathetic twit of a twenty-five-cents-more-than-me-per-hour boss, has been whining to the district manager whenever he drops by. Just because I pick and choose among clients, as to who I will kowtow to and who I will call on their bullshit. It's a good thing I'm so charming about it." He demonstrated the cute smile he usually reserved for women.

"Yeah," I said. "Let's blow this pop stand."

We headed along Columbus, walking up to Grant.

Manny turned to me. "I'm happy to assist you with the dance club piece when you're ready—take a look and help edit it. Hey, I almost forgot my big news! *Creem* called. With a rewrite, they say they'll consider a cut-down of the *Lifestyle* Blondie piece. I'm going national, Billy! Thanks for that line about 'Betty Boop meets Marilyn Monroe.' That's a keeper. The little blonde scamp in a nutshell."

"Congratulations," I said.

Wow, Manny was moving on. He wouldn't need menial employment. I was mired in it.

FOURTEEN

At the Savoy, Manny talked to the booker, the two of them standing there in matching black leather motorcycle jackets. I downed a gin and tonic and listened in on their chat-fest about the recent Ramones show. There had been barely a dozen of us to witness the band's first San Francisco appearance—Dee Dee's "One, two, three, four!" countdowns; Johnny's buzz-saw guitar; "Beat on the Brat," "Blitzkrieg Bop," and "Now I Wanna Sniff Some Glue"—the whole rapid-fire set lasting maybe 25 minutes.

As I waited for Manny to finish up, I achieved lift-off. There was the warm glow of the lude coming on strong, the personality shift to gregariousness, the mood-elevation rush.

We left North Beach in Kozmic, found parking a few blocks away from the Palms, and made our way along Polk Street. The sidewalks became crowded; lights shone from store windows; the bars and restaurants were doing brisk business. Fog was rolling in, the whole of it becoming a misty, light-diffused wonderland. At Buzzby's, two men kissed in line as if devouring each other. I thought about how I should include Buzzby's in my article, with its mix of gay and straight patrons and the Plexiglass DJ booth high above the dance floor.

Outside the Palms, we could see through the large plate-glass window to the bar running nearly the length of the place, and the boisterous crowd inside. Manny flashed his press pass to the doorman, and we were waved in. Leila and the Snakes were late into their set, making their way through the satirical "Pyramid Power." All three of the Snakes had on black mesh stockings and heels, a male drummer at the kit behind them and a guy on guitar off to the side. They looked like a Berlin cabaret act from the Thirties. We grabbed a couple chairs at a table as they finished up and left the stage to applause.

David and Monique welcomed us from the next table. Perhaps it was an illusion—accents, cigarettes, and clothes coming together as a phantom whole. There seemed to be a perfection to them: Monique, sophisticated, in a chair beside David who was wearing one of his crewneck sweaters that always appeared brand-new.

Shelley came over. "What can I get you?" she asked Manny.

"Any suggestions, my sweet?"

"My own favorite's Amaretto and soda."

"Okay, let's give that a try."

"Make that two," I said.

"We are going dancing later," Monique said loudly, bending forward to bridge the space between us. David huddled in as well, and I could hear him tell Manny he was going to set up an export-import business using his contacts back in France. Then, I observed the crowd around me, spotting a pair of nice-looking girls at the bar.

"Let me buy your next drink," David offered Manny. "Perhaps you will be able to write our press releases? Mention our business somewhere in an article? And Billy," David said to me, "do you have any cocaine?"

Even on the Quaalude, I made a shushing motion to him and shook my head no.

Shelley came back with our drinks. "Shell-EE," called David, smiling for her, "I will have another glass of wine. And Manny's drink is on me."

"I'll have another Scotch on the rocks," Monique said.

I stood up with my drink and cruised the place. I thought about approaching the two girls at the bar, but they seemed occupied with each other. Besides, I was mostly killing time before my midnight rendezvous. I wandered near the low stage, then back around the other side of the room. I examined faces but spoke with no one except to offer an aside to young, pretty Pearl E. Gates of the Snakes, interrupting her chatting with the bass player. But she brushed me off with a why-are-you-bothering-me look. Returning to Manny and the others, I found the tables merged as one, with everyone sitting closer together. Carlos had appeared out of nowhere.

I hung around as Manny talked to Shelley and David and others who came over to say hi, and I engaged them in my own lude-lubricated chatter. I heard Monique tell David that she wanted to go over to Dance Your Ass Off. David asked Manny if he wanted to join them, but Manny said no, nodding in the direction of Shelley and adding, "Waiting 'til my cutie gets off work." David smiled and winked at him.

Leila and the Snakes returned from their break for another set, and I got ready to leave. "Thanks for the ride," Manny said.

I walked back to Kozmic, drove over to Union, and began searching for parking. It being Friday night, I eventually had to park up the hill. I began the walk down to Adriano's, hoping she would appear.

FIFTEEN

"I'm getting so damn old, Billy," Lannie said. It was just the two of us outside Adriano's, on the other side of Union. The fog was heavier now, a fine drizzle falling as we stood together next to her used Chevy Malibu.

"We're the same age," I said.

"Wade and me—it's really over this time."

Tears ran down her cheeks, her mascara streaking, tiny beads of moisture in her hair. She eyed me sweetly, and I put my arms around her, facing Adriano's as we hugged. Through the windows, I could see Zora talking to someone I didn't know, Gina waiting on a customer, and Johnny Starr and Spencer drinking with Fat Stan. Thankfully, Ti wasn't around. She'd told me she would be out of town for a few days at a cousin's wedding. I was anxious to get things moving with Lannie just the same, but I didn't want to appear overeager.

"I almost didn't wait any longer for you," I said, acting tough about it.

"I'm sorry I was late. I'll make it up to you."

"Happy unbirthday to you," I sang, close to her ear. "Happy unbirthday to you."

"Oh, stop," she said, but she smiled as we broke apart. "Got any coke? My nose has that itch."

"Uh-huh."

"Let's go to my place."

"Where's Wade?" I said.

"He's not there. Don't worry."

"You sure?"

"He swore he wouldn't see me again, even if I begged him. Then he hit me, Billy." She started crying again.

"Okay, let's go," I said.

We got into her car and drove around the corner to Kozmic. I followed her into the night, Kozmic's headlights reflecting off damp streets, the worn wiper blades barely keeping the windows clear as we headed to Lannie's Twin Peaks apartment. Inside, it was modern and stylish, with exposed blond wood and thick, cream pile carpeting. I again wondered how she could afford it.

"Would you like some wine?" she asked.

"Sure."

"Red or white?"

"Red." I sat down on the black leather couch in the living room, taking off my jacket. Lannie returned, handing me a glass as she sat down and faced me.

"Billy, it's time for a lude."

I gave a half to her, and she swallowed it with the wine and eyed the remaining half, but I put it in my pocket.

"Hey, do you like my new guitar?" A flaming red Gibson rested in a stand near the fireplace, a Pignose amp beside it.

"Cool," I said.

"I'm taking lessons from Johnny Starr, and I'm learning chords! Forming a band's the next step. Zora and me are talking about it!

We wanna be rock stars!" Then, indicating the fireplace, she said, "Hey, can you make a fire?"

"Wasn't a Boy Scout for nothing."

"I'm going to change, if you don't mind. These jeans are killing me." I watched her leave—the sleekness of her walk in high heels—and I smiled to myself. When she was gone, I put loosely crumpled newspaper pages at the bottom of the fireplace from a stack next to it. Tightly-rolled lengths of paper followed; then, pieces of kindling, and finally a couple of logs placed up against the back of the hearth. A box of old-style wooden matches sat atop the mantelpiece. Striking one against the box flint, I lit the scrunched newspaper in several places, and the fire sprung to life. The guitar glowed sapphire in the flames. I wondered if Johnny Starr and Lannie had been having sex. Of course, they'd been. Who was I kidding?

Lannie reappeared, barefoot in a lavender negligee.

"You look very nice," I said, rising.

"You have the coke?" she asked.

I removed the vial from my jacket pocket, and we sat on the couch. Unscrewing the cap, I scooped up a pile of crystals and placed the spoon under her nose. She put a finger against a nostril and snorted it up hard, then did the other side. As I did the same, there came the sound of a key in the front door. Certain it was Wade, I tried to figure out how I would handle the situation. At least I still had my clothes on.

"I have a new roommate," Lannie whispered.

The door opened, and in walked a pretty girl I guessed to be Eurasian.

"Dana, this is Billy," Lannie said. "We go way back to my earliest days in Berkeley. He had a girlfriend who was a really good friend of mine."

"Nice to meet you, Billy," Dana said, eyeing the vial of coke. She wore pressed slacks, a print blouse, and penny loafers, and carried an attaché case. The way she dressed reminded me of the coeds my freshman year of college, before everything changed.

"Billy runs a T-shirt store in Haight-Ashbury," Lannie offered.

"Aquarius Shirts, at the corner of Clayton and Haight Street," I said.

"I'll remember that. If I ever need a T-shirt, I'll be sure to come by," Dana said with a trace of a southern accent. "Well, it was a late night at the law school library. Got a paper due in Contracts and Copyrights. Goodnight."

She retreated into the kitchen, and I heard the sound of her bedroom door closing.

"She seems nice," Lannie offered. "She paid me an extra month's rent in advance. She works part-time as a paralegal to help pay for law school. I think she's reliable, and she spends a lot of time away from the apartment, which is good. I sure could use some more coke."

We repeated the snorting ritual. In her haste, Lannie bumped the spoon, and some coke fell to the couch. Then, wetting a finger with her saliva, she pressed it to the leather to gather up the errant flakes, and sucked the finger.

The fire roared and crackled, and we picked up the wine.

"To our special friendship," I said. We clinked glasses, and our first kiss was clumsy.

"You sure know how to make a great fire," she said.

I put down my wine and, placing her face between the palms of my hands, stared into her luminous brown eyes. She just looked so damned beautiful.

"Hi, Lannie," I said. "It's good to be back."

We kissed again, and this time it was perfect. God, in that moment, it did feel like love.

"Should we go smoke something?" I said. "Maybe in your bedroom?"

She smiled and stood up as I followed. She must have lit the candles while changing, one on each bedside table, scenting the air strawberry. She turned down the red comforter, exposing pink satin sheets, and climbed onto the bed. Putting an arm against the headboard to maintain her balance, she laughed and said, "Could you turn on the radio?"

I went over to the stereo system on the dresser and turned the knob. Rock music blasted, and I lowered the volume.

"No! Keep it loud!"

I turned the knob back up and walked over to the bed.

"Okay if I make myself more comfortable?" I asked.

"Sure," she said.

I took off all my clothes, got onto the bed and lit a joint. Together, we traded hits.

We kissed and embraced, and I stroked Lannie's hair, her face, the back of her slim thighs, her ass. She sat up and raised her arms, and I lifted off her negligee as if unveiling a work of art. She smiled, eyes closed. I lingered at her breasts, teasing the nipples into revealing themselves. Then, she lay on the bed as my tongue traveled between her thighs. I sensed her moans were not real.

I went back to my things for a condom, returned to the bed, and started to put it on. But she said, "I can't get pregnant. I had surgery once. Don't ask—female problems."

I put the condom on anyway. Lannie hugged me as I moved inside her. I kissed her neck, her mouth, her face. Her hugs became tighter, her eyes closed, her breathing tense as I tried to coax it out of her.

SIXTEEN

I sat on my stool in the store and wrote about Dance Your Ass Off. My big notebook now contained five pages of the dance club article in longhand. Soon I would use Noel's typewriter to pound it out for submission.

I got up and placed the notebook under the counter. Outside, I noticed the trash basket had begun its weekly migration from Abe's flower shop to the T-shirt store, but at least it was not yet filled to overflowing. A Deadhead came over to me with a couple T-shirts to ring up.

"Coffee break!" Ti announced, traipsing into the store, her boot heels clomping against the wooden floor, as the Deadhead at the counter looked startled. I gave him his T-shirts in a bag, along with his change. Ti stood behind him, wearing jeans with a long-sleeved maroon top, a leather handbag slung from a shoulder, a Dixie cup of coffee in her hand.

"Thanks for shopping with us," I said to the Deadhead.

"Keep drivin' that train," Ti said to him as he left.

"Hi . . . on cocaine!" she said to me. "Here, have a capp—my treat!" She placed the cup on the counter.

"Thanks. So, how were the relatives?" I took a sip of the cappuccino.

"They suck. Not to mention spending all that time with my mother. *And* my fucking father who I hadn't even seen since I was eleven. We had to take a goddamned Greyhound bus for the last part of the trip. My mother couldn't even afford a frigging rental car. Jesus! Thank God I got out of there when I did. Going back was horrid, even for a few days. Anyway, what have you been up to?"

"The usual."

"You know, I called you a couple times at home at night. No one picked up."

"Out researching the dance club article."

"Really?" She eyed me from across the counter as if she didn't believe me. "So, how's Manny doing?"

"Why do you ask?"

"I don't know. Maybe sometimes I feel guilty about breaking up with him." She examined the sample T-shirts displayed on their cabinets behind me as if she'd never seen them before.

"He's fine," I said. "Writing music reviews regularly."

"Yes, I saw something in *Lifestyle*. So, is he dating anyone in particular?" She left the counter and began to pace. I noticed she had a trace of a sniffle, and I wondered if she'd been doing coke, and if so, who it came from.

"Are you having second thoughts about 'breaking up with him?'"

"No. Just it would be nice to know what he's doing. Stay friends." She stopped in the middle of the store and turned to me. "I so rarely run into him. I saw him at Raffe's once, but I was with Karen, and they just don't hit it off, so we didn't really get a chance to talk. Plus, there's some weird hostility thing going on, and he made a joke about Karen's boob job at my expense."

"Manny is Manny."

"Meaning?" She walked to a display table, ran her fingers over a stack of T-shirts, and looked out the window. A silver necklace dangled against the fabric of her top, reflecting the sun. Stepping back towards me, she said, "What do you think?"

"About your boobs?"

"No, silly! Manny."

"Well," I said, "what do *you* think is up with Manny?"

"He's seeing several women and nobody special?"

"You got it."

"What about you?"

"What about me?"

"Tits. Do you care about the size of mine?"

I switched on the radio and chose my words carefully. "It's more about the overall aesthetics," I said, sipping the cappuccino. "Thanks for the capp, by the way. I—"

"Don't change the subject, mister. What the hell is 'overall aesthetics' supposed to mean? We're talking about my breasts."

"Sometimes," I allowed, "I actually prefer them on the smaller side."

"*Them?* Can't you say the word?"

"Here in broad daylight and all? Gee, I don't know."

Ti glanced around the empty store and over at the door. With both hands, she yanked the maroon top up to her neck. In the bright sunlight coming through the window, I especially noticed how the little upturned nipples were not so much sand-colored as I remembered, but rather pink.

"Okay. *Tits.* Nice perky *tits*," I said.

She pulled down her top, looking pleased with herself.

"There, that wasn't so hard, was it, darling? By the way, that was a lot of fun, our last night together. The dancing and, you know, back at your place."

"Yeah, the 'you know.'"

She laughed, no doubt at herself, for giving me shit about my propriety.

Two older women walked in.

"Can I help you?" I said.

"We're just looking," one replied.

Ti watched them and turned to me. "I wondered if you had any," she dropped her voice and mouthed, "lude-treats."

The two women poked around, then headed for the door, and I let them leave without any attempt to engage them further.

"To sell you?" I asked.

"Yes."

"Oh, I don't know." I opened the register and broke open a roll of quarters with a quick strike against the coin tray, spilling them in, emptying the thick paper cylinder. "We could just go out again and split one."

"You want me, don't you?" She hoisted herself onto the counter. Sliding around, her boots on the wood, she reclined perpendicular to me, propped on her elbows as if posing, her head thrown back. "Did I ever tell you about my first modeling job?"

"Yes. I think the Sears Catalogue. Are you on something?"

"*Moi*? Only a cappuccino. Haven't you heard? If you only do drugs at night, it's not a problem."

"Do you do everything I say?"

"Oooh. That depends. By the way, it was actually JC Penny, I was twelve, and it was a really big deal. But then I stopped growing, which put a crimp into things. I could still become famous, you know, dahhhling. Hollywood awaits." She pulled out a pair of sunglasses from her purse and put them on. Then, she stood up and catwalked the counter. After a pivot and some twirls, she came back toward me, giving a little wave to an imaginary crowd and blowing kisses.

"Okay, I believe you. But why don't you get down? If Miranda shows up, she'll be unhappy. It'll look like I'm not taking the job seriously. What's more, she won't like scuff marks."

Ti sat down facing me, crossing her legs as her hands gripped my side of the counter. "Miss me? There are other guys interested. Besides, does Miranda screw you standing up in the dressing room in the middle of the afternoon?" She covered her mouth with a hand, her eyes going wide with mock horror. "Oops! Did I just say that?" She broke into laughter.

"I don't think that's a good idea," I said.

Her eyes searched mine intently, and she grabbed my shoulders, pulling me to her, kissing me on the mouth. Slipping off the counter, she pressed up against me. I put one arm around her; with the other, I attempted to keep my coffee from spilling.

"Just want to make sure you remember me," she said. "Especially in case what's-her-name comes around. The one from Adriano's."

"Lannie?"

"Yes. Isn't she a little long in the tooth for you?"

"She's twenty-seven."

"My point exactly."

"I think you're confusing me with your last boyfriend, although even he makes exceptions."

"Oh, really?"

"Besides, I don't think we've set anything off-limits. We're not exclusive. Remember?"

"Listen," she said. "Lock up the store for five minutes, and I'll make sure you forget all about her. Put down that fucking coffee."

She took the capp from me and placed it behind us on the shelf, next to the radio. Smiling, she hugged me harder and grabbed my ass. "I dare you."

"I can't," I said, pulling away. "I'm working."

She lifted up her face to mine and kissed me on the mouth, pushing her tongue between my lips. She tasted of cigarettes and wine. "Ooh!" she said, squirming against me, peeking down at my crotch.

"Okay," I said.

"Okay what?"

"Let go of me for a minute, and I'll close up."

"Are you serious?" She started to laugh. "How about I crouch behind the counter and just give you a handjob while you wait on the next Deadhead?"

I jumped up onto the counter and slid over it, walked to the door, shut it, threw the lock, and turned the sign in the window to "Closed."

"You're serious!"

I walked toward her and slipped back over the counter to rejoin her. "Let's go," I said.

"No!"

"*No?*"

"I was kidding. I was flirting. It's the middle of the fucking afternoon. Like you said, suppose Miranda shows up?"

"She's already come and gone."

I reached over and tickled her.

"Don't you dare!" she said.

I tickled her again. Shrieking and laughing, she ran along behind the counter as I gave chase. At the heat press, she raised the countertop and made a run for the door, skirting the display tables. I followed her, the both of us laughing, and caught her at the door as she tried to unlock it. Grabbing her from behind, I carried her to the dressing room. "Put me down!" she said without conviction and she burst into giggles.

I closed the curtain behind us as we kissed. She took off her top, removed her boots, then pulled down her pants and stepped out of them. Together, we undid my belt as I snagged a condom from my pocket, placed it on the little sitting bench beside us, and dropped my jeans.

"I don't believe we're doing this!" she said as she stood up against the wood slats of the wall and I sucked her upturned nipples, first one then the other. I saw her watching us in the changing mirror. Then, I pulled down her panties, and worked my way to her groin and onto my knees. Ti's breathing quickened. I felt the rumble of a truck as it passed. Ti gasped and placed her fingers around my head and guided me harder against her. She began to tremble, and then I heard her start to cry.

SEVENTEEN

After Ti left, I sat on my stool behind the counter with one of Noel's journals open before me. Outside, a parade of Hari Krishnas danced past with their saffron robes and shaved heads. They spilled out into the street, disrupting traffic, chanting, chiming their finger cymbals, and handing out brightly colored pamphlets to anyone who would take them. The small children with them concerned me—miniature versions with their own shaved heads and their robes, enigmatic expressions on their faces.

I went back to my reading:

January 3rd

I recall being a small child of seven or eight, and Mother put me to bed. As she tucked me in, I posed a question:

"Mother, where's the Universe?"

"I don't know what you mean, Noel," she replied, and sat down on the edge of the bed beside me.

"Well, we live in New Hope."

"Yes."

"Which is in Pennsylvania."

"Of course."

"Which is in the United States."

"Yes."

"Which is on Planet Earth."

"Okay."

"Which is in the Solar System. Which is in the Milky Way Galaxy. Which is in the Universe."

She watched me, saying nothing, and got up from the bed.

"But Mother, what's the Universe in?"

I caught a panicked look flash across her face. After a deathly pause, she said again, "I don't know what you mean, Noel. Now go to sleep." She bent down and kissed me quickly on the forehead. Even as she hurried from the room, I was insistent and called after her. "But Mommy, what's the UNIVERSE in?"

I considered that, shut the journal, and closed up for the day. As I walked along Haight Street, an open-top sightseeing bus passed me going in the opposite direction. The guide looked like the Good Humor man as he stood in the front of the bus, dressed in white, speaking into a microphone: "Next up is 710 Ashbury, the former Grateful Dead house."

Aquarius Shirts serviced tourists coming to Haight-Ashbury to see where the hippies had been. I would stare out the store window as the invaders walked warily and snapped their photos. Others took the open-top double-decker bus tour like the one that had just passed me, with the guide pointing out the sights, as if it was the jungle boat ride at Disneyland. Sometimes, the bus made a stop outside our little row of stores, disgorging passengers. They flooded the sidewalk. Some shot pictures of the various storefronts decorated with psychedelic remnants of color, and Abe's Flower Power sign with its rainbow letters. Some went into Feed Your Head next door. But more of them came into Aquarius Shirts and made their purchases as I operated the decal press at a fast clip.

I continued walking up Haight, crossing the street beneath the parallel overhead wires for the electric-powered buses of the Stanyan 33 line. Dobro Girl, in her faded jeans and purple stretch top, was playing for tips, her instrument's case open on the sidewalk beside her. A pair of speed freaks panhandled me at the corner of Shrader, their hair dirty, their manner jittery. Nearby, Zora was selling her jewelry alongside the other street vendors. She looked out of place in daylight with her makeup, her pale complexion, her dyed black hair, and her tattoos. She was engaged with a customer but gave me a smile and a "Hey, dude!" I waved to her as I passed.

Right before the park, a building stood with ragged spray-painted graffiti on its facade, the letters black except for the first word of each line gone over with bright red:

LOVE WITHOUT RESERVE

ENJOY WITHOUT RESTRAINT

LIVE WITHOUT DEAD TIME

I heard the steel drummers starting up at the Stanyan Gate—a cheery, high metallic din growing louder as I approached. I passed the drummers with their lightning hands and dark, smiling faces, a smell of ganga in the air.

I entered Golden Gate Park, heading down the steep-sloped path alongside Hippie Hill which was full of freaks publicly toking away on their joints. I continued past the lily pond at the bottom and on through the rock-lined tunnel under the Kezar Drive overpass. Strolling across the lawn on the other side, I sat down at my usual spot in Sharon Meadow. My copy of *Demian* rested on the grass, along with the big notebook and Noel's journal.

I opened *Demian* and examined the marked-up pages. The first time I'd read it I was on speed in college, and the pages had come alive with meaning. I'd underlined whole sentences in blue ink and scribbled comments in the margins concerning what the book told me about life. After that, I read everything Hesse wrote. It wasn't the only time I did that: reading a writer's books back-to-back, trying to replicate revelation, no matter that the second, third, or fourth book could never achieve the magic of first-time excitement and initial truths.

Just then, a girl walked by who reminded me of Honey. I watched her and became lost in my thoughts. I put aside the book, rolled over on my back, and gazed up at the clouds. Maybe I should take some speed to get the article completed. I had a few Preludins and a couple Dexedrines back in my stash box.

A face was suddenly between me and the sky and the vanishing light.

"Hey, dude, how's it going?" Rudy said. His blonde hair hung down above me; he looked like he should be carrying a surfboard and living in Southern California.

"Take a load off, man," I said. He sat down beside me, retrieved a joint from his jacket pocket, struck a match, lit the doobie, and took a long hit. His voice sounded strained as he fought to hold the smoke inside his lungs and talk at the same time. "You know," he said, and then he stopped and smiled as if remembering something. He took another hit and proffered me the joint.

I shook my head. "Got something on my mind," I said.

"All the more reason."

He eyed my notebook, Noel's journal, and *Demian* split open on the ground, its spine held up in the air by the grass against the pages.

"Whatcha doin'?" he asked.

"Writing an article about the dance club scene."

"More into Zeppelin myself."

"I like lots of music," I said. "Punk. Rock. Abba."

"Abba? You're shittin' me."

"A hook is a hook is a hook."

"I think you *really* need some of this," Rudy said, and he offered the joint again.

"No, thanks. You know, I just saw one of those tourist buses," I said. "The guided tours. Bugs the crap out of me. It's like we're on display for the yahoos, along with what's left of the Haight."

"I was here from the beginning," Rudy said. "Those were the days. The excitement in the streets, the newness of it all, the smell of revolution in the air."

I looked around the park as Rudy rested on an elbow. I thought how it had once seemed the world was about infinite possibility and that we had the power to change things.

"You know," I said, "on second thought, maybe I'll take you up on that weed."

"Sure, man."

Rudy took another hit and passed me the joint. It was almost the diameter of a cigarette, very professional-looking, and had clearly been made with one of the rolling machines he sold in his shop. The joint was wet at the tip from Rudy's mouth, and I wrapped my lips around it a little further up and took a hit. The smoke filled my lungs. I exhaled and took another hit. Lying there in the endless sea of grass flowing through the park in great long stretches, it was as if I was an organic part of it: the surging mass of green and trees, the people playing Frisbee and running with their dogs, the path winding through it.

"Pipes," said Rudy.

"Pipes?" I asked, exhaling.

"Handmade ceramic pipes. I started out with a stand on a corner of Haight and Cole. Now I got my own store. Something I love to do. Still make my pipes, and still smoke my dope every day."

I said nothing at first, thinking about Rudy and his store and his happiness as we passed the joint between us. "You're a lucky man," I said.

"You'll find something. Things always turn out in the end. Besides, it's a beautiful day. We got some righteous weed. Get Zen with it. Baba Ram Dass says, 'The quieter you become, the more you can hear.'"

"Uh-huh."

"Ever read *Be Here Now*?"

"Things aren't that simple anymore," I said.

"Don't be uptight, man," and he took another hit. Exhaling, he said, "It's still about peace and love."

I thought about that. "He's Richard Alpert, Timothy Leary's Harvard colleague and League of Spiritual Discovery fellow traveler. Always will be."

"He's Baba Ram Dass. You really should mellow out, man."

I took an extra-large hit and felt an immense rush as I released the smoke. I said nothing for a moment as I came back from it, staring at the park around me, disoriented. The sun was dropping low on the horizon, a chill was setting in; the path began rippling before me.

"What are we smoking?" I asked.

"HSD: Humboldt Special Delivery. Ten times stronger than any other shit around here. My brother farms it. Fluorescent grow-lights, hydroponics, foil reflectors, twenty-two-hour days indoors year-round. It's a science now, you know."

Rudy suddenly seemed a stranger. His hair wouldn't stop moving; it was shifting in the wind, shimmering, and changing colors. But there was no wind, and I knew his hair had only one color.

"Gotta go," I said. I got up quickly, gathered my things and began walking.

"Hey, Billy!" Rudy called after me.

As I set out to retrace my steps, I immediately became lost, unable to recognize where I was. I told myself not to panic. I was on some kind of acid flashback, triggered by Rudy's superweed. This had happened to me once before, when I was tripping in college. I did now what I'd done then. I stopped walking, closed my eyes, and I drew a map in my head of where everything was supposed to be: the park, the route out, the way back to Kozmic. I opened my lids. I knew I must walk according to the map in my head, not what I could see with my eyes.

I didn't want to run into anyone I knew and have to try to hold a conversation. Instead of taking Haight Street, I ducked out of the park on some steps up an embankment. I crossed Stanyan and walked east, paralleling Haight on the quiet of residential Waller Street. Alongside me were two and three-story apartment buildings with painted facades, and porches sporting columns and wooden balustrades, along with bay windows jutting out as if poised to land on my head. All of it was undulating before me and wouldn't stop.

A man came towards me. It was just the two of us on the deserted sidewalk. Our footsteps echoed as we approached each other. I debated whether to cross to the other side of the street to avoid him. Who was this man? How could we possibly occupy the same piece of narrow sidewalk without acknowledging one another in some fashion? What if he suddenly talked to me and posed some unexpected question? I should have crossed to the other side while I still had the chance. Now, my boot heels clip-clopped impossibly loud.

The man drew closer.

Jesus. I didn't know what to do with my eyes. I stared down, then up, then looked away. Whatever I did, I must not make eye contact. It was the law of the jungle and of the street.

We were almost upon each other.

I should take control of the pending confrontation. Perhaps say "Good evening" to him in the most normal of ways. Or maybe just "Hello." Or "Top of the evening, gov'ner!"

I smiled stupidly.

At the last minute, I looked at the stranger and acknowledged him with a nod. He was an older man wearing a tie and jacket. He ignored me. There was a sensation of passing each other at high speed, the air parting as if it was a physical, tangible thing. I looked back and could see wavy lines all around him, like we were now fish in the sea, the water put into motion as we transited through it.

I looked ahead. I should be finding Kozmic at any moment. It felt like hours had elapsed since I left the park. Where the hell was he? God, could he have been stolen? Shit. That would be the end of everything. Everything depended on me finding him.

Finally, I spotted Kozmic up ahead, facing me: the twin split windshield, the bumper in a Sphinx's smile, the swirls of multi-colored paint everywhere.

Thank God. Thank God, Kozmic was where he was supposed to be. Thank God, he wasn't stolen. Relief flooded over me as waves of emotion. I almost cried. I approached Kozmic and patted his driver's side door. "Found you, damn it. Wouldn't want you to get lost."

The engine turned over on the third try. Everything would be okay. I just needed to focus for the drive to the apartment. I shut my eyes for a moment before we started off, and mapped the route out in my head, block-by-block, street-by-street. Then, I pulled out slowly, surrounded by the unrecognizable buildings and avenues.

EIGHTEEN

The sax player was a middle-aged black man with lines on his face and an easy smile. He was the only one in the ensemble who was wearing a suit jacket. The rest of the band members were white, ancient men playing in shirtsleeves. The drummer used brushes on his kit for most of the set, and you could talk while they were playing.

I was sitting beside Constantina in the Starlight Lounge showroom, getting off on one of Noel's Libriums, enveloped in its cozy cocoon as I attempted to leave the day and my psychedelic freakout at the park behind.

"This one's 'Stardust,'" Constantina said. "Before that was 'Jersey Bounce' by Benny Goodman."

"Very nice," I said, as the band took a break. "Would you like to split a lude?"

"No, thanks. I prefer my poisons one at a time."

"Two, actually." I indicated the cigarette in her hand, then the drink in front of her.

"Well, yes. That's a good point. I'll also make an exception for blow anytime you're offering." She said it, smiling, showing a dimple on one side of her mouth that I hadn't noticed before. "And I'm always out of pot," she added.

"I'll remember that."

"Gee, maybe I should just make you a list," she said, laughing.

I broke the Quaalude in half as she watched, her cigarette held at the ready. I noticed how high and prominent her cheekbones were. She looked for a moment like a miniature Marlene Dietrich. If she wore makeup, she could have been stunning.

I took the half-lude, washing it down with my drink.

Constantina put an elbow on the table, bending close to me. "Is my company so scintillating you need to fortify yourself? I know I can be tough, but I pride myself on that. I make an art of being an acquired taste. My men have to work." She sat back, blowing smoke rings.

I pondered her use of "my men." "I really enjoy your company," I said. "Quaaludes just make the whole evening more fun. I only do a half at a time so as to avoid getting too sloppy. There's a discipline to it," I added, half-seriously.

"Really?" she said, with a hint of derision.

"By the way, what you just did was really cool."

"What?"

"The smoke rings."

"Oh, that. A silly parlor trick."

"This place is different. How did you find it?"

"I know the sax player, Sam. He's a neighbor of mine."

"Where do you live?"

"In the Fillmore, but I watch my back. I share an artists' squat. It's cramped, but there's a special camaraderie. The guys"—she indicated the music stands and instruments sitting idle—"do it for the love of the songs. Since there's no cover charge, all they get is a small percentage of the bar. Sam works at a hardware store near me during the day. One time, I needed some keys made, and he told me about this place, and that was that."

"Happenstance."

"Yes, happenstance, I suppose. Or perhaps destiny."

She undid a couple buttons of her shirt in the warmth of the place. I saw the whiteness of her throat, and the taught edge of a collarbone. It was difficult to know what she wanted from me. I thought what I wanted from her was simply a night like tonight, sharing her erudition in music, the droll commentary, the barbed wit. But I'd heard somewhere that single men and women could never just be friends. Even now, truthfully, it didn't exactly feel platonic. I wondered just what it was, and which of us would be the one to ruin it.

"They have a woman who sometimes sings with them," Constantina said. "Sometimes she's here. Sometimes she's not."

This hung in the air like a confession.

She played with the stem of her wine glass, making circles on the black Formica table.

"By the way," I said, "did I tell you I'm working on an article? It's about the dance club scene. Mostly the straight clubs, but I'm going to include Buzzby's. Bisexual chic and all that."

For a few seconds, Constantina didn't respond. She surveyed the room, rearranging herself in her seat, using her free hand to toy with her hair. "Yes, Alexander mentioned he saw you at Buzzby's. Next time, you should ask him to dance. He's a marvelous dancer. Really, he is." She smiled at me, but there was an edge to it.

"I was there . . ." I searched for the words carefully, ". . . as an observer, taking notes for the article—and showing Ti a good time."

"Jesus. She's a *child*."

For a moment, I wasn't sure what to say.

"Truthfully, Alexander is very pretty," I said, throwing it back at her. I gazed around the room; my legs stretched along the black Naugahyde bench of the booth. Near us, some people chatted, ordering drinks, getting up to find the bathrooms.

"Isn't he, though," she said.

"Buzzby's has a mixed crowd, actually," I said.

"Mixed? As in gay men and fag hags?"

There was a silence again between us. I thought about going to the men's room.

"Okay," she said. "If I remember correctly, there were hetero-sexual couples. At least one or two anyway."

"It's a fun place," I said, starting to feel the lude on top of the Librium. The night would be fine. I took a joint from my jacket pocket. Covering it with my hand, I slid it across the table to her, revealing it like a magician showing a playing card.

She smiled, picked up the joint and stuck it in her shirt pocket.

"Thanks," she said. "Listen, I wasn't making fun of you. Actually, I'm quite proud of you for doing the article. I only tease people I like. So you should be flattered. I would love to read it when it comes out."

"If it comes out."

"Alright. If it comes out."

The band returned from their break. The sax player passed by our booth and stopped next to Constantina. She presented the side of her face to him as he bent down and gave her a kiss on the cheek. I thought maybe he was in his forties or even fifties.

"Hey, angel," he said. "We could use your voice in the next set. Still want that ride later?" He gave me a sideways glance.

"Sure," she smiled up at him, then turned to me. "Sam, this is Billy."

"Nice to meet you, Billy," Sam said. But he was frowning at me, not extending a hand.

I stood to leave. Perhaps Constantina had a whole life I knew nothing about.

★ ★ ★

The burglar alarm sat in its spot far above my head, housed in its faded red casing, a small window with grimy glass located next to it. Down below and facing me at street level, the rear door to the building was metal and impenetrable.

All was still in the after-hours dark as I stood in an alley around the corner from Union Street after leaving the Starlight Lounge. Dimly lit by a streetlamp atop a nearby telephone pole, the alleyway was lined with the backs of businesses, mostly two-and-three-story structures. Some had apartments above the stores, with a few rear windowpanes illuminated.

I directed my flashlight beam at the window next to the alarm and took a closer look. There were no protective bars on the outside or on the inside. There also didn't appear to be wire mesh set into the glass for added strength in order to make it shatterproof. The opening would be just large enough to accommodate me with some room to spare. Based on the window's position and my previous in-store reconnoitering, I'd determined that it provided access to the stockroom located behind the pharmacy's prescription counter where white-smocked staff went each time they had an order to fill.

I imagined the stockroom lined with shelves filled with drugs. Sure, there would be the benign ones: antibiotics, prescription ointments, medications for this and that. But there would also be the only pills that mattered: Quaaludes, Percodans, Phenobarbs, Dalmanes, Libriums, Black Beauties, Preludins, Dexamyls, Dexedrine. Perhaps even the pot of gold: pharmaceutical cocaine. A one-ounce bottle of pure fluffy white that could be stepped on to produce God knows how many grams of still-potent blow. Maybe there would be more than one bottle.

So how was this break-in going to work? I took a few steps back from the building and surveyed things, almost tripping in the process. I steadied myself, concentrated hard, and looked around the alley. It was just me, alone on the uneven asphalt.

How did you disable a burglar alarm? I could see that the pharmacy's electricity came from the pole in the alley, connected to a clump of wires clustered in a corner of the building, adjacent to the alarm.

I could pull Kozmic into the alley, park under the alarm, open a door and use it to hoist myself up. Standing atop Kozmic, I would be at eye level with the alarm, the window, and the bunched wires. I just needed to procure some sort of wire cutters to eliminate the power to the building and neutralize the alarm. I would then use Kozmic's lug wrench—meant for changing tires in some more innocent time—to punch out the window. I'd climb inside with my flashlight to illuminate the stockroom and bring a pillowcase to carry away the loot.

But what if a marauding police cruiser was to appear in the alleyway as I stood on top of Kozmic, wire cutters in hand, lug wrench beside me, flashlight and pillowcase at the ready. My mind raced. There would be no escape. Years in prison stared me in the face.

I turned away and started walking back down the alley, picking up speed as I went. Hurriedly taking the turn to the street, I banged hard into the corner of the building. Losing my balance, I dropped the flashlight and fell to my knees. I cursed out loud. At myself. At my life. At my circumstances. That I had considered breaking into a drugstore for goddamned pills and a hoped-for cocaine mother lode. Was I out of my fucking mind? What if the police indeed showed up in the middle of the crime? I would be ordered down from Kozmic at gunpoint by a pair of cops, taken into custody, and sent away to prison.

No, I could never go to prison. Ever.

I retrieved my flashlight and struggled to my feet. Then, I lurched along the deserted street, making my way back to the apartment.

NINETEEN

Nick James moved slower than I did and was bigger and taller. His straight brown hair hung past his shoulders, and his eyes were dark, his features handsome in a way that women found appealing. He was also a man's man, I supposed, with the way he talked and his anecdotes, a bit of a macho bent to his words.

"Billy, you need a life plan," Nick was saying as we walked along Haight Street in the brightness of a sunny afternoon. "Mine includes moving to L.A. and becoming a stockbroker. I'm going to be a millionaire by the time I'm thirty."

"Watch out for the dog shit," I said, and we separated and walked around a fresh pile.

"In the words of Ben Franklin, 'Wish not so much to live long as to live well.'"

"Can't relate to it," I said. "I was in L.A. for Christmas a few years ago. The temperature hit 83 degrees on Christmas Day." I wondered why my relatives lived in Los Angeles—my Uncle Bernie and Aunt Francine and some cousins—why anyone lived there. "Besides," I added, "it's awfully materialistic. Selling out. Living in the land of smog."

"What do you mean? You're working for a capitalist enterprise. You just aren't making any money at it. So that makes you more noble?"

"I don't know. I'm still sorting things out."

"Billy, it's tough being a moral absolutist."

"Who said that one?"

"Nick James."

"Well, the last thing I am at the moment is a moral absolutist," I said as I thought about casing the pharmacy the previous night; the rest of everything. "I was once, you know, back in college. It was nice while it lasted. There are some things about it that are easier and some things that put you in a corner."

The sidewalk was crowded with vendors selling their crafts: handmade jewelry, leather goods, tie-dyed T-shirts, incense holders in all shapes and sizes, hats festooned with feathers, hand-carved wooden totems and other trinkets. I stopped in front of a girl selling stained glass doodads. I picked one up. It wasn't really anything in particular, just something you could put on a windowsill, or a mantelpiece, or a shelf. It might make a nice gift for Lannie. I'd been trying to call her, but instead, I got her roommate Dana who sounded annoyed and said only, "I'll tell her," and hung up on me.

Nick and I began walking again. At the restaurant, I peered through a window and spotted Ti waiting tables. "Hey, just a second," I said to Nick, and I tapped on the window. Ti glanced over just as I placed my mouth against the glass and tongued it lasciviously. I could see her laugh and mock swoon, bringing the back of a hand to her forehead and fluttering her eyelids. A woman at a nearby table regarded me with disgust.

With a wave goodbye, I rejoined Nick, who was standing there watching me.

"Why Ti?" he said.

"She's fun. I don't know. I like her. She really cares about me. She might be the only girl I've met in a while who does."

"She's awfully young, and you guys have nothing in common. Although you do have Manny in common." Nick laughed. "And that Lannie seems like trouble. Besides, it's not like we're going to stay with any of them."

"Even Summer?"

"Even Summer."

At Belvedere, two Children of God street preachers in dirty brown robes and sandals—one of them clutching a Bible—yelled at us about sin and salvation. We passed the usual ragged row of street people spare-changing in front of what used to be a Diggers free store. I'd done welfare once, food stamps for a time, and even donated blood for ten dollars a pop as often as they'd let me at the clinic behind the Safeway on College Avenue in Berkeley. But I never spare-changed.

"You think you'll be working in the Haight forever?" Nick continued. "The Haight, Berkeley, the Village, Cambridge—they're all repositories of transience. You drop in for a while. You enjoy it. You leave when it's time."

"But I love San Francisco."

"Or just move on, metaphorically speaking," Nick said. "You know I'm working on my MBA. You should consider going back to school. You're a bright guy."

"You're younger. School feels like ancient history. Besides, my undergrad grades suck. Sex, drugs, and the revolution pretty much took care of that." I felt something graze my arm. Crazy Poetry Lady had wandered near us. As usual, she had on her thick black woolen jacket and an orange-and-black Giants baseball cap.

"Support the arts?" she said, trying to sell her slim, self-published volumes for a dollar.

"Not today," Nick replied. She walked away, blowing bubbles from a child's kit while continuing to hawk the little stack of poetry books to passing strangers.

"Life is about making choices," Nick said as he nodded back at Crazy Poetry Lady. "Consider grad school, or maybe go into business. We can open a dance club if that's the hot thing. I can round up some investors. What's that place on Columbus you're writing about?"

"Dance Your Ass Off."

"Yeah. Raise some capital, find a warehouse space, and give it a shot. There's nothing wrong with making money. You only go around once. You gotta grab life by the balls, Billy, and squeeze. Figure in fifty years—sixty tops—we'll both be dead."

My jaw clenched at that.

We reached the shop. "Thanks for lunch," I said, and we headed to where Nick was parked next to me. There was no mistaking his vehicle. The VW Beetle was painted orange with headlamps mounted on top of the front wheel fenders. The car had been in a collision, and someone sought to salvage it by pounding out the front end, leaving hollow uneven receptacles where the lights should be. The bumper looked to be jury-rigged, kept in place by means of wire and a couple judicious nuts and bolts.

Looking at me, Nick said, "One day I'll be driving a Mercedes." He opened the driver's door, got in, and rolled down the window. "Hey, did you get the stuff for my roommates?"

"Just a sec." I unlocked Kozmic, reached into the walk-through space between seats, grabbed the small brown shopping bag with the six lids, and got in the passenger side of the Beetle. "It's an even hundred."

Nick passed me five twenties below dashboard level, looking around, appearing nervous as I handed him the bag.

"Listen, I can't be a stockbroker with a felony arrest for dope if I get stopped by a cop. And I've got a tail light out," he said. "You sure you couldn't just bring this by the house?"

"Okay. After I close up."

"Hey, thanks," Nick said, returning the bag to me. "Good luck on the article. And think about the rest of what I said."

TWENTY

After dropping off the dope at Nick's place that night, I returned to the apartment. I said hello to Tim who'd just moved in and was lounging half-naked on the living room couch, watching TV and smoking a fat joint.

"Hey, wanna a hit, Billy?"

"No thanks," I said without stopping.

"You sure? It's good shit."

"Sorry. I've got something important I need to get done."

I went into my room, closed both doors, put Nick Drake on the stereo, and sat down on the waterbed. I turned to the typewriter on the nightstand, the large notebook open beside me. Inserting a sheet of paper, I began to type, transcribing the notebook's handwritten pages.

I paused in my typing. I was having difficulty getting Constantina off my mind after our time together at the Starlight Lounge. I imagined a visit to her tiny room at the artist squat: an unfinished painting perched on an easel; other canvases leaning against a wall, none of them framed. For how could she possibly afford frames with her Bohemian lifestyle? I wondered when I would next encounter her, and where it might lead. But I had other things to deal with first.

Manny put a forkful of pasta into his mouth, appearing to relish the moment. We were sitting at a sidewalk table at Enrico's, Manny facing the street and staring past me at people walking by as cars honked and cops cruised on motorcycle patrol.

"So, pal, how's it going with Ti?" he said, between bites.

"It feels kind of strange talking about it," I said, reading the little drink card mounted on a metal stand in the middle of the table. The tall, thin waiter brushed me with his ass as he tended to the table behind me. I'd finally agreed to take Ti out for dinner, and naturally, we'd run into Manny. Well, I told myself, at least things were finally out in the open.

"It's okay, chum. I dumped her," Manny said. "It's all about a certain morbid curiosity at this point. Rest assured, I could care less about the little marginal miss. Besides, David told me about you two a few weeks ago. I was waiting to see if you'd come clean."

"It's going alright, I guess," I said, surprised at the revelation about David. "Nothing too serious. Besides, I wouldn't even be seeing her to begin with if you hadn't brought her by the store that day."

Manny paused mid-chew and gave me a sharp look.

"Oh, so you're saying it's my fault you're screwing my leftovers and have no scruples?"

"No. Just that it's not like I pursued her. She kept coming back, bringing me coffee and food from the restaurant, inviting me to go out with her. She practically threw herself at me."

"You just couldn't resist her feminine wiles?"

"Listen, man. I'm sorry. We split a lude and did some blow one night. One thing led to another. She was just so damned aggressive about it."

"Yeah, that's her general man-strategy. But you know she can't be trusted. It's you today, and then—especially if you don't respond fully and completely to her rather desperate ardor—any Joe Blow tomorrow. Actually, make that any Joe with blow." He chuckled.

"Yeah, well, I try to keep it on hand for the women," I said.

"It's a waste of money. Some of us don't need it to snag the fairer sex. Anyway, my memories of her are merely semi-fond. Or," Manny leaned over the table, "is that semi-fondle? Her boobies are rather small."

He smiled and took a drink of his Amstel. I sensed that underneath it all he was only mildly annoyed.

"You know, truthfully," he continued, "screwing her from behind—my favorite position—you could mistake her for a boy. That short haircut, that little white ass, her titties out of sight. Kind of threw me for a loop the first time. Hopelessly hetero, I'm afraid." He looked at me as if expecting a reply.

"We haven't done it that way," I said.

"Missionary only?"

"Not exactly."

Manny seemed to be waiting for more. I felt, under the circumstances, I needed to oblige.

"Actually, I kind of like her on top."

"*Really*," he responded intently. After another forkful of pasta, he added, "I don't know. I read somewhere that liking the woman on top is supposed to be a gay thing." He sat back and took another drink of his beer.

"I don't think so," I said. "And it makes her breasts look sexier."

"Yeah, I know what you mean. I schtupped Constantina, speaking of tiny tits."

I wondered when this had happened.

Manny bent further over the table, masticating the food in his mouth and punctuating the air with his fork. "We were smoking this joint of hers," he said, "and all of a sudden, it's like her nipples turned into pacifiers. Very primal just to suck on them."

Over Manny's shoulder, I saw Brigit from Café Le Petit emerge from the back of the restaurant. Next to her was Ti, the both of them returning from visiting the ladies' room. Who knows what they had talked about?

"When was that?" I asked, hurriedly.

"Last night. It wasn't my idea. She was just so 'damned aggressive about it.' Hey, when Brigit and Ti get back, what say we blow this pop stand and go to the Mab? The Damned are in town. With my press pass, I think I should be able to get us all in for free."

"Well, maybe after we get something to eat. Hey, are you and Constantina going to be—"

And it was right then that Brigit and Ti rejoined us. "Are we having dessert?" Brigit said in her accented English, sitting close to Manny and opposite me.

Ti sat down at my side. "Hope you two boys had a nice chat," she said, a playful smile on her lips.

TWENTY-ONE

The next morning, Ti headed off to her waitress job, but not before we tussled.

"How about tonight?" she wanted to know as she put her clothes on.

"I don't know. I think we could use some time apart," I said, still in bed.

"Did Manny say something to you? Is it a him or me choice?"

"No, nothing like that. Just give me a few days. Some space."

She gave me a hurt look. "Even after last night?"

I had to think for a moment. Had I done or said something? I decided she was only referring to the release of inhibitions—what seemed like emotion, real or not so real—from the Quaalude. Lovemaking with abandon.

"Yes, it was really nice," I said. "We'll see each other again soon."

"I'm going to trust you on that," she said, finishing getting dressed. "Aren't you going to walk me out?"

I got up and put on some jeans. As we emerged from the bedroom, I could hear Tim out in the kitchen.

"Morning, guys!" he called over.

At the door, Ti initiated a long kiss, giving Tim a wave with one hand as she and I embraced. Then, she reached down and grabbed me as I tried to scooch back at the meeting of our hips.

"Hey!" I exclaimed.

"Oooh, somebody doesn't want me to go! Couldn't we maybe . . ."

"You've got the restaurant, and I've got stuff to do."

We finished with another kiss. I kept it short this time.

"Okay. Ta-ta," Ti said, more subdued than usual. "Bye," she called to Tim, and he responded in kind. Finally, she left, but not before looking back with a poor-me expression on her face. As she headed down the stairs, I gave her a little wave goodbye and shut the door.

I tried to dodge engaging with Tim over breakfast, but without much success. He attempted to grill me for information about my life, until he left for his latest contracting job.

After feeding Cat, I spent the rest of the morning retyping pages, proofing my article a final time. Then I headed over to *Lifestyle*.

"Here it is," I said to Debbie, who sat at her desk outside Ed Bernstein's office.

"I'll call you if he decides to go with it," she replied in business-like fashion, taking the article from me. The office door behind her was closed, saving me from any forced pleasantries with Bernstein himself. I realized I should curry favor with Debbie like Manny did, but I couldn't think of anything to say to her.

I left and drove to Café Le Petit, double-parked out front, and pressed the horn. After a few minutes, Manny emerged just as a cab squeezed by me, the driver yelling something out the window.

"Hey, pal," Manny said, carrying his big notebook and some comics as he got up and into Kozmic. "So, you have the article?"

"Already turned it in," I said, and I accelerated.

"I thought you were going to have me read it first. Provide you with my expertise."

"It's like I told Bernstein. It's about dance clubs, the music, and what type of crowd each place attracts."

"You don't even have a copy with you?"

"Nope."

"I thought that's why I was joining you in the first place."

"I do have another idea I'd like to run by you. That, plus I've got work to do with Miranda in Sausalito, and it's a fine day for a drive."

"I don't want to see Miranda."

"I'll be quick. Lunch on me at the Trident. I can drop you off there first."

"Okay, I suppose." Manny opened a comic book and began to leaf through it. I took a left down the hill and worked my way to Lombard. Where the street made the big S-curve near the Palace of Fine Arts, with its distinctive Beaux-Arts rotunda and dome, we rose up the slope of the 101 and drove above the rooftops. It was one of those crystalline San Francisco days. Off to our right, sailboats dotted the bay, articulated at sharp angles in the wind, their sails reflecting sunlight with flashes of bright white. Perhaps there was some sort of regatta, I thought. It was Saturday, the day for such things.

At the Golden Gate Bridge, I paid the toll, and we made our way past joggers, cyclists, and tourists walking across the span from the parking lot on the other side.

"Keep your eyes open for any jumpers," I said.

"You're in a fine mood."

"Maybe some of those tourists should make the leap," I said, watching them taking their photographs.

"With the railing that low, it's like the authorities don't really care."

"Democracy in action."

"Thinning the herd."

Crossing into Marin, we drove up the long incline toward the twin tunnels with their hand-painted rainbow-encircled entrances.

I stayed all the way over and kept the gas pedal to the floor as Kozmic fought to maintain fifty-five. We entered the tunnel on the right and burst out the other side. Marin opened up before us: the blue of the bay off to the right, some houses sprinkling the lush landscape, all set against the backdrop of Mount Tamalpais looming majestic up ahead.

Zooming down the broad curve of highway, Kozmic hit sixty, sixty-five, seventy. At the bottom, I slowed, brakes squealing, and hooked us around the Sausalito turnoff. The road was low and flat beside the bay. We passed houseboats moored in a ragged row, covered in weathered wood, paint fading, and home to a collection of diehard hippies. Beyond the houseboats, the water sparkled in the sun, pleasure boats visible.

Manny browsed through his comics, saying nothing. There were times when even Manny, after filling up the social space around him with conversation, checked out if you were alone with him enough.

Near the center of Sausalito, we drove past the yacht harbor with its flotilla of ivory hulls, varnished wood, and a stick forest of masts. On the other side of the road, houses rose above us, scattered about the steep hillside. The small downtown was crowded with weekend traffic, and the driving became slow going. Manny glanced up. "So, you're dropping me off at the Trident?"

"Right. I'll come back after I load up."

"Don't give Miranda my regards."

We sat behind the long string of cars at a light. I looked around at Sausalito and the bay, and suddenly didn't mind being stuck in traffic.

"I'm thinking about doing another article," I said. "One about the sexual underground."

"What do you mean?"

"Like the Cockettes party and some other stuff."

"Shouldn't you make sure Bernstein takes the dance club piece first?"

"Well, I was just thinking ahead, and I—"

"So, let's get this straight," Manny said, making quotation marks in the air with his fingers. "Something like, 'Cross-dressing: For Art, for Commerce, and by Compulsion'?" He chuckled.

"Something like that. And there's the Black Door—"

"Oh! Wait! How about, 'Oops, I Seem to Have Tripped and Fallen into an Iron Maiden'," he said, laughing.

"No, more like—"

"How about, 'Damn, These Nipple Clamps Hurt!'" Manny laughed harder. I shut up as the light changed and we lurched forward. Reaching the Trident, I made a sharp turn across Bridgeway Avenue, aiming Kozmic for the restaurant's parking area as I tried to beat a car approaching from the opposite direction. The other driver hit the horn hard, his car screeching to a stop. Pulling at the wheel to avoid him, I missed the restaurant entrance as Kozmic banged up and over the curb and I jammed on the brakes. Manny pitched forward, barely getting a hand up in time to keep from slamming his head into the windshield.

"Jesus Christ!" he yelled. "Are you trying to get us killed?"

I said nothing and allowed the car to pass behind us. When the coast was clear, I backed up slowly off the sidewalk and down over the curb. Kozmic plopped hard into the street, and this time I turned carefully into the parking area. We pulled up at the restaurant, and Manny got out.

"I'll be back in about a half-hour," I said.

"Fine." He slammed the door.

I drove to Aquarius Shirts, taking it easy. I noticed a pull to the right that required me to compensate with pressure on the steering wheel to the left. I wasn't unhappy I'd put a scare into Manny, but if I'd damaged Kozmic I'd be pissed.

At the Crafts Cooperative, with its boutiques, jewelry stores, and art galleries pressed up against the hillside, I turned and entered the parking garage. I found a space near the stairway. Taking my flashlight from the wooden storage box mounted behind the passenger seat, I crawled underneath the chassis to inspect things. I spotted the problem immediately. Two of the four bolts holding the rear axle to the frame on the passenger side had been sheared off by the force of ramming the curb.

"Shit." I put away the flashlight and headed up the stairs.

Aquarius Shirts Sausalito was crowded with tourists. Miranda came out from the storeroom, bright in a canary top, her skin tanned to the point of almost changing her race. She wore jeans too tight for her, a pair of black ankle boots, and aviator sunglasses, her eyes barely visible through amber lenses.

"The boxes are in back" was all she said. I carried two large boxes of shirts at a time, taking them from the storeroom down the stairs to the parking garage. Each time, I thought how I really should lock up Kozmic—but didn't. This was Marin after all; nothing would happen. After a couple trips, I said good-bye to Miranda as she busied herself with customers. "See if you can get to the Haight and help out Laurel for the rest of the afternoon," she said as I departed.

I drove back to the Trident, taking the turn slowly into the parking area out front. Walking through the restaurant, which was mounted on pilings out over the water, I found Manny at a table on the deck surrounding the outside of the place. I took a seat opposite him and looked around. Some of the tables were empty, others filled with people eating, drinking, and lounging about.

"Want to go over to Muir Beach?" I said.

"Why would I want to do that?" he said, rocking back on his chair, putting a foot on the wooden railing. A seagull flew close, suspended in mid-air, eyeing the tables for untended plates. "Got all the nature I want right here, Mister A.J. Fucking Foyt. And with other sights to boot." Manny nodded behind me. I turned and spotted a young waitress in a sheepskin vest, green suede boots, and hair down her back. A garland of tiny white flowers adorned her head.

"Look at her," Manny said. "A veritable Marin hippie goddess."

"She's hardly a hippie," I said.

"Let's not fall prey to linguistic subtleties."

Just then the waitress came over.

"So, how is everything?" she asked Manny. I saw her take in his partly consumed sandwich and an iced coffee reduced to some half-melted cubes.

"Tasty," he said. "What's your name, by the way?"

"Mysti. With a 'y.'"

"At the end?"

"No, it ends in 'i.'"

"I'm Manny. Ends in 'y.'"

"Mine's closer."

"Closer to what?"

She shrugged and looked at me. "Want anything? There's supposed to be a minimum."

"I think we were just leaving."

"You know," Manny said, "if you add a 'c' to the end, it becomes 'Into the Mystic,' like the Van Morrison song."

"He's my boyfriend's neighbor."

"Or, if on the other hand you drop the 'c,'" Manny continued, as if she had said nothing of a boyfriend, "it becomes, 'Into the Mysti.'"

He gave her his cute smile, and she giggled.

"I'll be back with the bill," she said, sauntering off.

"Isn't she adorable? At first, I thought my odds were looking pretty slim here in the land of moolah, musicians, and mellow."

"Think you might be deluding yourself," I said. "She mentioned a boyfriend, and he lives near Van Morrison. Maybe he's got a lot of money. Or he's a musician. Or both." Then, I tried to get us back to what was on my mind. "While we're over here, it would be nice to do."

"Do what?"

"Drive over to Muir Beach. Just for a little while."

"I know to you it's 'where some of all of it began,' Billy-boy, and well put by the way. But acid tests, the Dead and all that—not real meaningful today."

"It's not so much that . . ."

Manny watched Mysti, then gazed out over the bay, San Francisco visible in the distance. "Anyway," he said, "I have a piece due on the Damned, and I'd like to get back to the city. A trip to Café Le Petit for a cup of Joe, jocularity with Joaquin and Felix. Enjoy the simple things."

This time, I made quotation marks in the air with my fingers. "'A latte, a looker, and my friends?'"

He stared at me, and his eyes narrowed. "Actually, the girl's optional. My friends come first." He tossed a piece of bread to a seagull, and the bird caught the morsel in midair.

A pleasure craft went by. It was a good-sized yacht, and I saw a few people on deck. A girl in a white bikini was sunning herself, and a guy in a sailor cap stood at the wheel.

"I used to want to move to Marin," I said, not thinking of the pleasure boat, but everything else.

"Yeah, it does feel like paradise, but lacking the excitement of the city," Manny said. "I think I'd be bored shitless in two days."

"I don't know. I could see it. It's easy enough to drive into the city."

"I need to be awash in the energy of urban life," Manny said, and he took his feet from the railing. "I'm just getting myself established, Billy, and on my way to becoming a veritable bon vivant of San Francisco. An *enfant terrible* covering the arts."

Mysti came over. "Sure I can't get you something else?"

"My dear," Manny said, "is there a way to reach you in your off time?"

I felt embarrassed for Manny and leaned away, making as if I wasn't with him, my arms folded while I looked at the bay.

"I told you, I have a boyfriend," she said sweetly enough.

I observed the pleasure craft, the girl in the bikini now standing, looking sexy and perfect. Then, I thought about how Manny had no control over it. How that could be a good thing at times when I was in the mood and wanted to meet people, and annoying at others. As I watched the girl in the bikini, she bent over the side of the boat and puked.

"You know, that seagull's name is Johnny with a 'y,'" Manny was saying to Mysti, as the bird perched on the railing a little way down from us. "You know, short for Jonathan Livingston." He gave her his cute smile again.

She laughed. "I read that book," she said, tallying up the bill with a pen. "Deep stuff." She deposited the bill in front of Manny, picked up his plate and glass, and left.

"Well, it would have been a hassle coming back and forth to see her anyway," Manny said, seeming unfazed by the rejection. "Schlepping and schtupping, schtupping and schlepping. No car. In the city, who cares? But here, you have rock stars with Porsches. Isn't that Paul Kantner over there?"

I turned. "Think you're right."

Manny picked up the bill as we got up, then laughed out loud. "Yes!" he said, sounding triumphant. I looked and saw a phone number written in blue ink. Then, he gave me a nod, and I took a ten from my wallet and put the money on the table. Manny waved to Mysti on the way out, and she smiled back. He made a call-you motion with his thumb and pinkie to an ear.

"Schlepping and schtupping doesn't sound so bad after all," he said as we walked outside. "Maybe she's got a car. She can do the schlepping, and I'll do the schtupping!"

TWENTY-TWO

Manny and I got into Kozmic and headed out of Sausalito. This time, I drove south on Bridgeway, parallel to the low sea wall, the bay beautiful beyond it with Angel Island's rocky coastline and pristine hillsides rising out of the water. On the opposite side of the street, a charming row of restaurants, cafés, and small shops faced the bay. At the end of Bridgeway, we turned up the hill. Streets became lanes, winding their way up the mountain. We drove past homes with large bay windows, juniper trees out in front, bougainvillea in vibrant colors. I slowed and stopped between two houses. You could see all the way to Berkeley, the air so clear that even the clock tower on the Cal campus was visible. It had only been six months since I lived in Berkeley, but already it seemed so long ago.

"Can we turn on the Giants game?" Manny said.

"Sorry, the radio died."

I got us going again. We reached the cars streaming by on the 101 roadway above. As we paused at the stop sign to the freeway entrance, I realized I had no desire to return to the city anytime soon.

"I want to go to Muir Beach," I said. It wasn't a question this time.

"Okay, nature boy. Perhaps you could do me a lude or two in return for my patience. More freebies for Shelley, or Brigit, maybe Heather, or even," he said with a smile, "Mysti."

We got onto the 101 and drove down the slope of the mountain again. This time at the Sausalito turnoff, we headed north on Route 1. At Tam Junction with its hodgepodge of artsy touristy craft stores and run-of-the-mill commercial ventures, we turned west and soon began the ascent. Kozmic climbed steadily, the windows open, as we drove through tall Eucalyptus groves, the air filled with the sweet tang of their nuts. Then came the Redwoods, arranged in their primal circles of sibling giants, along with ferns, hanging vines, and the lushness of plants growing along the roadside.

We reached the top and the stop sign for the Panoramic Highway cutoff to the right that was the inland route to Stinson Beach. A smattering of houses covered in weathered wood crested the ridge: a geodesic dome and a few regular framed homes, surrounded by low scrub and grasses. Just beyond to the north, much closer now, stood Mount Tamalpais and its Redwood-encased lower flanks.

We descended the switchbacks on the other side in silence, curving back and forth, the ocean visible, the horizon a knife-edge. I clung us against the hill, and carefully navigated the blind curves of the road, adjusting the steering to compensate for Kozmic's new pull to the right.

The summer dry season had yet to set in, and everything around us was rich shades of green. Across the way, horses dotted the hillside. Below, nestled in the crease that split the ridgeline, was the Zen retreat with its wooden buildings and bucolic gardens. Snatches of half-remembered audiotapes played in my brain: Alan Watts and his talk of Nirvana and Nothingness.

Reaching the bottom of the mountain, we turned left onto the road leading to Muir Beach. No one yet manned the wooden shack to collect the day-use fee. That started Memorial Day week-end. I pulled Kozmic into a space up against one of the logs mark-ing the edge of the dirt parking lot. I sat and looked out the split panes of the windshield, taking in the sand, the water, and the sky.

"You want to get out and walk around?" I said.

"I can see fine from here, chum. You go for a walk. Maybe I can get a jump on this article," Manny said, the large notebook open in his lap.

"How about for just a bit? Come on."

"Jesus Christ," he said.

We got out and wandered the path from the parking lot, cross-ing a small wooden bridge over Redwood Creek. On the other side of the stream, we sat down on a huge log at the edge of the beach. The air smelled of the ocean; there was the sound of the waves, and seagulls flew close around us with the whumping of their wings.

"Honey and I used to drive over here from Berkeley on beauti-ful summer days before you moved out here," I said. "It was our favorite beach."

"Yeah, it's not bad."

"Sometimes it was just the two of us—plus Cat, who was just a kitten back then. Sometimes we'd bring friends like Asher, who always had killer weed. Once, we hiked up Mount Tam and smoked some really great dope and saw a bobcat. Then we just sat at the top of the mountain for hours. You could see forever."

I picked up a stick of driftwood, bent down, and drew formless patterns in the sand at my feet. Turning to Manny, I said, "Honey and I used to think maybe somehow we could find a way to rent a house over here, along with a few people."

Manny sat silently staring at the ocean, his chin resting in a hand, his elbow on a knee, wearing his black leather motorcycle jacket and beret as always.

"You know," I continued, the stick smooth in my fingers and the sand moving easily to the touch, "to escape the funkiness of Berkeley and leapfrog the bay to Marin, where hippies lived in paradise and there were Redwoods and mountains everywhere." I laughed as if it were a silly fantasy and meant little to me now.

Manny remained quiet. The ocean hissed and carrumphed against the beach in front of us.

"Hey, what's that giant insect thing?" he said.

I looked over and a large black beetle was approaching along the log.

"Just a beetle."

"Jesus." He stood up. "Do they bite? It's fucking huge!"

"No. It's harmless."

Manny placed two fingers over each other in a cross, as if the beetle was a vampire to be vanquished. The beetle continued its slow, long-legged, jerky walk along the top of the log.

"I'm going back to the bus and work on the article."

"Oh, come on."

"I'm heading back, pal. You can stay here and be at one with the vermin."

"It's unlocked."

I turned and watched Manny walk back, propelled forward as if launched with each stride of his black Converse high tops. Then I stared at the ocean and the waves and the sky. There was a breeze coming off the water.

I looked at the beetle. When it was inches away, I took the stick and put it lengthwise in front of the pincers. The beetle climbed aboard, and I set it down behind the log, among the grasses and dirt.

After a while, I got up, took off my shoes, and walked south along the beach, my toes curling into the sand. Cutting back through the trails in the scrub, I came upon Redwood Creek again, and I stepped onto another small wooden bridge. I stopped in the middle, stood against the railing, and looked out at the sunlight reflecting off the sea. Then, I gazed down at the stream and remembered how the rains came hard that winter and the water had swollen and raged. Honey and I discovered that the stream had broken through the beach to the ocean, and wild Coho salmon ran for the first time in years. We walked parallel to the rushing water as flashes appeared, the fish jumping, fighting their way upstream to spawn. Excited, Honey pointed out each one, keeping count.

We stopped and hugged, her hair soft against my cheek, patchouli oil scenting the air, beads colorful against her neck, the water gushing. "Honey and Billy forever," she said into my ear, swearing her undying love the way she always did. Half a question, the way she said it this time, as I thought about it now.

I raised my head from staring down at the creek and looked around. Today, it was the same beach. The same sun. The same gentle curve of sand. The same, but completely different.

I walked slowly back toward the dirt parking lot. Manny had Kozmic's passenger door open, his head bent in concentration.

I opened the driver's side door and got inside, brushing the dirt and sand from the soles of my feet and putting my shoes back on.

"So," Manny said, glancing up from his big notebook, "hypothetically speaking, at the end of the Damned show, what do you think Rat Scabies might say to Captain Sensible? You know, some amusing capper to a night of punk, a droll *bon mot*."

I gave him a look. "How about, 'Go fuck yourself'?"

Manny furrowed his brow. "That could work." And he started to scribble in his notebook.

3

TWENTY-THREE

I sat on the floor of my bedroom, nursing a cup of coffee. The remaining words about the final eighteen months of Noel's life lay open on my lap. Tim was gone for the day on a contracting job, and I had the apartment to myself. I turned the page and read the next entry:

October 10th

I remember when I was still living in Berkeley. Late one night, as I lay awake in my bed waiting for the Librium and the alcohol to take effect, I heard it pierce the floorboards from above: a series of muffled blood curdling screams emitted in rapid succession by Suzanne in her bedroom overhead. I listened for any sounds indicating something dangerously amiss, such as an intruder. But there was nothing.

"Pillow Death Screams," I thought to myself.

Now for the first time, my own such panic attacks had a name.

I was interrupted by the ringing of the doorbell. I went into the living room and buzzed in whoever was there. I pushed open the door to the landing and heard the sound of several people mounting the stairs. I bent over the banister and saw a woman in a gray pants suit, two men in brown work clothes plodding behind her. Each man carried several unconstructed cardboard moving boxes.

The woman looked up and fixed her eyes upon me. As she arrived at the landing, I stepped back into the doorway as if in some vaguely defensive gesture. Astride black pumps planted wide apart, she faced me, dark hair pulled back from her face, her hands on her hips. The two men remained behind her.

"I'm Evangeline, Noel's sister. I know about the journals. The family wants them and the rest of his personal papers and effects that you were supposed to ship. I'm an attorney, so don't give me any shit."

She reached into the chest pocket of her suit jacket and handed me a business card. As I took it from her, she brushed past me into the living room, trailed by the two men. I turned and followed and managed to get in front of her. The men were dressed like movers but stood on either side of her as if they were bodyguards; large tape dispensers hung from their belts like sidearms.

"You know," I said, my voice trembling, "I think we should at least try to get the poetry from the journals submitted for publication. Maybe even the journals themselves."

Evangeline stared back at me as if I'd just said something incredibly stupid. Sensing it might be futile but feeling I owed it to Noel—to myself—I persevered. "Then at least," I continued, "in death, Noel's dreams might be realized."

My voice cracked at "realized," and my heart was pumping almost as hard as that morning I'd found him dead.

"You've been reading them, haven't you?" she said.

"Well, yes. His father—your father—sent me a telegram asking me to pack up his things for shipping. I stumbled across the journals in his bedroom closet. I figured, in a way, I had the family's permission."

"You figured wrong. The family has no interest in anything other than getting them and the rest of his things returned. They are personal effects in your possession illegally. Where's his room?"

The fact she wasn't immediately sure which room was Noel's told me that she'd never been in the apartment before today.

"It's been rented," I said. I nodded to the brown cardboard cartons stacked in twin piles in a corner of the living room. "The boxes are already packed," I said, as if they were on the verge of being shipped any day.

Evangeline walked toward them. The two men put down their unconstructed boxes and followed her. "Where are the journals?" she said.

I pointed to their box atop the pile. Evangeline lifted the flaps and picked up a spiral notebook. She leafed through it, pausing to read portions as I watched. I knew from the journals that she was two years older than Noel, and that he loathed her with a passion. In that moment, I felt closer to Noel than when he was alive.

"Where's the novel?" she said, her eyes glued to the page.

"What novel?"

"The novel he's been writing all these years."

"I didn't find anything."

She turned to face me. "You're not holding out on me, are you?"

"There was nothing else in his room."

"You mean, this is it?"

"This is it."

"God, that is so pathetic and just like him," she said, seeming at once both irritated and smug with satisfaction. Then, with a motion of her hand, she indicated for the movers to carry the boxes away. The two men removed their tape dispensers and ran them against the flaps, sealing them. Evangeline continued to read the journal in her hands as I stood watching.

She turned to me. "You think I'm horrible, don't you?"

I just looked at her, my arms folded. Then I stared at the floor.

"Do you know what it was like growing up with him? His anxiety attacks, his weakness, his sicknesses, the doting by our mother, not to mention the money wasted on him for Yale."

I kept looking down, powerless and angry.

"What's this?" She walked over to where Noel's framed cover hung on the wall, his journal now tucked under her arm. "Well, well," she said. "'Failing to Fly' in the *Paris Review*. You weren't going to send it along with his things, were you?"

"Well, I was thinking of it as a memorial to him and his time here in in this place."

"Hold this," she said, and she handed me the journal. "It belongs to the family." And with both hands, she ripped the frame from its place on the wall. Then, she took the journal from me and followed the two men trooping down the stairs with a couple boxes each, the framed cover in one of her hands, the journal in the other.

I called after her. "Please think about trying for publication— at least the poems."

Evangeline gave me a dismissive wave with the back of the hand holding the journal.

I still held her business card. I wondered if she worked with their father, since he was also an attorney. Yes, the address of the firm appeared familiar. Would it be worth calling him to see if he would somehow intercede? No, I doubted it. There was, after all, nothing in the journals to indicate Noel and his father had much of a relationship. In fact, to the contrary.

Evangeline and the family would probably place the journals and their box in a basement, along with the rest of Noel's things, ignored and forgotten. I wondered if his father or mother would read them. No. But Evangeline would. Yes, of course. She was behind it. It was all about getting her hands on the journals, the rest subterfuge. She had to see what he'd written and pick it apart to feel superior to her mother's favorite.

The movers returned for the remaining boxes and their unconstructed ones. I watched them leave and walked into Noel's room, which was now full of Tim's things. I went to the window that overlooked the street. With a quick twist of the hanging rod to level the slats, I opened the Venetian blinds and witnessed a truck parked at the curb, the two movers shutting the rear doors. A taxi with its engine idling sat behind it. Evangeline stood against the taxi, reading the journal. I saw her laugh at something, and I thought about how she'd gained control over the only thing left of Noel—the essence and the truth of him. Then, she dashed off what I presumed to be a check and handed it to one of the two moving men. The truck pulled out as she got into the cab, still reading the journal. The cab followed the truck out of sight around a corner.

I returned the blinds to their closed position and moved away from the window. I felt as if I'd let Noel down. But what else could I have done? Noel should have handled things while he was alive, making better preparations, trying harder for his own publication, keeping his family at bay, especially Evangeline.

For that moment, just one moment, I despised Noel and his weakness with a totality that surprised me.

TWENTY-FOUR

January 20th
Sometimes I think I am my own version of the Self-Taught Man:
A serial reader and counter of volumes consumed but not truly
mastered, all in a vain attempt to add some worth to myself. Yet always
doomed to my isolation, peering out from my dark corner at the happi-
ness of others. I am like Meursault in his cell, clueless about my life and
how I arrived at this point.

I was glad I'd kept the final journal from Evangeline. It was the one I'd started to read again, sitting in my bedroom, as she rang the bell. It was a thick notebook, the thickest of the bunch. Noel hadn't begun a new volume when he reached the end. Instead, he had started over, as if surprised he was still alive, writing entries in reverse order on the backs of pages.

Tim was gone again on another of his contracting jobs that were frustratingly lucrative, given my own financial status. But I enjoyed the solitude his absence provided, the freedom to do as I pleased. I didn't have to open the store today with Miranda on the job. I hadn't heard from Ti since I told her I needed space, and Lannie still hadn't responded to the messages I left with her roommate.

I returned to the notebook, feeling much like when I first read the journals, examining every page and every line. I told myself I could send this one to Evangeline eventually, especially if she realized it was missing and contacted me. But Noel had not even had her phone number posted in the kitchen. It would likely give him great pleasure I'd kept the journal from her. Noel and I were now in league through death in a way we could never have been in life.

I marked my place with a fold in the top right-hand corner of the page, got off the waterbed, and put the journal back into the nightstand drawer.

"So, you bastard, where did you hide it?" I muttered.

I went into Noel's former bedroom. The closet was the first place to check. With a pull of the hanging string, I turned on the closet light and stared up at the shelf where I'd found the journals. Tim had left the shelf alone. There was even Noel's old can of spray starch still standing in its spot. Once again, I rolled the desk chair from its place on the other side of the room and gingerly stood on it, propping myself against a wall with a hand. With the other hand, I reached to the very back of the shelf and recesses that were difficult to see. A daddy long-legs in a corner made a run for it, going past me before it ran out of shelf space and drifted lightly to the floor. I pulled back my hand and brushed away spider webs and some dust. Then, I directed the light bulb on its cord into corners like a spotlight.

I started thinking crazy things about where to hide a manuscript: hidden panels, a secret piece of the floor that lifted up, a false bottom of a dresser drawer. I got down from the chair and checked the floorboards. Nothing. I pushed the chair on its rollers back to the desk and pulled open drawers. Noel's neatly organized writing supplies were replaced by the jumble of Tim's contractor materials: pens embossed with his name and business phone number, keys to who knew what, blank contracts, and various construction manuals. The row of hanging files in the large bottom drawer now all related to Tim's job and its paperwork requirements, tags reading: "Invoices," "Leads," "Truck Receipts," "Taxes," "Signed Contracts," and the like.

I went over to the dresser, becoming mildly interested in exploring Tim's life. All the while, I kept an ear peeled for the sound of his pickup truck returning. Clothes lay strewn inside each drawer, making me appreciate Noel's pristineness.

Taking a break from my search, I turned on Tim's color TV and sat on the living room couch with its cigarette burns, coffee stains, and holes in the fabric. Merv Griffin was interviewing Eva Gabor. She said "darling" a lot and sounded like her more famous sister Zsa Zsa who'd I'd seen on the same show the week before. Both women appeared to be great pals of Merv's.

I used to watch all sorts of TV as a child: old game shows such as *Beat the Clock* and *Queen for a Day*; half-hour series like *Ramar of the Jungle*, *Sky King*, and *Tarzan*; Warner Brothers cartoons; movies on Saturday morning, especially *King Kong*, *Mighty Joe Young*, and *Godzilla* anytime they ran.

"I always knew I would be famous, darling," Eva was saying to Merv, "even as a child growing up in Hungary."

How many other actors once thought the same thing? Or writers, painters, and poets? Or people with more vague creative aspirations, such as myself, and who were now stuck in dead-end jobs and failure? Or even worse, what happened to Noel.

I kept watching Merv, for lack of anything else to do. There was the boredom of daytime on a day off. I was finished with the dance club piece; wondering when I would hear from *Lifestyle*; thinking about the sexual underground idea; awaiting the coming of the night.

Cat jumped up into my lap and purred. I stroked him from a spot near the base of his tail to the top of his head. I heard the sound of Tim pulling up in his truck. I moved quickly to turn off the television, partly out of embarrassment at doing something so wasteful during the day and partly to avoid being indebted to Tim for using his color TV.

I went into my bedroom and mixed my usual one-part vodka to two-parts Kahlua in the glass I still kept in my closet. I hurried into the kitchen to add some milk and a couple ice cubes. Returning to my room, I closed both bedroom doors, played the stereo low, and took a half-lude with my White Russian, no matter that it was barely approaching early evening.

There was the noise of the garage door closing below, followed by the sound of work boots on the stairs. I heard Tim enter the apartment, go into his bedroom, then into the kitchen as he whistled something tuneless. Next came sounds of dinner being prepared. There was the opening and closing of the refrigerator, dishes striking the counter, knives and forks retrieved from their drawer. Then, the TV went back on, and the theme from *Star Trek* played as Tim took over the living room.

As I listened to Tim and his activity, I made my own preparations: pills placed into the front pocket of my denim jacket, along with a couple condoms, a book of matches, and two pre-rolled joints, and my little coke vial sequestered in a side pocket of my pants. I put on my jewelry and went into the bathroom to brush out my hair.

The half-Quaalude was starting to come on. I smiled at the face in the mirror; I was ready to deal with Tim. I walked back into the bedroom, turned off the stereo, and opened the door to the living room.

"Oh, hi," Tim said, corpulent on the couch in his underwear and smoking a joint. There was a partially consumed sandwich in a plate on the coffee table.

I looked at the TV but didn't sit down.

"Wanna hit?"

"That's okay."

"So, Billy, what happened to the pile of boxes? And that magazine cover on the wall? You finally ship them out to your old roommate?"

"Yeah, well, about that—"

"Man, wouldn't it have been groovy to have Captain Kirk as your dad? My dad was okay, but kind of boring." He inhaled again from the joint, and when he exhaled, he farted. "Oops. Hey, I should get my lighter. Ever light farts? It's really funny, especially if you're stoned and turn out the lights. Once, when I was—"

"Noel didn't move out. He committed suicide."

"What? Really?"

"Uh-huh." I looked at the TV. Captain Kirk, McCoy, and two crew members no one had ever seen before were transported down to a mystery planet.

"Where? Here?"

"In the bedroom."

"My bedroom?"

"Well, technically, it wasn't your bedroom at the time." I sat down on the other end of the couch from him.

"How?"

"What?" I said, thinking about what I was going to do that night, and drawn into the TV.

"How did he kill himself?"

"A quart of gin and a lot of pills." As I watched the TV, the first of the two unknown crewmen bit the dust. Strange octopus-like suction marks covered the guy's corpse which was found hidden behind a large boulder. Funny, I thought, how all these alien planets generally looked pretty much like Earth. Just with some weirdly colored prop plants, and sometimes not even that.

"Were you the one who found him?"

"Yep. His stereo had been playing all night," I said. The Quaalude was really kicking in. I couldn't shut up. I didn't even mind that it was Tim I was talking to; practically anyone would do. "It was Prokofiev's '6th Symphony'—the Peter and the Wolf composer. Noel listened to classical music all the time. He was very erudite. I heard once from Gerold across the hall that Noel was somehow tied to the Beats."

"I liked Maynard G. Krebs. He was my beatnik growing up. I loved *Dobie Gillis*. Did—"

"And that morning the music was playing. It kept repeating, Finally, I knocked and then opened the bedroom door, and there he was, naked and dead."

"Naked and dead on the mattress I'm sleeping on?" Tim said, looking away from the TV as the second nameless crewman met his blotchy fate.

"Well, yeah."

"Jesus. No wonder you threw in the bed for free."

"Don't forget I also gave you the desk, and that's a decent piece of furniture."

"I don't know. The whole thing makes me feel creeped out."

"You could always flip the mattress," I said.

"Very funny."

"I was being serious."

"Okay, let's do it."

Tim got up from the couch and walked toward the bedroom.

"It's not like he slit his wrists," I couldn't resist saying as I followed him.

We hoisted the mattress, a bulky old queen, unwieldy and without any straps along the sides to hold onto. When we had it all the way up and ready to flip, Tim said, "What's this?"

I couldn't see, since the mattress was up against my face. But I could sense Tim bending down, the weight of the mattress shifting.

"Holy shit!" he said. "It's two guys—"

"Can we just do the mattress first?" I said. We finished flipping it, dropping it back on the box springs. Tim lifted a corner of the mattress and pulled out a couple photos from underneath that I must have missed. In one, a naked guy was being led around on a leash by another guy with ruddy cheeks and a mask across his eyes. His complexion and build convinced me that it was Gerold in the mask. The man on the leash was Noel.

"Yeah, I found a bunch of them when I stripped the old bedding," I said, trying to sound nonchalant.

"Jesus," Tim said, and he trundled off to the living room with the photos. He placed them on the coffee table. "What should we do with them?"

"I don't know," I said. "I'm heading out."

On the TV, McCoy confronted the pleadings of the Salt Monster who was responsible for the two crew deaths. The creature was now on the Enterprise where, disguised in human female form and dying from lack of nourishment, it was attacking more crew members.

"Where you going?" Tim said. "Meeting Manny? Got a date with Ti? If you ever need any company—to go out drinking, smoke some weed together—just let me know. I'll treat."

I briefly considered inviting him along.

"Maybe some other time." I walked to the front door, turning back as the Salt Monster, shot by McCoy wielding a phaser, devolved into its true grotesque self. I felt sorry for the creature and guilty about Tim.

Maybe it was because of the Quaalude.

★ ★ ★

The Mineshaft dance floor was thick with men, sweaty, young, many of them good-looking. Some wore tight white T-shirts and equally tight jeans. Others had on tank tops plastered to their bodies, hairless chest-flesh and bare shoulders exposed. Mustaches were trimmed, hair mostly short. Surrounding the dance floor, a handful wore their leathers: thick heavy motorcycle boots, black leather pants and jackets, Marlon Brando *Wild One* peaked motorcycle caps.

I stood behind a support column and watched, the warm rush of another half-lude opening me up. The bass line thumped. The mass of bodies throbbed. Sweat glistened and fell. Poppers were inhaled in dark corners.

In search of enough light to write in my pocket notebook, I located the men's room. Somebody was getting a blowjob in a stall. I could hear it, loud and sloppy. I felt myself sized up by two men standing at the sink. I left and returned to the edge of the dance floor. I found a spot and made notes in large letters, hoping to decipher them in the morning. Maybe I should add the Mineshaft as part of the dance club directory for the article. Or, I told myself, it was research for the sexual underground piece. A guy approached me and tried to make conversation, yelling in my ear over the music, wanting a phone number.

I headed out the door and up steep concrete steps to the street.

"Fancy meeting you here!" said a voice. It was Ti, with Karen, Alexander, and a guy I didn't recognize.

"Meet anyone interesting?" Karen asked, sarcastically.

"You want to come in with us?" Ti said.

"I was just heading out."

"Got any fairy dust?" she said.

The guy who was with Alexander extended a hand. "Gregory. I'm a dance instructor." His palm was slippery.

"Terrific," I said to him. Alexander whispered something into Gregory's ear.

"Let's go," said Karen, grabbing Ti's hand.

"Fairy dust?" Ti asked me again. She sounded tired. "Come with us. And then maybe you and I can—"

"I don't know. It's late. I'm working on something."

"Didn't you already finish the dance club article?"

"I'm working on another piece."

"But I want to spend time with you! *Why won't you let me?*"

"Maybe it's good to have a few more nights off."

Karen pulled on Ti's hand.

"Got any pills? Poppers? I've got cash." It was Gregory.

"I don't know you from Adam," I said.

"Hey, everybody make nice," said Alexander.

"Billy, it's been *days*," Ti pleaded. "You had your space! I thought I was your girlfriend."

Karen looked exasperated. "Jesus, honey, come on!" she said, pulling Ti's hand harder. Then, Karen glared at me, her eyes flashing. "Why don't you just leave her alone!"

TWENTY-FIVE

I heard the phone ringing. It was morning.

"It's for you," Tim called from the kitchen.

I struggled to get out of bed, trying to shake off the effects of the Phenobarb, the ludes and the alcohol. I went out and took the phone from Tim. It was Debbie. "We're running your article," she said.

I tried to contain myself. "Great!"

"A couple things," she said. "Payment is seventy-five dollars. You can come by, and we'll cut a check. Or I'll mail it out."

"Oh, I can come by."

"Alright. And your byline—do you want Billy or Bill? Or, I suppose, William."

"I'm not sure. Can I tell you when I come over?"

"Okay. By the way, congratulations. Mr. Bernstein wants to run it as the cover story in two weeks. He's calling it 'Dancing Your Ass Off,' and we'll need to shoot a cover photo. You know, a guy and a girl dancing. Got any ideas who could be models? We're on a shoestring budget, so there's not much pay."

I thought for a second. "I know somebody who works at I. Magnin, and she does some modeling for them. And I also know a good-looking bartender who could do it."

"Okay. Can our photographer talk to you about it?"

"Sure."

"So, lunchtime today? We'll see you, say, noon."

"I'll be there."

That morning at the store, I played the radio and sang along. I was extra helpful to customers. I didn't mind when a Deadhead spent twenty minutes trying on shirts and then didn't buy anything.

At lunchtime, walking through the *Lifestyle* offices, I passed people doing layout, pasting up pages, selecting headline fonts, determined expressions on their faces. Others moved briskly and with purpose as phones rang and conversations rose. I was surrounded by all the activity, taking it in, feeling more a part of it this time.

"Here you go," Debbie said, handing me a white envelope. She adjusted her glasses, and I peered into Bernstein's office, but he was speaking with someone. I lingered for a moment at Debbie's desk, but she took a phone call and sat there talking, paying me no heed.

The envelope wasn't sealed. Once outside, I looked at the check. I walked up Ashbury, passing people all around me. I felt different from the rest of them as usual, but this time in some more tangible way. I thought in that moment, this is how my life was supposed to be.

Back at the store, a bulldog dropped a large steaming turd in the middle of the sidewalk, just outside the front door. The dog's owner pulled the leash and continued on her way. In the next ten minutes, five other dogs sniffed it, numerous people walked around it, and one guy stepped right in it. Scraping the bottom of his boot on the curb, he scowled at me inside the store as if I was in some way responsible.

After watching the smooshed pile a little longer, I went next door to Flower Power. The air inside was fragrant and moist from flowers and plants being wetted down. In a refrigerated display behind the counter, varieties of roses sat fresh and pretty.

"Hi," I said to Abe. He prepped his newest arrivals, trimming stems and removing fading petals. "Do you have a garden hose I could borrow to clean off the sidewalk?"

"Sure, young man," he said with his Eastern European accent. "Just do me a favor. Could you also do the sidewalk in front of my shop?"

"Okay," I said. He passed me the garden hose, and I ran it out his door. He followed me, handing me an old paint scraper attached to a broom handle by duct tape.

"It works real well for scraping the dog shit," he said. "Just be sure to rinse it off after."

This was becoming a bit of a production. But I said, "Thanks," and adjusted the nozzle of the hose, directing the jet of water at the offending pile of dog shit. Slowly, it broke into pieces, and I sent it over the curb. I began cleaning the entirety of the stretch of concrete at hand. The hose reached just far enough to include the sidewalk in front of Feed Your Head. Rudy threw me a peace sign from inside, and then twirled a finger around an ear as if I was nuts.

I kept at it, hosing down the cement until it glistened in the sun. With the paint scraper on its broom handle, I attacked the wads of old gum and the encrusted dog shit, and things began to take shape. Abe waved a couple times, yelling out his door, "Yes! What a good job!"

I eyed the T-shirt store as I worked, just in case a customer entered. After a while, I inspected my efforts, looking along the whole of the expanse of spick-and-span sidewalk. I returned the hose and scraper to Abe.

"Doesn't it look respectable now?" he said. "Just because the hippies have taken over doesn't mean we can't have pride in our neighborhood. Martin at the deli and Jerome at the hardware store, we were all here before the hippies, and we will be here after the hippies are gone. Being merchants is a noble occupation. And the sidewalks should be clean. In Europe, they have street sweepers do it. Here, no one does it if we don't!"

"It feels good to see it so spotless," I said as he walked with me outside and we admired the results together.

"You have long hair, but you are not a hippie. You are responsible. Your clothes are clean. You have a job."

"I'll do your sidewalk again next week," I said.

"Our sidewalk."

"Okay. Our sidewalk."

"You are a fine young man. What's your name, son?"

"Bill." We shook hands.

"You got a girlfriend, Bill? You did good work. I will give you some nice flowers for free for her."

I was surprised. "You don't have to."

"No. No. No. You got a girlfriend, a nice young man like yourself?"

Seeing how much he wanted to do this, I said, "Yes."

"Now, let's find those flowers for your girl. So, what does she appreciate? Roses? Girls always love roses."

"Roses would be swell."

As he prepared the flowers, retrieving them from the refrigerated case, cutting their stems, and pulling green wrapping paper from a roller at the end of the counter, I peeked out the door to check on the T-shirt store.

Soon, I headed back, carrying the dozen long-stemmed roses nestled in the green paper. Miranda came by just after I had walked in and put the flowers down on the counter. She wore her aviator sunglasses, designer jeans, and a tight red top. She paused outside the door for a moment before entering, noticing the sidewalk.

"Alright! Looks sharp! Did you do that?"

"Yep."

"Borrow a hose or something?"

"Yes, from Abe."

"The *tsoris* next doorus?"

"Today, he was okay."

"How's business?"

"Kind of slow."

"Crap. Oh, for me?" She picked up the flowers from their place on the counter, smelled them, and added, "Ah, young love. Got a hot date?"

"Well, yeah, I guess."

A couple strolled by outside, and Miranda walked briskly to the door. "Hi, guys!" she said. "Beautiful day, isn't it? Honey, you look like a medium. Let me show you something we just got in that's perfect for you."

Miranda always said, "Never, I repeat, never ask someone 'Can I help you?' Don't give them a 'yes' or 'no' question. Just start talking to them like you're friends." It was training I found hard to follow in practice, and only did so when she was around. But in the end, she sold the young couple two T-shirts each as I watched her turn idle passersby into paying customers.

After a while, Miranda left to go to the Fisherman's Wharf store. The sidewalk had dried in the sun. Just for good measure, I went out and picked some litter out of the gutter and placed it in the trash basket. While I was there, a guy tossed a wrapper from a candy bar onto the sidewalk. I picked it up, threw it in the trash basket, and called after him, "Hey, please don't litter."

He stopped, turned back, glowered at me, and yelled, "Fascist!"

TWENTY-SIX

At Adriano's, I watched Gina serve someone across the room. Lannie had called me finally, grateful for the *Lifestyle* cover shoot and promising to see me soon. I wondered if it would be tonight.

Turning to Constantina, I said, "I have friends telling me to consider going back to school. Pick up a Masters in something."

"Friends? Like who?"

"Okay, truthfully, one. Nick James."

"Oh, so it's that friend. Isn't he younger than you? Besides, he's not one of us."

"He's just a few years younger," I said, ignoring the rest of it.

"And what degree would you pursue?"

"That's the problem. Or at least one of the problems. On some level, it feels like school would be a dodge."

Spencer came over to us. Behind him, Zora stood in silver lamé pants, a tight black top splashed with glitter spelling "Rock Slut," and a choker with a pentagram mounted in front. Spencer bent down and spoke into my ear. "Got any?"

I passed him a couple Percodans, and he gave me some ones. "Thanks, man," he said, and they drifted off.

"Yes, school is perhaps a stalling action at this point," Constantina said, exhaling cigarette smoke as if blowing into a flute. "It's a path but not the answer."

"What's the question?" I asked.

"I think you know."

"Sometimes the truth is hard to find," I said.

"Sometimes the truth is hard to accept," she said.

We sat in silence, and I watched Spencer at the bar with Zora. They were arguing about something.

"And," Constantina continued, "unless you give me some blow to loosen my tongue, that's all I have to say about it."

"My company is so scintillating you have to fortify yourself?"

"Oh, turnabout is fair play. That's very good!" She put out her cigarette hard in an ashtray. "One day soon, I'm going to quit these damnable things." She lifted her drink to her lips, holding it between white tremulous fingers. After a sip, she placed it back down on the table between us. Seeming not sure what to do with her hands, she rested them on the knees of her paint-splattered black jeans.

"I turn thirty next week," she said. "Trust me, I don't plan on celebrating."

"Oh. You seemed different tonight."

She looked at me with alarm. "I'm wearing a little makeup, you bastard, if that's what you mean."

"No," I said, taken aback. "I don't know . . ."

She lit another cigarette and took a deep puff, holding it between her thumb and a forefinger, unusual and inelegant for her. Then, she stubbed it out virtually unsmoked.

"I've resolved to stamp out bullshit."

"That's a pretty ambitious goal," I said.

"Not all bullshit. Just the bullshit in my life."

I wasn't sure how far to take this. Gina arrived with my drink, a rum gimlet. I slid it across the table to Constantina and ordered another for myself.

"Whoa, big spender," she said with a small tight smile. "Business is good?"

"It's a living," I said with mock seriousness.

She gulped down half the drink before placing it back on the table. For an instant, it appeared as if she might cry. Then, she looked at me long and hard as if probing behind my eyes, unnerving me. She leaned across the table. I wondered if I wasn't going to want to hear what she had to say.

"I marched like we all did. What did it mean? My older brother was killed in the fucking war. I was in a commune at one point. There were the liberation movements, of course. Black, gay, Latino, the one inside your own head. But that was then. This is now."

I thought about what she was saying and debated how to respond. Gina brought me another rum gimlet. I slipped her a lude, and she smiled back at me.

"Long hair has become pretty much meaningless as signifying anything," Constantina went on. "Take your friend Nick James, for example. His hair is halfway down to his ass."

"Well, yeah. But—"

"It's not exactly the age thing. Then again, perhaps that's part of it." She picked up the drink and almost polished it off. She brought the glass down a bit too hard on the table.

"We hang out in this place with these people," she said, and she glanced around the room. "They should call it the Bar on the Edge of Fucking Nowhere." She looked at me directly. "You know, it's time to move on."

She was quiet for a moment. There was only the noise of the people around us and the music from the speakers overhead.

"It would be unseemly to do," Constantina said. "But I will beg for a little blow if you don't spare me that embarrassment. Alexander has been giving me some, on and off, but he's out."

"Isn't it a bit out of his price range?"

"He has his ways."

"It's in my jacket pocket," I said.

Constantina covered what was left of her drink with a napkin, and I did the same to reserve our seats. "Follow me," she said. She gripped my hand as we got up. Perhaps she had done it instinctively, I thought, not sure it meant anything, her hand small inside mine.

We reached the restrooms. Constantina tried the handle to the women's, but it was locked. I tried the men's, the result the same. Constantina stood beside me, our backs to the wall.

"*Merde*," she said. "Fuck!" She slammed a fist hard against the door.

"Be out in a minute!" called a female voice from inside.

We remained there in tandem, arms folded.

Gina came out of the women's bathroom. "Sorry. Glad you're in my section. Love those special tips." She beamed at me. Constantina glared after her.

"Subtle. She just wants you for your drugs." Then, Constantina laughed. It was a raw laugh of self-aware embarrassment, I thought. I followed her into the women's bathroom, and she locked the door behind us. I took out the vial and held the spoon heaping with white powder to her nose. She placed a finger against one side and snorted it. I gave her a spoonful for the other nostril.

She touched my arm. "What about you?"

"It's okay. I have other things I like more."

"Well, I feel badly. Can you at least do *some*? Join me. Come on! Live dangerously!"

Someone jiggled the door handle. I put away the vial. "Just a second," Constantina called out.

I took one of my remaining Quaaludes from my pocket as Constantina looked on. At the sink, I bent over, got some water with a cupped hand, put the pill into my mouth. I broke it up with my teeth, the taste chalky, and swallowed the pieces with the water. Immediately, I was annoyed with myself. Doing a whole instead of a half wasted a night.

"That's living dangerously?" Constantina said.

"I already did a half."

A voice called in from up close against the door. "Hey, can you hurry up? I really gotta go!"

"Zora's getting impatient," I said.

Constantina opened the door and walked through. I followed her as Zora squeezed by up against me, our faces inches apart, her eyes thick with makeup, her breasts pressed to my chest.

"Naughty, naughty, naughty!" Zora teased, wagging a finger at us.

Constantina and I returned to the main room and around the partition to our chairs. She didn't hold my hand this time.

"You know," I said as we sat down, "it's really hard not to think about going back to school." I removed the napkin covering my drink and took a sip. "Besides, what I really have to do is be productive in ways that matter."

"Yes, I guess dealing doesn't really count."

"Well, it does mean I get coke at cost."

She smiled. "An employee discount of sorts."

"I prefer to think of myself as an independent contractor."

"Yes, I suppose that's true."

As I put down the drink, the glass fell over in Constantina's direction. I grabbed at it, but what was left of the cocktail spilled.

"Maybe doing that lude *was* living dangerously," she said.

"I'll be okay."

"Is that coke any good? I don't feel much."

"Yes, it's fine." Truthfully, I knew it was stepped on.

Constantina fidgeted with her hair, twisting and braiding it between her thumb and a finger, eyes darting.

"By the way," I said, "my dance club article was accepted at *Lifestyle*, and they're going to run it as a cover story."

"That's fantastic news!" she said, smiling at me in a way she never had before.

TWENTY-SEVEN

I drifted in and out of *Go* and stared off into space. It was peaceful up in the Beat room. It was nice to feel good in the middle of the day. Nice to have no commitments. Nice to have freedom. Nice to be straight and okay with it.

I took in the book spines on the shelf before me, and the photos of Beat luminaries on the walls. Kerouac in black-and-white, young and impossibly handsome. God, the standard they set. Heroic achievements against all odds in a time so hostile to their art, to their lives, to their very existence. Such creative gifts seemed worlds away from me and my labors just to get the dance club article done.

The wood of the chair grew hard against my ass, the copy of *Go* in my lap now an afterthought. I bent the new corner, returned the book to its shelf, and walked down the stairs. I left City Lights and headed up Grant to Caffe Trieste and ordered a cappuccino. As I waited at the counter, I examined the fisherman mural covering the wall to my left, then looked around at the patrons. They talked and read as an opera aria came from speakers. Some appeared to me to be Beat survivors, sometimes dressed shabbily, a few of them writing where they sat. I wondered if any of them had known Noel. I sat down at a small table, had a few sips of coffee, and decided I needed to get going.

I walked down Vallejo to Columbus and took a right. I strolled up the avenue in the bright breeziness of a Sunday afternoon, the air cool and crisp, the sky cloudless. At Washington Square Park, I stopped and watched old Chinese people clumped together on the grass, an elderly man leading them in Tai Chi.

I crossed Columbus. I could see Dance Your Ass Off up ahead. The club seemed forlorn in the light of day, minus its colorful neon and waiting crowd. I turned left and began the trek up the huge hill. The exertion felt good, my lungs filling with the fresh air, my legs getting a workout. With effort, I made it to where the street hit a dead end at the top. I came down the narrow, zigzagging steps on the other side, taking them in loose, plunging strides.

Below me, a family occupied the small cobblestone square. Mother, father, young boy and little girl, an infant suckling at the mother's breast. As I passed, the boy pointed out to sea, the view today clear and distant. The little girl sang and twirled in carefree circles, her head back, her arms extended, her long hair flying as she whirled. I watched them as if from across a chasm, thought about them far too long, then finally reached the bottom of the stairs and cut left.

Manny was supposed to be spending the day ensconced in Café Le Petit, tackling a new project. "Hack work" was all he'd said. I opened the door to the café, feeling the heft of the wood as Joaquin and Felix nodded greetings from behind the counter. Manny sat at his usual table. Sunshine streamed through the windows. All was cozy warmth. The aroma of brunch foods floated out from the kitchen. Bacon sizzled. I smelled mushrooms and onions cooking. I heard the sound of someone using a chopping board. My mood rose, and I reached Manny's table and sat down with him. He had his big notebook open.

"Hey," he said. "Congrats. Debbie told me. I haven't done a cover story for *Lifestyle*. You got it on the first try."

"Just lucky, I guess. And it's not like it's a competition." Truthfully, that's exactly what it felt like it was. "Thanks for that introduction in the first place," I added.

"Sure. Just let me do these revisions for a sec, and I'll be right with you." Manny picked up his pen and went to work.

I stepped up to the counter for a Cappuccino Royale. Felix prepared the oversized cup as I gazed around the room which was filled mostly with couples. I was particularly envious of a guy talking to a smiling brunette. She held a cup of coffee at her chin and looked at him intently as if about to respond with some earnest thought of her own. I imagined her to be the perfect girlfriend. Nice-looking more than beautiful, intelligent and capable of sustaining not just conversation but a serious relationship, happy with her life. I stared after her as I headed back to the table. In my distraction, I almost collided with Joaquin delivering food.

"Sorry," I said as he dodged me smartly.

I sat down. Manny leaned back in his chair and in a loud voice, as if no one else was present, announced, "Okay, pal, here goes." He cleared his throat like a politician preparing to give a speech. "'San Francisco is the only truly European city in America, and just as everyone should have the opportunity to travel to Paris, everyone should enjoy a visit to America's own city of lights. The panoply of restaurants with their varied cuisines. The sleek modernity of downtown, with the Transamerica Pyramid rising as if a monument to the future. The parade of houses in the Sunset District, marching in tight formation to the Pacific as if an advancing army of white stucco. The ubiquitous neighborhood markets, bakeries, bars, and cafés of North Beach, inviting one to drop in and sample their wares. The Victorians of Haight-Ashbury . . .' something else, I'm not sure what."

I noticed a couple at the next table had begun listening.

"What's it for?" I asked.

"Just bear with me here. What'd you think?"

"Well, it sounds nice enough, but—"

Manny placed a finger to his lips.

"Okay. How about this? 'San Francisco is a truly great city for walking, with its eclectic mix of architecture and vibrant neighborhoods. The Italian delicatessens and restaurants of North Beach. Chinatown nearby, but a world away. The faded Victorians of Haight-Ashbury with their bedraggled charm, as some begin to receive new coats of bright, colorful paint restoring them to their former glory. The Transamerica Pyramid rising like San Francisco's own *Tour Eiffel*. Look north from Coit Tower to Marin's Mount Tamalpais looming in the distance, the magnificent Redwoods of Muir nestled at its base like—' God! Who would have thought hack work could be such a pain?" Manny was interrupted by applause from the couple next to us.

"That was so good!" the young woman said. Her male companion, wearing a T-shirt with "Fisherman's Wharf" spelled out on the front below a grinning fish, nodded in eager agreement. Platinum hair cascaded past the woman's shoulders and down a fire engine-red top with "I Love San Francisco" stretching across her chest.

"Thank you, thank you," Manny said, acknowledging them.

"That just *so* captures what I've been feeling while visiting here with my fiancée," she said. "Are you a writer?"

"Yes, we try," Manny said grandly. "But it is such a struggle. My garret is high above the street on the fourth floor, and there is no elevator."

She sat there for several seconds, and then she laughed. Her boyfriend watched with dull eyes and a confused smile.

"Well, folks, back to the artistic struggle," announced Manny. "Enjoy your stay in our fair city."

"Oh, we will," said the young woman.

Manny turned to me. "So, what do you think?"

"I liked the second a little more than the first, I suppose."

"Okay, pal, here's the scoop. My agent, the weasely but top-notch Larry Feldman—introduced to me by the almost equally weasely editor of the rag paying for my writing, the one and only Ed Bernstein—says I can make some real money if I do a San Francisco guidebook. You know, crank out some introductory descriptions, divide the tourist sights into concise sections with comments and commentary. Or," Manny laughed, "as Feldman put it, 'Think in clichés!'"

"You have an agent?" I asked.

"Yeah. My agent—hey, I like the sound of that—wants to get me doing some more commercial stuff. He says the guidebook can net me a substantial advance, maybe a grand."

"Wow."

"Yeah, that's what I said. It's a ton of work, but I could quit the copy center. Buy that mean motor scooter I've been wanting."

I glanced down at my coffee, wondering what the hell to say. Without looking up, I asked, "Shouldn't you be writing a novel instead? You know, incorporate all that witty observational—"

"A novel! Are you kidding?" Perhaps deciding he should be flattered, he added, "Well, maybe that's something for the back burner. W-a-a-a-ay back. Right now, I need the bucks and legitimacy of being a paid writer full-time. Plus, long-term, Feldman says, I'll set myself up as a new local raconteur. Maybe land a column with the *Chronicle* and become the next Herb Caen. The copy center will, thankfully, be history. I will quit, announcing that with glee, I might add, to young Myra as I finish my final shift. So, can you just be happy for me? Jesus Christ!"

"Okay. Sorry. I just don't want to see you waste your talent."

"So long as I'm getting paid, I'm not wasting anything, chum."

I remained silent, playing with my coffee cup. "Like I said," Manny continued, "it's hack work. But Feldman says, not only can I make some real dough on the advance, these things are perennials. You update them every year or two, and they practically sell themselves."

I continued to avoid his eyes, gazing around the room.

Manny frowned. "Oh, I forgot. I am so conflicted. But is it 'art?'"

I would try to be more careful this time. "No, it's fine, Manny," I said, looking at him squarely. "Congratulations. But you know, you could put all that repartee, your writing ability, and that observational humor of yours into a novel. Other people talk about it. Other people want to do it. Other people wish to hell they could do it. But you have the goods. You could deliver."

"Well, pal, be that as it may—and it's very flattering and all—perhaps one day. But frankly, it's too much work with no guarantee at the other end of anything beyond a very long dark tunnel full of toil and sweat. Besides, something has to pay the bills."

"There's always the copy center."

"Minimum wage and being treated as a toady? Like I said, I'm quitting as soon as the ink is dry on the deal. My plan is to support myself with my writing, regardless of who it's for. You work in retail, pal, assuming you can find another job when the store closes. I'm moving on."

"Manny, how can you do this?" I said, raising my voice. "You have this gift you are going to squander on some fucking tourist guidebook!"

Manny looked surprised. I could feel people around us staring, conversations silenced. "I think perhaps you had best concentrate on your own life, pal, and worry a little less about mine—and everyone else's, for that matter," he said, tersely. "I don't see you doing a whole hell of a lot. You watch, Billy. You suck energy from everything around you like some black hole. You hold everyone else to a higher standard. You ride my coattails. What's 'Dance Fever' but a nightclub guide—tourist or otherwise? Maybe you're just jealous this isn't happening to you."

"'Dancing Your Ass Off,'" I corrected.

"It was a joke, oh literal one. Now, if you don't mind, I have fuckin' work to do."

I slumped back in my chair, defenseless. Manny bent over the table, writing on the notebook sheets before him.

We sat like strangers.

TWENTY-EIGHT

Gina smiled at me from the bar, giving a thumbs-up with one hand, holding a copy of *San Francisco Lifestyle* with the other. The cover was a color photo of Lannie dancing hip-to-hip with Jerry the bartender, her hands in the air, his in motion above his waist. Bold purple letters emblazoned above the both of them announced: "Dancing Your Ass Off," and in smaller lettering below, "by Bill Johnson." I sat on a couch with my own copy, procured for fifty cents from a newspaper vending machine down the street. I would also pick up a few free from the *Lifestyle* offices.

Manny was at the bar, standing near Gina and talking to Jerry, ignoring me. Zora was there, too, while Spencer was seated up the couch from me. David and Monique, after congratulating me, now sat at a table with Carlos and a woman I didn't recognize.

Zora came over to me, her cleavage on display in a V-necked black top. She held a bottle of beer in one hand and a small, lit cigar in the other.

"Want some company?" she said.

"Sure."

She sat down beside me. A large silver bracelet in the shape of a serpent adorned one of her wrists, and a ring with a skull caught my eye.

"I'm putting together an all-girl band," she announced.

"Terrific," I replied. Spencer leaned back at his end of the couch, his eyes closed as with yellowed fingers he took a drag off his cigarette. I figured he'd shot up. Johnny Starr sat in a plush chair opposite us, casting his mascara-thickened eyes about the place.

"What are you going to play?" I asked her.

"Bass. Maybe you can give us a write-up after I score a gig, now that you're getting so plugged in. I want Lannie to play rhythm guitar. We're gonna to call ourselves 'Bitchin.'"

"That's great. Have you seen Lannie lately?"

"She might be dropping by tonight."

"Is that definite?" Johnny wanted to know.

"Maybe." Zora smiled at him. "Can't wait, huh, lover boy?"

"I can always wait," Johnny replied. He got up and went over to the bar and started talking to Val, the prettiest waitress in the place.

Zora scooched closer, drinking her beer as Spencer snored so loud I could hear him over the noise of the place.

"Hey," she said to me. "I don't suppose you got any Percodans or ludes or—"

"Okay if I squeeze in?" Nick James interrupted, easing into the space on the other side of Zora, between her and Spencer. He reached across her lap and shook my hand. "You did it, Billy. You made it happen. 'The only person you are destined to become is the person you decide to be.'"

"Who said that one?"

"Ralph Waldo Emerson."

"Nick, you're getting all literary on me."

"Fallout from undergrad electives."

"Billy, who's your friend?" Zora wanted to know.

"Zora, this is Nick James," I said. "By the way, he plays some jazz guitar."

"Really? Maybe you could give me some lessons, handsome, to sharpen my playing," she said to him, placing a hand on his thigh.

"Sweetheart, I don't think you could afford me," he said, lifting her hand away.

"Oh," she said, "believe me, I could find a way."

"Hey," I interrupted, "is Spencer okay?"

Zora peered down the couch at Spencer, his head back, his mouth open, his cigarette at risk to set the sofa on fire. She got up and went over to him.

"So," Nick said, moving closer to me, "what's next?"

"What do you mean?"

"The next article."

"Oh. I'm considering some ideas."

"Well, kudos on this one. And don't forget what I said about maybe going into business together. Listen, I'm heading over to the bar to say 'hi' to Jerry and maybe trade barbs with Manny. Summer and I are going out after her shift's over. You have fun with Zora." He stood up.

"Still breathing," Zora called out, standing in front of Spencer as she shook him. She frowned as she watched Nick go. "Nice meeting you," I heard him say to her in passing. She walked back to me and sat down, just as Ti burst through the front door with Karen. Ti had on her pale green flapper dress and black flats. She split off from Karen who shot me a nasty look as Ti came my way.

"Congratulations," Ti said icily, standing before me.

"Thanks," I responded.

"Hi, sweet cheeks," Zora said. Ti ignored her.

When it became clear Zora wasn't moving, Ti sat down on the armrest of the couch, her face close to mine.

"Is something wrong?" I said, looking up at her.

"Where the hell have you *been*?" she said. "And why didn't you use me for the *Lifestyle* cover? I am a fucking dancer, you know."

"Lannie and Jerry seemed to have worked out pretty well. I'm sorry, you just didn't come to mind."

"Yeah, that pretty much sums it up," she said, and I could see her eyes moisten. "Why are you *doing* this to me?" When I didn't say anything, she gave me a hurt look, got up, and headed across the room.

"I'll call!" I yelled after her.

Zora patted my arm. "She's such a skinny thing, don't you think?"

I watched Ti as she sat down with David and Monique, along with Carlos, Karen, and the other woman. Ti smiled at David, and I could hear her laugh girlishly when he spoke. It had already occurred to me that David could be the source of the cocaine I'd suspected Ti to be on that day we had sex in the dressing room—which meant they likely had sex also. There could be other explanations, but I'd settled on that one.

Just then, Manny came over to me. "Don't know how you stand that Nick James. King of the buzz kills." Looking at Zora, he said, "Hello, oh Queen of Darkness." Glancing down the couch to Spencer, he added, "You seem to have lost your royal consort."

Zora took that in and gave a hoarse laugh.

"Well, I'm off to the Mab," Manny said to me. "Mysti and I are going to meet up. By the way, too bad young Ti appears unhappy with you. Sometimes, what goes around comes back around, pal, and smacks you in the face."

As he left, Lannie passed him coming in.

TWENTY-NINE

Illuminated by the candlelight, Lannie rested a bare foot on top of the Redwood plank of the waterbed frame. She lifted her dress, revealing a thigh-high stocking. It was as if her slim leg were perfect, the nylon held in place by that perfection rather than the elastic band. As I watched, she slipped the stocking down the smoothness of her skin and dropped it to the floor. She did the same with the other leg and then removed her dress. Wearing ruby panties and a matching bra, she got onto the bed, the water like ocean swells, lifting us. I kissed her on the lips and exhaled hash smoke into her mouth. She laughed, lost her balance, and fell beside me. I kissed her again, ready.

"Give me some more coke, Billy," she said, pulling away. "Let's celebrate the cover shot!"

"You sure?"

"Yes, I'm sure!"

I picked up Noel's old hand mirror that I was using for coke these days. Lannie sat up and did a line with the rolled-up dollar bill I gave her.

"Whoosh!" she said, laughing. She polished off the drink from the nightstand where the dozen red roses from Abe lay on top, wrapped in their green paper. I'd tried to keep them fresh for her in the refrigerator, but the petals had withered at the edges, some falling off completely. Lannie didn't seem to mind, or maybe she couldn't tell. The Quaalude was really hitting her. I had only wanted to give her a half, but she'd insisted on a whole one in a way that told me everything depended on it.

"Another line!" she said.

"I don't know, Lannie."

"One more line, goddamn it! I want to go to the sky!"

"Okay. Okay. Relax, and please keep it down." Tim was out in the living room with the TV on.

Lannie grabbed the coke vial, pulling it from my fingers. She unscrewed the top and poured the remainder of the white powder onto the back of her hand, snorted it into a nostril, then licked the rest off her skin.

"Man, that's some strong shit!" She grinned. "Kiss me!" she said, her smile loopy.

I knew I was losing her.

"No! Wait! First let me put on more makeup. I want to be beautiful like a cover girl should. Where the hell is my purse?"

"You look fine," I said. "Really." She crawled over me, found her purse on the floor next to her clothes, and went into the bathroom, slamming the door behind her. Before, she hadn't been my responsibility when she got like this. Wade or someone else had to deal with her.

After an inordinate amount of time, she opened the door and came back into the room, accidentally dropping her purse on Cat who scooted into the closet. "I'm sorry, little kitty," she said, trying to find him, searching where he'd been. Crouching on bare haunches that seemed to be getting thinner, she reached down to keep from falling over. Then, she stood up and turned to me. I could see her face in the candlelight, a garish mask: thick eyeliner, too much mascara and rouge, lipstick not just on her lips but surrounding her mouth. Getting back on the bed, she lost her balance again. She began laughing uncontrollably as, on the stereo, Bryan Ferry crooned about love and loss.

I tried to kiss her, but she reached up to my bare chest, holding me at bay.

"Billy, I want more coke."

"You finished it."

"You must have some more."

"No. But I can get a gram tomorrow."

"I want it now."

"There isn't any. I'll get it tomorrow."

"I know you have some. You're holding out on me. Or else just call the guy, and let's go get it tonight."

"Lannie, he's all the way over in Berkeley. I promise, tomorrow. And I'm really out."

"Likely story. I need it, Billy. I need it, and I need it tonight! I know you can find us some!"

"No, it's true. I'm out," I said as I tried to embrace her. She pushed harder against my chest.

"You're not Wade!" she screamed. "Get off me, you son of a bitch!" She began hitting my chest, forcing me to grab her hands and hold them together at the wrists.

"Lannie, please. Shhhh!"

"I want Wade! He'll have some coke. I'm leaving!" She struggled, trying to wrestle her hands from my grip until I released her. "You used to be my friend, Billy. Now you just want to fuck me!"

"You're in no shape to drive," I said, grabbing an arm as she started to get off the waterbed. She hit me hard across the face with her other hand. Stinging pain seared my cheek. She stood up and began to put on her dress, crying as she struggled with it.

"Please relax, and come back to bed," I said, trying to keep the night from falling apart completely. Lannie worked at getting into her dress, but only one hand found an armhole. Trying to put on her stockings, she fell to the floor, going to her knees against the record player, knocking the needle off the album with a loud scratch. I got up and held her from behind, smothering her in my arms. She struggled, groaning and crying. I could feel her shaking.

She broke free, lurched over to the dozen roses and grabbed them, pulling the flowers from their stems, cutting her hand, her wrists, her arms as she tore at them. She let loose with some guttural noise I'd never heard before. "I hate you!" she yelled, and then, she turned and threw what was left of the roses at me. "Honey was my friend! She loved you! What am I doing here?" She cried some more while I tried to comfort her, as she let me hug her now.

Tim knocked on the door. "Is there anything I can do, folks?"

"Yeah," I yelled. "Get fucking lost!"

I put my mouth close to Lannie's ear. "Do you want something to feel better?"

I sensed Tim lingering at the door.

"I want to leave. Now! I don't love you, Billy! *I'll never love you!*"

I winced and clung to her. "You're in no shape to drive," I said again. "Take something to relax first."

"Then I go?"

"Right. After you calm down."

"Okay. Just make the pain go away, Billy," she said, slumping in my arms.

I continued to hug her, my cheek against her face, her hair soft, perfumed scents rising from her neck.

"Will you stay right here for a minute if I let go?"

She sobbed quietly. "Okay."

I got up, keeping an eye on her. She rocked back and forth, sitting on the floor, grasping her knees that were drawn up tight, her head down. I moved around the bed, reached for the stash box, and found a Phenobarb. I grabbed my White Russian from the nightstand, then kneeled naked beside her.

"Here's something to make you feel better."

She took the pill as I put the glass to her lips. Then, I held her around her shoulders and shifted behind her, rocking us both slowly back and forth.

"It'll be okay," I said. "It'll be okay. Everything's going to be all right."

She began to hum a melody I didn't recognize.

"That song's nice," I said. She continued for another verse, then stopped. We stayed together in the candlelit semi-darkness. She hummed the tune again softly. The sound of the television in the living room crept under the door. The stereo turntable spun around and around, making a "whisk, whisk, whisk" noise as the length of the needle arm hung useless.

"Let's get you more relaxed," I said, lifting her gently by a hand and leading her onto the bed. She closed her eyes, the motion of the water subsided, and her breathing slowed. I stroked her hair and kissed her cheek. Then, I went into the bathroom and retrieved a towel. Back in the bedroom, I wiped the blood from the thorn cuts and scratches on her hands and arms as best I could as she lay there. Finally, I blew out the candle, and the waterbed grew still. At some point, Cat jumped up onto the bed, and I pulled the covers over the three of us.

★ ★ ★

In the morning, Tim had gone to a job. I made us some instant and brought the cups into the bedroom. Lannie sat on the edge of the bed, dressed in last night's clothes, the scratches on her hands and arms visible. I gave her a cup of coffee, and she took a sip.

"I'm a little worried about getting you presentable for work," I said. "Do you at least want to brush your hair?"

"I got fired from I. Magnin," she said, her voice flat.

"You promised this time would be different."

"I know. But the clothes were so beautiful and too expensive, even with the employee discount. And they paid me almost nothing for that little bit of modeling I did for them. I just couldn't resist taking some stuff home." She took another sip of coffee.

"I hate myself," she said.

"Don't say that."

"I'm such a fuck-up. And I can't play guitar worth a damn." She reached into her purse, opened a vial, put a couple blue Valiums into her hand, and before I could say anything, took them with the coffee.

I finished getting dressed. I had to hustle, as I needed to open the store. I drove behind her to her apartment, alarmed when she narrowly missed hitting a pedestrian. At Van Ness, she almost ran a red light, coming to a sharp stop, me up against her bumper.

Her roommate Dana was home when we arrived. At first, I thought that was a good thing, as Dana could help take care of Lannie rather than me leaving her there alone. But Dana gave me an accusing look as if it was my fault Lannie appeared such a mess.

"I'll call and check in," I said to the both of them, and I headed for the Haight.

THIRTY

I strode into the *Lifestyle* offices and found Debbie.

"Mr. Bernstein says he wants to stick to the deal," she said as if she enjoyed cutting me down to size.

"But I'd like to pitch him on an idea I have for another article," I said. To pique her interest, I added, "'Exploring the Sexual Underground.'"

She raised an eyebrow. "You have to sell advertising to get in the magazine again. Mr. Bernstein's at lunch. He left this for you."

Reluctantly, I took a folder from her. The cover had the *San Francisco Lifestyle* logo. I opened it, and inside were rate cards for ads of differing sizes.

"Oh, and Billy? Mr. Bernstein says, 'Wear a tie, and be professional.'" She picked up a cup of coffee on her desk, took a drink, and wheeled around to her typewriter.

I left. I walked up Ashbury, navigating the sidewalk crowds. The sky was darkening, clouds moving in. I jaywalked Haight Street, ditched the *Lifestyle* ad kit into the trash basket that was filled almost to overflowing in front of the store, and opened back up. A Deadhead came in and bought a New Riders T-shirt in a large. I didn't ring it up and pocketed the cash. As he left, I took the little notebook from my pocket. I added five dollars to the running tally I'd started keeping, working from the back of the notebook forward. I'd told myself that this way, one day I could repay Miranda. It made me feel better.

I thought some more about other possible articles. Maybe I would say to hell with Manny and write one about the arrival of punk to the city. I couldn't sell it to *Lifestyle* now anyway. Maybe the *Guardian* would take it.

Then, I opened *Siddhartha* and read for a while. There were none of my underlining's on its pages, and despite its slimness, I had yet to ever finish it. Soon bored, I made notes for the sexual underground article on the blank page at the very back.

After a while, cars splashed by in the street. I sat on the stool behind the counter, watching the rare late-spring shower, the front door open, the sweet smell of rain permeating the store. I was making plans for my life in my head when Ti rushed in without an umbrella. "Damn it all to hell!" she said. "Who thought it would rain? Got an old T-shirt I could use to towel my hair?"

I passed her a "Steal Your Face" Dead shirt that had been returned.

"I was at the restaurant," I said. "They told me you don't work there anymore."

"Could you give me a ride home after you close up?" She took some lipstick and a hand mirror from her purse.

"So, are you working at the Black Door now with Karen?"

"Listen, Billy, don't do this. I don't want to talk about it. What I want to talk about is us."

"I just want you to be honest with me."

"That's rich. Like you are with me?"

"I know about you and David," I bluffed.

"Get real! Like you haven't been trying to screw anything that walks? You couldn't be faithful if your life depended on it."

"What about you?"

"It's a moot fucking point. You know, if you had been ready to commit to something instead of pushing me away, that would have changed everything!"

"Gee, maybe I didn't want to come between you and Karen."

"That's low. At least she cares about me."

"Besides, I couldn't trust you. I found out about Carlos."

"Are you kidding? You and I didn't even know each other yet, and it was just one night. He had some great blow, and it was before I was seeing Manny even!"

"Hey," I said, "can you keep it down and avoid making a public spectacle?" I turned up the radio on its shelf behind me.

"The store is fucking empty!" She put the mirror back in the purse and straightened her new-looking brown leather jacket. "And there's that Lannie thing. What do you see in her? And getting her on the cover of *Lifestyle* instead of me. She's dumb as a rock. Speaking of which, I've seen how you ogle Zora. Jesus. Is she next?"

"You and I are both free to see other people. 'Fuck buddies,' I believe you called it."

"That was your idea, mister! You could have had me, you know. Really had me. What the hell did you expect me to do? I got tired of guessing what you're thinking, what you're feeling. Make that not feeling." She started to cry.

"I talk to you."

"Yeah, that's you, Mister Chatty. Mister Open-and-Honest. Mister Loquacious. Only on Quaaludes, Billy, and even then, it's mostly about you. David bought me perfume. And he took me to dinner at Chez Noire. And he's fucking French!" She laughed through the tears when she said that last part.

I stood there, my arms folded. She reclaimed her handbag from its place on the counter.

"You never said you love me. I can feel you backing away all the time. Your cat gets more attention than I do. I'm done trying to get you to value me!"

"Go then. Have your fun with David. I hope his coke is good."

"I will! Don't you fucking worry about that! And his coke *is* good by the way, you prick!" She said it really sobbing now, distraught, her tears pushing me further away. I was glad no one walked into the store in the middle of this.

"Anything else on your mind," I asked, "as long as we're clearing the air?"

Part of me was trying to hold on to her, but it was too late. She headed for the door.

"It would be nice if I didn't have to see you at Adriano's," I said.

She turned around and faced me. "You don't own it, mister!"

"I showed it to you. Okay, to hell with it. Whatever. It's copasetic, Ti. We can wave at each other across the room. Or if you'd like, make faces."

On another day, that would have broken the tension. We would have laughed and gone on. Or I would have done something goofy like stick my tongue out at her. But she just stood in the doorway as if gathering her strength, glaring at me.

"Fine!" she yelled, storming out into the rain, which came down in buckets now. I picked up *The Myth of Sisyphus* from my little collection under the counter and perused the underlined pages, turning down the radio, trying to regain my composure. I caught Ti through the window, dumping the trash basket onto the sidewalk.

Terrific. I would have to clean up the mess.

I went back to Camus. Let Abe come out and yell at her, I thought. When I glanced up again, she was dragging the trash basket across the sidewalk toward the store. With some sort of supreme effort, she swung it with both arms, sending it hurtling against the window, and the glass shattered in an explosion of noise.

"Are you fucking crazy?" I yelled through the opening.

"You're playing with people's lives, Billy!" she yelled back, and she gave me the finger.

I vaulted over the counter. Outside, I found her breathing hard, bent over, her hands on her knees in the rain.

"Happy, fuck-face?" she asked. She stood up, crying. "Look what you made me do."

Then, she took off running. After watching for a moment, I sprinted in pursuit. I dodged people with umbrellas as I tried to catch up.

Ti dashed ahead, passing vendors with plastic sheeting over their wares; Zora was among them, looking up with surprise as I went by.

At Cole, I almost collided with Crazy Poetry Lady.

I stopped and watched Ti disappear from view.

4

THIRTY-ONE

Asher pushed an oversized prescription pill bottle across the counter, along with a bindle of coke. The cash register blocked them from the view of anyone entering the store.

"Next time, I'll have some more Percodans. And hash, too, if you want it," he said, staring past me at the display shirts mounted on their cabinets.

"Pick one," I said. "On me."

"Alright, my man. Been to fourteen Dead shows. I'll take a 'Tiger Rose' in a large."

I turned around to pull the shirt from the stack in the cabinet.

"Shit!" Asher said, and I glanced at the door, but no one was coming. I looked at Asher and saw blood dripping from his nose. He tried to stop it with a hand, bright red oozing between his fingers.

"Jesus," I said. "You scared the crap out of me."

"Sorry, man. Got anything to help?"

I tossed him the "Steal Your Face" shirt Ti used to dry herself a couple weeks earlier. I hadn't seen or heard from her since. I'd tried calling, but nobody picked up. The window had been replaced. I told Miranda a crazed speed freak had heaved the trash basket through it, and she bought it.

Asher placed the T-shirt over his nose and held it there. I passed him the money. With his free hand, he stuffed it into a pocket.

"Let's see if I can hang onto this cash for a while. I keep snorting up my profits," he said with a jittery laugh. "Goddammit. Gotta get this bleeding under control."

I picked up the coke bindle from the counter and dropped it into my shirt pocket. Just then, out of the corner of my eye, I caught a cop coming through the door. I grabbed the pill bottle and slipped it under the counter, just as another cop followed the first into the store. Asher's stricken expression said it all.

"You William Johnson?" the first cop asked. He had a handlebar moustache and acted as if Asher wasn't there.

"Uh-huh," I said.

"You need to come with us."

My mind raced. "Can you tell me what this is all about?"

"That's up to Detective Miller down at the station."

"Am I under arrest?"

The cop rested both hands on the counter, his fingers thick with black hairs, a tattoo peeking out from one of his short sleeves. "You're not under arrest—not yet anyway. But I'm sure we could arrange something if you'd like." The second, smaller cop stood behind him, hands on his hips, sunglasses on his face. He blew a bubble with a wad of gum and sucked it back in, popping it with a sharp snap.

Asher was making as if to examine the shirts on display, while backing away from the cops.

I pulled my denim jacket from the shelf next to my books and came around the counter through the lift-up top. Another hour and the cops would have missed me. On another day, I wouldn't have been there at all. And on any day but today, I wouldn't be carrying a gram of coke. At least I'd stashed the hundred Quaaludes.

"This will make me need to close up early," I said, stopping in front of the cops. "My boss won't be happy. I could lose my job."

The shorter cop glanced over at Asher making his way to the door, the T-shirt held tight to his face.

"Friend of yours?" he asked.

"Customer," I said. "Nosebleed."

Asher maneuvered the rest of the way past the cops and out of the store, still holding the T-shirt against his nose, drawing curious looks from both cops.

"Soak the shirt in cold water. You might be able to get all the blood out," I called after him. It was becoming difficult to speak. My pulse pounded worse than the day I found Noel dead. I flipped around the "Closed" sign. I couldn't think of what else to do. Even though the red plastic hands read "Back at 1:30," I left them that way. The three of us stepped outside, and the cops watched me lock up.

I spotted the police cruiser just up Clayton; there was a tow truck parked behind it. The shorter cop opened the back door of the squad car and said, "Get in."

"Where's your vehicle?" asked the other cop.

I pointed to Kozmic across the street.

"Keys?"

I hesitated.

"We've got a warrant." He flashed a piece of paperwork at me.

I took the key off its ring and gave it to him. He took it to the tow truck driver and returned as I got into the cruiser. I started to worry they were going to also search the apartment, in which case I was screwed for sure.

The bigger cop with the moustache did the driving; the shorter one mostly talked. I sat in the back, a prisoner, as we turned left onto Haight Street. Outside the patrol car window, stores and people slipped by. I spotted Nick James walking past, Summer pretty at his side.

As the cops talked, my mind began to focus. The two of them seemed to ignore the squawk and static coming from the two-way radio: scrambled bits of code numbers, cops talking to what I guessed must be a dispatcher. I considered my options. I needed to think about ditching the coke.

The cops were talking restaurants.

"I like Gino's."

"My wife says it's too fattening."

"The food at Dominic's is pretty good."

"I'm happy being single again myself," said the shorter cop. "Been dating a chick from Alameda. Pounded that pussy last night."

I could try to squeeze the bindle into the crease in the back of the seat. I felt around behind me with my hand. It could accommodate the coke, but I was having trouble with the idea of getting rid of the gram. It was for Lannie, and I knew she'd be unhappy if I didn't have it next time I saw her.

We turned right on Stanyan. I looked at the entrance to Golden Gate Park. The steel drummers were playing, colorful in their bright clothing, their hands flying. I wished like hell I was entering the park and about to lie down in the cool grass.

We crossed Page, then Oak, and the Panhandle as some people walked its paths. I moved the coke bindle from my shirt pocket into the sock of my right boot, after first checking the rearview mirror to make sure the cops weren't watching. I hoped that I could find a way to ditch it at the station if I had to.

At Fulton and the University of San Francisco, the car stopped.

"You want to first check that place we staked out yesterday?" the taller cop asked, and the shorter one nodded.

They hung a right and then another right until we got onto Hayes and headed east. I saw a few people sitting outside the Blue Unicorn Café. It was said to be the original coffee house in the Haight. I'd been there once with Honey.

The cops pulled over and stared at a building on the corner of Hayes and Masonic. A guy, perhaps a student, came out.

"Is that him?" the shorter one said.

"Yep. Let's come back tomorrow with a warrant."

I watched the guy head down the sidewalk. His hair was even longer than mine. We did a U-turn and soon were back on Stanyan, traveling north. We passed a school with a big asphalt playground. Kids on the playground appeared to be in junior high, all dressed in the same clothes: green tartan skirts with white blouses for the girls, green tartan pants and white shirts for the boys. Each child wore a blazer. There was such an innocence to them.

We pulled up to a light at Geary. I retrieved the coke bindle from my sock and placed it inside a pocket of my denim jacket which was on my lap. I figured if I had to ditch it, I needed easy access. We took a left, and after another few blocks, we arrived at a police station. It was a squat concrete structure with a small adjacent parking lot packed with police cars and motorcycles.

"Okay, pal," the shorter cop said, getting out and holding the door open.

I stepped out, carefully carrying my jacket bundled in a hand. The cops were escorting me on either side, the shorter one a little behind me, cunningly making it difficult to ditch anything. They led me up steps and inside, past the front desk, down a long hallway, and into a bullpen office area. I spotted a small holding cell and wondered if they were going to lock me up. But they took me to a desk. They both pointed to a metal chair in front of it, and I sat down. They walked away without saying anything.

A nameplate faced me: "Detective J. Miller." Alongside was a framed photo of a guy, probably my age or a little older, with short hair. Beside him was a nice-looking brunette holding a toddler.

I looked around the room. Cops not in uniform—detectives, I supposed—worked at their desks, typing, talking, smoking cigarettes, the place noisy and alien. I sat there, an index finger tapping the edge of the chair beneath me, my jacket in my lap, waiting. Finally, a guy came in from the same door I'd arrived through.

I looked at the photo. It was him.

THIRTY-TWO

"The name of the deceased is Nancy Klanowski. Age twenty-seven. She was from . . ." Detective Miller looked down at his flip-top spiral notebook. "Iron City, Minnesota. Her roommate, Dana Lindsay, found her yesterday morning in the bathroom. Everyone seems to have known her as 'Lannie.'"

I shouldn't have been surprised, but I was stunned.

"She changed her name a few years ago," I said. "She wanted everyone to call her Lannie. It was her stage name for when she became a star."

Detective Miller gave me a look. "It has all the earmarks of a drug overdose, including coke paraphernalia next to the body and an empty Quaalude prescription bottle from a doctor in Berkeley in somebody else's name. When did you last see her?"

"Maybe a couple weeks ago."

"Do you know who she got the pills from? And the blow?"

"No."

He fixed me with a steely gaze. "You sure?"

I stared back at him across the desk as blankly as I could manage. "Yes."

"Did she ever indicate to you why she might want to commit suicide?"

"She didn't commit suicide."

Detective Miller raised his eyebrows. Before he could speak, I added, "She didn't want to kill herself. It must have been an accident."

I thought about the cocaine in my jacket pocket and how I should have ditched it in the cop car. I was sweating now, and my hands trembled. I sat on them to make sure they stayed still, the jacket resting in my lap. I felt something crinkle against my hand under my left back pocket. In a flash, I realized it was Noel's journal page with its indictment. My sweating increased; my pulse pounded. I tried to hold it together.

Detective Miller stared at me. I had to say something, try to sound natural. "She was upset," I said. "Her boyfriend had broken things off. And she'd been fired from her job at I. Magnin." My voice quivered. I was feeling out of breath.

"Why so sure?"

"Just because—" My pretense of composure threatened to crumble completely. "She was probably just numbing herself. She didn't realize what she was doing." I sounded like I knew too much. "Listen, I'm just guessing."

Detective Miller wrote something in his notebook. "Did you know she was seeing a wealthy older guy? A William Fitzpatrick III? We found an uncashed check for a couple hundred bucks from him in her purse. He confessed to paying her regularly for—well, let's call a spade a spade—services rendered."

"But Wade was her boyfriend. Most of the time, anyway."

"Wade Trenton? He was clueless about the whole thing. Pretty upset when I told him."

I tried to process this new information.

"I suspect it was toxic buildup from the pills over days," Detective Miller continued, "plus maybe alcohol in her system, along with cocaine. Or else it was administered all at once as an intentional overdose. We'll know more when the toxicology report comes in." He leaned over his desk. "Don't you guys realize you're playing with fire? Coke is stepped on with anything from Inasatol to speed to any friggin' white powder. Take enough pills, and you can kill yourself."

"Excuse me. If we're finished, I'd like to go now."

"Yeah. Go. Fuckin' leave." He flung the notebook onto the desk. "But I might want to talk to you again if I have any more questions."

I took my hands out from under me and got up, holding my jacket carefully.

"Where's my bus?"

"It's parked out front now. Good thing for you it was clean. I did you a favor by not impounding it anyway. And if I ever see you in here again, we'll search your apartment too."

"Understood," I said, relieved.

"Here." He tossed me the key.

"Thanks." I started to leave.

"And hey, don't end up like Lannie," he added, almost friendly.

I stopped and turned to him. "Why did you come looking for me in the first place?"

"Her roommate told us about you. Don't blame her, though. She just thought since you knew the victim, you could help us out in the investigation."

I wondered about the truth of that, and whether Dana had more directly pointed the finger at me.

"What's going to happen to Lannie?" I said.

"The body? It'll be turned over to her parents."

"Yeah, guess that makes sense."

I walked back down the hallway, through the front door, and down the steps. I held the jacket tightly in my hands, my head low. It was still daylight, but I could barely see. My eyes were wet, my vision blurred. I walked over to Kozmic.

As I drove, I noticed the pull to the right was worse, and I had to tug the steering wheel harder to the left to compensate. I wondered if the cops had caused further damage with their towing. Perhaps they'd snapped one of the remaining bolts holding Kozmic to his frame.

At the top of Pacific Heights, I could see far out over the bay: Alcatraz on its rock and Angel Island beyond it; the beauty of Marin and Mount Tam further still. All of it meant nothing to me today.

I reached the apartment, drove into the garage, and parked beside Tim's truck. I got out and closed the garage door behind me. I was now in complete darkness, but I didn't want to turn on the overhead light. My eyes tried to adjust as I felt my way along the back of Tim's pickup. I squeezed between Kozmic and the wall that had the former bus mattress stacked up against it, then eased past the plywood sleeping platform that I'd also removed. Reaching the driver's side, I opened the door and got in.

I sat alone in the darkness. I couldn't remember the last time I cried. It was such a strange feeling, sitting there with tears streaming down my face. I pounded the steering wheel with both hands and yelled, "You stupid fucking idiot! You stupid fucking, fucking, fucking, fucking idiot!"

I caught my breath. My hands hurt. I wondered if anyone could hear me.

"Fuck 'em," I said. First Noel, and now Lannie.

My head rested against the steering wheel. My mind stumbled around. She hadn't meant to kill herself. You get one fucking life, and she'd accidently snuffed hers out. She'd just kept taking the pills, drinking, doing coke, self-medicating. What had she said that night she'd lost it at my place? "Just make the pain go away, Billy." I should never have sold her the Quaaludes. I would have given her a couple for free, but she'd wanted ten. The cocaine came from someone else. Some guy who'd probably walked out, leaving her comatose in the apartment. Maybe the rich guy the detective mentioned.

It was all such a goddamned waste.

I wiped my eyes on my sleeve and sat quietly. I remembered the Quaaludes back at the store. Shit. I couldn't risk Miranda discovering them in the morning when she opened up. I got out of Kozmic, raised the garage door, and squinted against the setting sun. Then, I drove back to the Haight and retrieved the ludes.

Returning to the apartment, I parked out on the street. I took the stairs two at a time, ignoring Tim's "How's it going?" as he sat on the living room couch, smoking a joint, watching TV, and petting Cat. Gerold was beside them. Pausing only long enough to take Cat, I continued into my bedroom and shut the door. I closed the other door to the bathroom.

I grabbed a Quaalude out of the amber pill bottle from Asher. I looked at the white pill with its smooth beveled edges, "RORER" in capital letters curving along the surface at the top, "714" at the bottom. I turned the tablet over and split it in half along the scored line through the center. I returned one half to the container, crunched the other half between my teeth, and swallowed the little pieces with Kahlua straight from the bottle. Then, I got on the waterbed, Cat jumping up and joining me.

I lay on my back for a long time, thinking about Lannie. I would remember her, slender beside me. Her luminous brown eyes looking up at me. Her vulnerable prettiness in the morning without makeup. I'd told myself she needed me in some special way. I never hit her like Wade and who knows how many other guys. She depended on me, at least sometimes. Someone who was more knowledgeable. Someone to advise her. Someone to try to keep her from becoming too self-destructive.

If we'd gone to high school together, I would have probably done her homework for her. Imagining that made me smile for a moment. But I knew if she'd ever come to me for a serious relationship instead of the dodging, the disappearing, and the lies, including the surprise about her selling herself, it would have been over in weeks.

Maybe days.

I checked the clock on the nightstand: 8:37 PM. I got out of bed, retrieved the bindle from my jacket pocket, and carefully emptied it into my coke vial. With the small silver spoon, I placed some of the white powder into a little pile on Noel's old hand mirror. I shaped it into a long row with a razor blade, then halved it into twin smaller ones. I rolled up a dollar bill and snorted a line. My nasal passages burned like hell. No wonder Asher's nose was bleeding. Who knew what this coke was cut with? I did more anyway, wincing at the sting, finishing it with the other nostril. I opened the bathroom door, and Cat followed me into the kitchen where I fed him from his bag of dried food.

Back in the bedroom, I armed myself with a joint, matches, the coke, various pills, and a couple condoms, along with a pen and my small notebook, all stuffed into the deep pockets of my leather bomber jacket. I grabbed *The Rebel* from its place on the bookshelf, taking cash secreted inside the pages, folding fifties and twenties into a wad, and placing it in a pants pocket.

I passed Tim and Gerold as I left but said nothing. Outside, I mounted Kozmic and drove off.

THIRTY-THREE

parked around the corner from Adriano's and went inside, the bell jingling. Carlos called to me from the bar. I ignored him. I heard the bell jingle behind me, and Manny walked in with Mysti. She looked lovely, with such a youthfulness about her. Manny and I faced each other.

"What's new?" he asked.

"Nothing good."

I looked over at Mysti and couldn't tell if she remembered me. She just stood there.

"What about you?" I asked.

"*Creem* ended up turning down the Blondie piece. On the other hand, the guidebook's going forward." He nodded out the window to where a sleek brand-new motor scooter was parked perpendicular to the curb. "Well, see you around, pal."

Gina gave me a little wave from across the room, and I nodded. But seeing nobody I wanted to hang out with and the place only half-full, I left. I began walking to Kozmic, pausing along the way to pick up a free adult sex magazine from one of the sidewalk vending machines. The machine next to it, now empty, had once held my issue of *Lifestyle*.

Back behind the wheel, I drove to Van Ness, then up and over the hill to Market Street, reaching the 101, taking the on-ramp, and heading for South San Francisco. At the higher freeway speed, Kozmic pulled even harder to the passenger side, listing more noticeably. I fought the steering wheel to compensate. He must have lost another bolt, for sure.

Shit.

The unlit mass of Mount San Bruno soon loomed off to my right. I exited the freeway, drove into a Shell station, and found a spot where there was enough light to double-check the ads in the back of the adult magazine. Then, I went into the gas station office and looked at the map on the wall.

I drove off, and soon enough, entered a parking lot manned by a valet. I went past him without stopping and parked in a corner. I carried my little notebook and ballpoint with me. The valet looked like he was about to say something, so I gave him a couple bucks.

Inside the place, I sat on a red vinyl couch and looked around. The wood-paneled walls of the room were hung with paintings of half-naked women dressed in black leather and what appeared to be latex. Some held whips. I studied them as I sat there, a coffee table in front of me. Next to an ashtray, a neat stack of glossy magazines gave the feel of a waiting room in a doctor's office. Piped-in classical music lent an air of respectability and sounded familiar. It could have been one of the records Noel used to play.

On the table, there was a button to push with a printed label reading "Hostess." I pressed it. After a moment, a woman came out from a door opposite me. She was dressed in a tight black dress and heels.

"Welcome to the Black Door," she said. "Have you been here before?"

"No."

"Are you here to see someone specific?"

"Yes," I said, taking a gamble. "Ti."

"I don't recognize the name."

"About five feet three, short red hair, kind of brash."

"Oh, you must mean Yvonne. She's not here anymore."

"How about Delaney?" I asked.

"Oh, yes. Who should I say is here?"

"Billy."

"She knows you?"

"Yeah."

"Okay," she said with what sounded like some dubiousness. As she headed back through the door, I had the thought that maybe I didn't look like the typical customer.

After a few minutes, the door opened, and Karen emerged. As Delaney, she was so different as to be almost unrecognizable: her hair slick with gel and combed straight back, her lips seething with red lipstick, her eyes thick with makeup, her breasts torpedoed against a black, skintight catsuit. She was much taller in the spiked-heel black leather boots going up past her knees. She appeared surprised to see me and strolled over slowly, twirling a small black purse by its drawstring around a finger. She stopped and stood in front of me.

I indicated the spot next to me with a hand. She ignored the invitation and remained standing, pulling a lighter and a pack of Marlboros from her purse. She lit one, holding it between her lips, taking big puffs against the flame.

"What the hell do you want?" she said, removing the cigarette from her mouth.

"Actually, I want to write an article about this place," I said, holding the little notebook and my pen at the ready. "The whole sexual underground and the S&M subculture. Profile some of the women who work here. Like you. And Ti."

She exhaled a cloud of smoke my way. "I'm not interested in being a part of some goddamned article. And Ti doesn't work here, asshole."

"Okay," I said, measuring my words. "If that's the way you feel about it. By the way, how is Ti?"

"We did a porno together. Has a great girl-on-girl scene." Her tongue came down from the roof of her mouth in exaggerated fashion as she added, "She loved it. So, unless you want to start dropping fifties, I think we're done here." She bent over, stubbed out the cigarette in the ashtray, and began to stride away.

"Wait a minute," I called after her.

She paused and turned back towards me. "Really? It's a hundred for an hour."

"Okay." I got up and placed the notebook and pen into my jacket pocket.

She appeared to hesitate, and I was concerned she would turn me down. But she shrugged and gestured for me to follow her through the door.

On the other side, the hostess sat behind a small desk with a phone, a brass lamp, and a large datebook spread open. A beefy guy in a too-tight suit was stationed on a barstool next to her.

"We need to see a driver's license," the hostess said to me. "We don't keep the information, just basic security when it comes to new clients. Protection for our girls, along with Frank," she said, nodding at the big guy on the stool.

"It's okay. Don't worry about this one," Delaney said to her. "We'll be in the dungeon." And to me, she said, "C'mon."

We headed past the hostess, turned and walked down circular steps. At the bottom, we made our way along a dimly lit corridor, past closed doors. I heard muffled noises. Groans, bits of conversation, the sound of something electric buzzing, a woman's voice barking commands, a man's voice pleading in the night.

Delaney stopped at a door. "I'm in here."

We stepped inside a room about the size of my bedroom. My eyes adjusted to a single, exposed, red ceiling bulb, the walls painted black. I looked around the space. The wall on my right was occupied by a floor-to-ceiling mirror, a narrow bed along-side it with lengths of chain and rope attached. To my left, items hung from hooks: a cat o' nine tails, handcuffs, and a zip-up black leather hood and nipple clamps like the ones Noel had; plus, ball gags, blindfolds, and a leather dog collar with a chain leash. In the center of the room, a black leather swing-like device with two openings for legs hung from the ceiling by means of four large chains, leather straps and a pair of stirrups dangling.

Delaney stood in front of me, feet planted, the spiked heels elevating her above me. "The hundred bucks is in advance," she said. "Anything topless costs an extra fifty—and no touching. The cash goes in that box." She pointed to a small silver treasure chest on a little table in a corner, a low stool beside it. The table was ar-rayed with vibrators and dildos, some graphic and cock-like, some strap-on.

I walked over to the table, lifted the treasure chest cover, placed two fifties inside, and put the rest of the cash back into my pocket.

"I see you came prepared," Delaney said. "So, that money was supposed to be for Ti?"

"I thought it was important for me and Ti to really talk, and I—"

"Oh, I get it! You were coming to 'rescue' her!" She laughed. "That's very funny!"

There were thuds against the other side of the mirrored wall. I wondered about it, but Delaney acted as if it was nothing unusual.

Exhaustion swept over me. It had been a hell of a day. I looked for a place to sit down and chose the stool.

"What else can you tell me about Ti?" I said.

"Maybe I don't want to tell you anything."

I eyed the treasure chest on the table beside me. I couldn't really afford this to begin with. Delaney caught me.

"Don't even think about it," she said, "or I'll have Frank pound you a new one."

I felt trapped down in this basement room.

"You know, as long as we're here, and you paid—" At this, she reached for the cat o' nine tails and removed it from its place on the wall. The whip had a black handle and braided cords several feet in length; lethal-looking metal bolts pierced the end of each strand and threaded through nuts on the other side.

She began to slap the handle rhythmically into a palm. Moving closer, she stared down at me. "Maybe you're a sub. A disobedient little sub who deserves to be punished."

Truthfully, as I sat there, I considered it: the lude, the coke, everything else that day, making me open to the night and whatever came along with it. I thought about losing Ti. I thought about Lannie. And there was my role in Noel's death. If anyone deserved to be punished tonight, it was me.

"I know I blew it with Ti," I said, resignation in my voice.

"Yeah, good luck finding somebody else to put up with your self-centered male bullshit."

She placed a stiletto-heeled foot on the stool between my legs, inches from my groin.

"Perhaps you'd care to lick a boot?"

There was more noise up against the wall behind the mirror. I winced, then I looked up at her hard, young face. "Maybe the other way around," I said.

Her nostrils flared, the jewel in her nose stud flashing red. "I don't think so."

"Aren't you a 'switch?'" I asked with a hint of sarcasm.

She removed her boot from the stool. Her eyes narrowed. "For Master Robert, I switch. But he tips me—a lot. And he drops a fortune here every month. Management wants us to keep him happy. For you, not likely." She brandished the whip.

"So why did Ti stop working here?"

"How is that any of your business?"

I thought for a moment. "Ti dumped you, didn't she?"

The whip froze in her hand.

"Fuck you," she said.

"Who'd she leave you for?"

She turned away and paced.

"I'd still like make things right with her," I said.

She spun around. "You're delusional. It's too late. She's gone."

"To David?"

"David's out of the picture."

"Where is she?"

"Wouldn't you like to know! Besides, is this only because you're on ludes or whatever it is that makes you even *think* you care?"

"Maybe I'll just go by your apartment and check."

"Won't do you any good. Like I said, she's gone."

"Where?"

"Out of the country." Her eyes appeared moist; her expression softened ever so slightly. She sat down on the edge of the bed and placed the whip beside her. "I treated her right," she said as if talking to herself. "I took care of her. You know how many times she cried in my arms?" Her voice trailed off. "Now she's . . . out of the country."

"I don't believe you," I said.

"Believe me."

"Where to?"

"Japan."

"Japan? Are you serious?"

"She left for a whips-and-chains dance tour with Alexander's friend, Gregory."

"Jesus."

We stayed silent for a moment. Then I got up. "Have fun with Master Robert," I said, and I headed for the door.

"When was the last time you made a hundred bucks an hour, asshole?"

I turned the handle.

"Hey!" she said, getting back on her feet and picking up the whip. "You want to know who Ti really wanted to be with in her heart of hearts?"

I paused and turned back to her.

"David?"

"No, not David," she said. "*Manny*! Yeah, fucking Manny—speaking of narcissistic assholes. She never really got over him."

I took that in. I didn't like it, but I thought it had the ring of truth.

"You and Manny have a lot in common," she said. "He's just a lot more entertaining."

I opened the door, headed down the hallway, went back up the steps. The hostess checked her watch and gave me a look, but big Frank let me pass.

THIRTY-FOUR

Outside, I got into Kozmic and headed back up the 101 to the city. I couldn't find parking near Adriano's. After driving around the block twice, I got so pissed I floored the gas pedal and almost crashed into a delivery truck. I said to hell with it and parked tight up against a car at a corner, ignoring that I could get ticketed.

Inside, Manny and Mysti were nowhere to be seen. Spencer sat at a table with Johnny Starr who looked sharp in a black velvet jacket with a scarf around his neck. I joined them. Spencer seemed to be dropping weight, and each time I ran into him lately, his eyes were duller, his walk slower, his clothes dirtier.

"Where's Zora?" I asked him.

"Fight. She's moving out."

I took this in. Gina came by. "Hey, nice to see you, Billy. Glad you came back tonight."

"I'll have a rum gimlet. Don't have anything on me for a special tip. Maybe I'll come back with something later, and I could give you a lift home at closing time."

She hesitated. "I usually go home with Val, but okay, I guess."

Johnny watched her leave and said to me, "Got anything you can front me? Maybe a couple of ludes?"

"Sorry. Running low, myself."

He got up and went over to where Fat Stan sat alone on a couch in his brown leather trench coat as always. Johnny dropped down next to him, leaned in, and said something close to his face.

Spencer stared at me. "You look like shit."

I thought how that was ironic, but said only, "Lannie's dead."

"Oh, man. What happened?"

"O.D. The cops pulled me in for a talk."

"They give you any details?"

"She had too much of this, too much of that."

"We should tell Johnny."

"How about we don't?"

Gina returned with my drink. I tried to think of something more to say to her, but she seemed in a hurry and left quickly.

"Listen," I said to Spencer. "I feel kinda restless. I'm gonna go someplace. You want to come?"

"Like where?"

I thought for a moment and polished off the rum gimlet in two gulps. "There's a really cool place over on Divisadero where this band plays tunes from the Thirties and Forties. Great standup bass player. And I've got some blow."

"Sure. What the hell."

We left together. I took the ticket from Kozmic's windshield, tore it into small pieces, and discarded it into the gutter. Then, I took Noel's journal page from my pocket and ripped it up as well. Spencer did some hits from the coke vial as we drove, and I watched for cops.

"Hey, be sure to leave some," I said.

We strolled into the Starlight Lounge. At the entrance to the showroom, I froze, Spencer hulking beside me. Constantina sat perched on a stool in front of the little orchestra. She wore the men's dress hat pulled low over her eyes, the striped club tie hanging loosely from her neck, her legs snaked around each other in black jeans. Her face was lit by a single blue spotlight, cigarette smoke rising up through it as she sang "La Vie en Rose" in French. She began the haunting chorus, her voice husky, the music soaring around her. Following a sax solo by Sam, she sang some lyrics in English about a kiss that could make heaven sigh.

The houselights came up. Constantina abandoned the stool as the audience showered her with applause. I watched her walk to the same booth we'd occupied a few weeks earlier. There she joined Alexander and some guys in bright clothing who I took to be friends of his.

I headed over with Spencer.

"Hi," Constantina said as we approached. She gave the hat a push to tilt it back, freeing her eyes to gaze up at me, her face aglow. "I'd ask you to join us, but things are kind of booked."

"It's okay, sis," Alexander said as he and his friends got up.

"Can I grab a ride with you guys if I stay?" she asked me.

"Sure," I said.

Alexander gave her a kiss on the cheek. "You better take good care of my big sister," he said, smiling at me. I couldn't decide what that smile meant. I considered bringing up Gregory and Ti but thought better of it. Alexander departed with the other boys. I sat down opposite Constantina as Spencer slid in beside me. I saw Sam watching from his place with the band.

"That was wonderful!" I said to her. "You're really good."

"Thanks." She took a sip from an almost empty wine glass in front of her. "How are you?" she asked me, finishing the last of the wine, no cigarette in her hand tonight.

Before I could respond, the band began something with a bouncy rhythm to it, one of the guys blowing a sparkling clarinet lead. I watched them play. Then, Spencer got up.

"I'm gonna hit the head," he said. "Can you order me a beer?"

"Sure," I said.

We watched him go, with his height, his leather hat, the tattoo on the side of his neck, the slow amble of his gait.

"He looks dangerous," Constantina said. "Be careful."

"I stay on his good side."

"So, how are you?" she asked again.

"Lannie's dead. An overdose."

"I'm sorry."

"Are you?"

"Well, I feel badly about it for you. Can't say I really ever knew her."

"Can't say I did either, it turns out."

She gave me a questioning look but didn't say anything. After a few minutes, she said, "Can you buy me a drink? Money's tight and getting tighter. Today is my great liberation from the running dogs of capitalism."

"Meaning?"

"I quit the store."

"Any particular reason?"

"We're pushing a decade since the Summer of Love. Like I said, it's time to move on. Maybe go further north, or even to the Sierras. A more natural and real world. Back to the land and all that. Ha!" She laughed. Looking more serious, she added, "Force myself into action."

"What about your painting?"

"I'll keep at it, I suppose."

"Aren't you concerned about some income? Can you collect unemployment?"

"No, the job was under the table. I'll come up with something."

I sensed a false bravado, the illusion of her resilience

disintegrating before me. Everything was different tonight. I looked over at her, seeing vulnerability. I guessed her to be very alone underneath it all, more so even than myself.

Then, I thought about how she had presented Manny with that delicate body of hers, which went along with the artistic fingers, the barbed wit, the keen intelligence. Maybe she'd gotten all she wanted from Manny: humor, a verbally adroit equal, perhaps even halfway decent sex. But I knew that from me she would want more.

"You know, men can be such shits," Constantina said.

I was startled.

"It's partly because of the owner," she continued. "The fuck keeps coming on to me. I have to go back and face him one last time to get my final check. Could you come with me?"

"Sure. As your muscle?" I laughed a little.

"As my friend," she said pointedly.

The moment felt awkward.

"We could bring Spencer," I said, joking but sounding more serious than I intended.

"He makes me nervous."

"I've got coke if you'd like some."

"Thanks anyway. I'm cutting back on my poisons, for real." She waved for a waitress, then began drumming her fingers on the table. She looked like she didn't know what to do with her hands without a cigarette.

The waitress came over, and we ordered drinks as the band played. I watched Sam doing a solo on sax. After a couple more songs, Spencer returned. "The music's cool," he said as he sat down. "Even if I have no fuckin' clue what the tunes are."

"This one's 'In the Mood,'" Constantina said.

Spencer nodded. "You pay for my beer?"

"Yeah," I said. "Don't worry about it."

We listened to more of the music. I bought Constantina another drink and paid for another beer for Spencer. At the end of the set, Sam came over, and Constantina spoke with him quietly as he bent down. Sam glanced at Spencer and me, shook his head, and walked away.

THIRTY-FIVE

Constantina, Spencer, and I left the Starlight Lounge together. I drove us to the Fillmore. Constantina gave me directions from the passenger seat, Spencer crouching in the walkway between us, holding onto the seatbacks on either side. We pulled up outside a building that had seen better days.

Looking at me with the passenger door open, Constantina said, "Would you like to come by and help us cook our communal dinner some night?" She gave me a soft smile. "Spaghetti's on the menu a lot, and we're always short on meat, not to mention wine."

"Okay, that would be cool."

"Think you'll be able to find it again?"

I focused on everything around me. "I think so."

"I'd give you my number, but we don't have a phone. So, see you around."

"Sure."

"Night, Spencer," she said, and she stepped down, closed the door, and headed for the building. I watched to make sure she made it safely inside. Spencer got up from his spot between the walk-through seats, and his leather jacket slapped me in the face. He took a place next to me in the passenger seat.

"Wanna stop at my place?" he said. "I'm just around the corner, and I've got smack if you'd like some. Besides, Zora's packing up, and I want to keep an eye on my shit."

Soon, I was walking down an alley with Spencer in the heart of the Fillmore after parking on a dimly-lit street even worse than Constantina's. I was anxious about leaving Kozmic there. We went through a ground-floor door and started up stairs that were covered with dirty carpeting, past walls filled with graffiti. Spencer's boots thudded in front of me, his silver spurs jangling. A black guy in a porkpie hat passed us coming down, and he and Spencer exchanged hellos.

Inside the apartment, chaos greeted us: a bass amp, a drum kit set up in a corner, old magazines strewn about, and some cardboard boxes that were apparently part of Zora's moving effort. We picked our way through it as we headed in the direction of the couch.

Zora came into the room wearing a Black Sabbath T-shirt and carrying a box of stuff. "Oh. Hi, Billy," she said. I was surprised to see that her thick eye makeup was smeared. She'd been crying.

"Lannie's dead," Spencer said to her. He swept the couch clear with a hand, spilling fast-food wrappers, a copy of *Musicians Contact* magazine, and God knows what else onto the floor to make room. I took a seat on the couch, and Zora sat down beside me.

"That is so fucked!" she said. "What happened?"

"O.D.," said Spencer, putting a Johnny Winter album on the stereo before going to the corner of the room that served as the kitchen. He pulled things from drawers and out of his pockets. Zora got up and joined him. I could see him make preparations, and then he shot her up.

"Your turn," he called to me.

I took off the bomber jacket and went over to him. Zora passed me, going back to the couch as I kept an eye on my jacket and its contents. I'd wanted to try heroin before, but the one time I'd gone looking for some with a couple college pals, we couldn't score any.

"Roll up your sleeve."

I did what he said and exposed my left arm.

Spencer tied me off with a length of thin rubber tubing, the works and packet of smack on the top of the stove beside him. He tapped some heroin into a spoon and added liquid from an eyedropper. Then he lit a gas burner and placed the spoon over it until the mixture bubbled.

"Great veins," he said, and he stuck the needle in my arm with a lancing sting. He did his task methodically, like a medical professional. I felt a rush. Warm floating sensations engulfed me. I walked back to the couch, sat down, grabbed my jacket, leaned back and closed my eyes. I'd heard that sometimes you got nauseous the first time, but I felt fine. Good, even.

Zora leaned against me. I opened my eyes and looked over at her. I gently pushed her away at the shoulder so that she sat up, her eyes closed. It was hard to tell what was intentional and what wasn't. I'd been surprised at her tear-streaked emotion tonight. She told me once that she grew up with her mother out in the Southern California desert near Barstow, only with a different name. And what that name was. I wondered if she would stay in San Francisco or return back south.

Spencer was moving over to his bass now, plugging it into the amp and starting to play along to the record. He played without a pick, his fingers dancing over the strings in melodic, running bass lines. He was very good. He should be in a major rock band, I thought. I wondered why he wasn't.

Zora was against me again. Her hand came around the side of my face as I sat there with my eyes closed, resting my head against the couch, absorbing the bass as it accompanied a wild Johnny Winter guitar lead. I felt Zora kiss me. Her lips were surprisingly soft—softer than they should be, I remember thinking, for someone who looked so rough with her jet-black hair and her tattoos.

I was jerked to my feet by two strong hands as Spencer threw me over the couch. He came around behind it as I was getting up and slammed me against the wall. He ripped a fist across my face. I stumbled sideways over the amp.

"Motherfucker," he said. I got up and staggered away from him, making it to the door, retreating quickly down the stairs, clutching my jacket and walking fast in the night to Kozmic. I climbed in and looked back to make sure Spencer wasn't following me. Then I checked my face in the rearview mirror. I was lucky. The punch had gotten me on the cheek, missing my nose and not knocking out any teeth.

I remembered I was supposed to pick up Gina at closing. I grabbed a rag from the storage box behind the passenger seat and held it to my face. I hoped the bleeding would stop. After a couple minutes, I turned the ignition and headed out of the Fillmore.

Inside Adriano's, I saw Monique with a guy I didn't recognize. He was good-looking and well-dressed like David. She and I mouthed hellos across the room. Then, I saw a look of concern cross her face, no doubt at my appearance. I went into the bathroom and examined the damage again. I splashed some water on my cheek and did my best to remove the blood. The cheekbone was red where Spencer's fist landed, and it was starting to swell.

When I came out, Jerry the bartender called over to me. "Hey, let's take care of that."

I walked over, and he pulled out a first-aid kit and came around from behind the bar. He worked on my cheek with surprising tenderness and applied some stinging antiseptic.

"What happened?"

I left it at "Spencer."

"Bad news, that guy." After he applied a large Band-Aid, he said, "This should hold you." Then, he added, "Hang on a sec." He made a rum gimlet and passed it to me. "On the house."

I said, "Thanks," went around the partition and sat by myself, waiting for Gina to get off work. I took a half-Quaalude, not even sure why. When she was ready, we walked out together, just the two of us. Gina stood tall and straight beside me, an inch or so over my own height, despite her wearing flat shoes.

"What happened to your face?" she said.

"Little accident." I handed her a lude and, while doing so, tripped over the curb but regained my balance. Glancing around, she said, "Hey, this isn't cool out here on the street." Then she slipped the lude into her purse and asked, "Are you okay to drive?"

"Sure. No problem."

"Alright, but take it easy. I'm in the Marina."

We reached Kozmic, and I unlocked the doors. She stepped up and in on her side, and I did the same on mine. I focused behind the wheel as I drove, staring straight ahead. Kozmic pulled hard to the right at a stop sign, brakes squealing.

"Is this bus okay?" Gina asked, holding onto the dashboard with a hand.

"I'll take it slow." It felt like Gina and I were far apart tonight, which was too bad. I worried about the impression I was making. Things seemed like I was on a date back in high school. I tried to remember dating protocol. Should I get out and open her door when we arrived at her place? No, she would likely just get out herself.

As we drove along Pierce and crossed Chestnut Street with its sports bars and restaurants filled with the Marina crowd, I thought how maybe tonight didn't really matter. I knew nothing about Gina, just that she looked healthy and appealing. I'd always liked her long straight hair, her smile, and the intelligence behind her brown eyes.

"God, these hours are killing me," she offered, breaking the silence. "I mean what with school and all."

"You're in school?" I said.

"I hope you didn't think I just cocktail-waitressed."

I tried to cover. "What year are you?"

"I just graduated San Francisco State. You take a right here."

I turned onto one of the looking-all-the-same streets of the Marina that were lined with upscale two-story apartment buildings.

"You seem surprised," she said, looking over.

"Well, I thought maybe you were a little older."

"Gee, thanks!" she said, but she laughed. "Must be my great maturity. This is my street over here."

I took the turn. "You just seemed to fit in with everything at Adriano's." Even as I said it, it didn't seem to exactly make sense.

"Well, the girls are great. But I'm going into a graduate program for hotel and restaurant management in the fall. This is it," she said, pointing to a smooth stucco building coming up on the right. "I share it with a couple other girls. Val and a waitress at Perry's."

I double-parked out front. She opened the door, and I leaned over to kiss her goodnight, but she was already beyond my reach.

"Thanks for the ride," she said, standing on the sidewalk with the door open. "See you around. Listen, be careful. Drive nice and slow, and please go straight home. And you should get this thing fixed." She eyed Kozmic, her face a frown. Then she said, "Night." I called the same back, and she slammed the door.

I took her advice, but only because I couldn't think of anywhere else to go. Inside the apartment, Tim's bedroom door was closed. In the kitchen, I took a glass from the cabinet and poured some milk. I took it to the bedroom as Cat followed, and I added some vodka and twice as much Kahlua.

I swallowed the last of Noel's Libriums with the White Russian. Then, I lit the candle on the nightstand. I took off all my clothes and collapsed onto the bed. As the sloshing subsided, I reached across and turned on the old black-and-white TV and caught some of *Morocco*. In her tuxedo, a young Marlene Dietrich sang to an equally young Gary Cooper. She made me think of Constantina.

The next thing I knew, the television had gone to snow. I was sweating for no reason. I couldn't sleep. My mind whirled away, despite the alcohol, despite the heroin, despite the Quaaludes and Noel's Librium. The coke had burned my nostrils and was likely cut with speed. Pot might help relax me, I thought. I got up and opened the window to cool the room. By the glow of the snow of the television, I retrieved a partially smoked joint from the ashtray on the nightstand; then, I sat cross-legged, smoking, naked on the waterbed, gently rocking back and forth.

When there wasn't enough left to smoke, I put the roach back into the ashtray. I stared into the candle flame. Outside, a tree rat squeaked, leaves rustled, crickets chirped. The candlelight danced, making for strange patterns on the walls. Inside my head, a noise began and wouldn't stop. I got up and took a Percodan, crunching it between my teeth as I polished off the White Russian.

I was back on the waterbed, Cat beside me. The pills should have slowed everything down to the usual fade-to-black. Instead, everything sped up. The room became formless, my thoughts random and confusing. Images came and went. My mind hurtled as I lay there and thought about Lannie. I thought about Gina and her distance tonight. I thought about Constantina, hiding behind her sarcasm and aloof bemusement. I thought about Ti and how I'd blown that. I thought about Noel's suicide and how he got to that point. My own role in his plans. I thought about myself. How I needed to find my place in the world and what that place was. How there was an unstoppable clock ticking away on my life.

Next, I was screaming, my face buried deep into my pillow, my legs climbing an invisible ladder. Just when the panic felt like it would never end, it subsided. I raised my head from the pillow; I could hear the muted sounds from the garden below.

Then, I felt it coming on again. The noise in my brain grew louder as I lay in bed, fighting it, my breathing an audible panting, my teeth clenched so tight my jaw felt wired shut.

I got out of bed, threw on my boots, a shirt and some jeans, and headed out the front door. I continued down the stairs to the garage, where I dragged the plywood platform and my old mattress into Kozmic. I made a few trips up the stairs for more things: Cat's litter box and his food; a few books, clothes, and records; the last of the cash; stuff from my stash. All the while, I kept as quiet as possible to avoid waking up Tim behind his door. I returned to my bedroom one last time and grabbed Cat who was meowing as if afraid I would leave him behind.

I hit the road. I needed to just *go*. I tried to get Cat to curl up in my lap like the old days, but he remained in a crouch on the passenger seat. I reached the Gough Street entrance ramp to the 101 and flew up. Kozmic made noises: groans and moans and creaks. Handling him was more difficult than ever. He was pulling so hard to the right it felt like he was trying to commit hari-kari into the fucking guardrail. Like he'd had it, like he was lost without his days of supplying living space for Honey, Cat, and me during our cross-country runs.

And now, as we began to cross the Bay Bridge, there was a new noise somewhere behind me. I cocked my head, and it struck me that if that last bolt holding the axle and the frame together were to snap, the resulting accident could kill not only me but also Cat. I reduced my speed and hugged the slow lane. But still, something was happening—a heavy thud, then a careening spin-out that looked slow but sounded faster than hell. A bridge buttress slammed into the passenger door; everything shifted; Kozmic rolled, and the windshield shattered and sprayed my face with bits of glass. My head hit something hard as metal screeched against and seemingly into pavement.

Then a strange voice was forcing me to open my eyes. Stretched out on my back on the bridge in the night, 1 saw orange traffic cones and a couple flares spitting white-hot fire. A police car with twirling red flashers was parked nearby. Blood flowed down my face. The roadway thumped against me as cars passed. A cop was watching me as he directed traffic. I tilted my head and saw Kozmic lying on his side, chassis facing me, one wheel angled cruelly away from me, the rear axle separated from the frame.

"Try to stay calm," another cop shouted in my direction. "An ambulance is on the way." He was cradling Cat tightly, and soon, very soon, other people were kneeling near me, strange people, talking to me, too.

5

THIRTY-SIX

The sun was incandescent. Around me, an alien landscape revealed itself: curved soundstage roofs, a few low modern buildings, swaths of concrete and blacktop everywhere, people moving about below. I was standing against Aunt Francine's Chevy Caprice on the top floor of a parking structure open to the sky. The HOLLYWOOD sign stared back at me from its hillside perch, the smog a low brownish line on the horizon. A lizard stutter-walked on the low wall in front of me and disappeared over the edge.

I reached into the car and retrieved my blazer, slipped it on, and adjusted my tie using the driver's side door mirror. I was still trying to get used to seeing myself reflected back with the haircut I got from Carlos in exchange for a couple lines of coke. I looked like I did before college, except for the moustache. But I was keeping that nice and neat now, carefully running a razor over it when I shaved and trimming it along the bottom with Noel's scissors.

The tie constricted unnaturally around my throat. Uncle Bernie insisted it was more appropriate than the one I'd brought with me. The blazer was my old one from high school that I'd asked my parents to ship out. It was tight across the chest when buttoned, so I left it open. I'd bought khakis at Macy's on Union Square in

San Francisco, along with some cordovan loafers and dress socks. The loafers had been on sale and hurt my feet.

If I combed my hair just right, it almost covered the shaved strip on the top of my head where I received twenty-eight stitches. If I was careful not to tilt my face down, they wouldn't show. I checked the Sears Timex on my wrist. I was nervous as hell. Uncle Bernie had helped me land the interview, but said, "After that, you're on your own. It's entry level with a lot of hours, so be ready to work."

I had copies of my resume—a half-fabricated document that Manny had helped me compose and printed off before he quit the copy center—accompanied by tear sheets of "Dancing Your Ass Off" and "Punk Arrives in San Francisco," the latter eventually accepted by a free handout publication in North Beach. It was just as well I hadn't done the perverse "Exploring the Sexual Underground" piece. On the passenger seat was an oversized how-to paperback about screenwriting that I picked up from City Lights Books and had been reading while waiting for my appointment.

I glanced at the watch again. The guard at the gate had given me a little map that now was folded inside my blazer pocket, my destination circled by him with a ballpoint pen. I walked past parking spaces filled with employee vehicles and descended the concrete stairwell.

Soon, I sat in a room opposite a genial, heavyset African-American woman; photos of her and another woman hugging faced me from a shelf behind her desk. Both women wore sweatshirts and jeans and looked happy together. The office door said, "Vice President Production," in small, dull, gray metal letters.

That night, to celebrate my new job, I borrowed Aunt Francine's Caprice again and drove to the Rainbow Bar and Grill on the Sunset Strip. The Rainbow was next to the Roxy, a showcase club for bands and part of a music industry nexus. The Whisky was just down the street, the Troubadour not far away.

I did a half a Quaalude along with my first drink at the bar. Some coke was in a jacket pocket, along with a just-in-case condom. Soon, I was in a friendly conversation with the bartender, a guy named Terry who said he was really an actor. I noticed members of Black Sabbath sitting in a booth behind me—Ozzy and the ones I didn't know by name, girls in spandex draped over them.

I wondered what Zora would have thought.

I gazed around the room some more, starting to feel the half-lude, feeling good, better than I had in a long time.

ACKNOWLEDGEMENTS

First and foremost, to book doctor Mark Wisniewski for his invaluable contributions. Second, to Michael Snyder—culture blaster, journalist, broadcaster, and screenwriter—for his copyediting, and for being a creative sounding board. There are some final decisions relating to grammatical choices made by me, which should not reflect negatively on his efforts to keep me on the *Strunk & White* straight and narrow.

Richard Lewis Mater
Los Angeles, California 2021

AUTHOR BIO

Richard Lewis Mater was born in Pinner, England, and grew up in California, New Jersey, and Munich, Germany. After college, he travelled the U.S. extensively in his VW bus. Along the way, he did some freelance writing. Eventually he settled in Los Angeles and began working in local television news and programming, earning an Emmy nomination. That was followed by a long career in network television. He was formerly married and has two 20-something daughters.

Website: Richardlewismater.com

CPSIA information can be obtained
at www.ICGtesting.com
Printed in the USA
LVHW111652270322
714534LV00002B/286